City Secrets

edited by Cathy Bolton
& P-P Hartnett

Acknowledgements:
file>>corrupted by Rosie Lugosi was first published under a
different title by *Cadenza*.

First published in 2002 by Crocus
Crocus books are published by Commonword Ltd,
6 Mount Street, Manchester M2 5NS.

Crocus Books are distributed by Turnaround Publisher Services
Ltd, Unit 3, Olympia Trading Estate, Coburg Road,
Wood Green, London N22 6TZ.

Cover photograpy by P-P Hartnett, design by Ian Bobb.

Printed by Shanleys, 16 Belvoir Street, Tonge Fold, Bolton
BL2 6BA

British Library Cataloguing-in-Publication Data. A catalogue
record for this book is available from the British Library.

CONTENTS

INTRODUCTION

P-P H: You start.

CB: Putting this collection together has been more fun than I expected. How was it for you?

P-P H: The writing exceeded my expectations in both content and style. We set out to find work which was somehow 'real' and very much connected to now, and...

CB: And we got it. The secrets theme did the business. I guess us queer folk have a lot of shady experiences to draw on.

P-P H: So why is there so much formula drivel out there?

CB: Why's the moon round?

P-P H: I'm pleased that this collection has integrity to it, selection depended on the quality of writing from the 100+ submissions received and that alone.

CB: That sounds contrived! You've got notes haven't you?

P-P H: Might have.

CB: Go on anyway.

P-P H: Many of them explore less than wholesome lifestyles and not-so loving relationships. I think it's a sign of maturity that we can own up to being as obsessive, vindictive, manipulative and downright perverse as straight people.

CB: Mm. There's been one fuck of a lot of blinkered thinking and self-censorship in the past. Here people are just doing their own thing, rather than playing to a formula or working a really obvious commercial angle for a market that is long dead.

P-P H: And?

CB: And I was worried we might be inundated with all that grope by numbers stuff that's supposed to be a turn on. Although there's lots of references to sex, especially in the boys' stories, they probe more into the psyche and relationships of characters.

P-P H: Er, I was hoping for a bit of the grope stuff actually.

CB: You were? You sod.

P-P H: In terms of an intro that's probably enough.

CB: Oh, okay. Over and out.

** CB has left **
** P-P H has left **

JACK BERRY

Jeff Stryker in a Box

'J.Lo's on *Parky*, can't wait!'
He's the straight acting one. He's tall and very
thin, a bit like bamboo, same rich skin colour too. He's
just eighteen, with dark 'curtains', hair that makes him
look three years younger. He reminds me of myself
when *I* was a bit younger, nervy and unaware of the
effect he has on people – mainly men. Everybody takes
the piss out of his haircut, but he seems to be sticking
with it. Says he doesn't want anything too racy - for
racy, read gay. He *is* the straight acting one after all.
Not a very convincing act though. Why are they all so
desperate not to appear queer in here? Except
Brendan, he's like this neon camp fluff puff. Air kisses,
those huge Spice Girl boots and a too tight t-shirt. The
name of our gay superstore is punctuated by his left
nipple [and ring]. He's like me, we are what we are.

And what we are is an illusion.

'Girls though, I mean, *yuck*.' The weekly
debate rages on. It's like being back at school. Luckily,
though, I'm always spared having to contribute my
thoughts on the matter because someone always steps
in with, **'You're just as bad as straight men.
Women aren't just sex objects you know!'** Or,
**'It's not right for us to judge other people's
sexual habits! Think how much suffering is
caused by homophobia.'** If I had to state my
position, I fear that they might all get a bit freaked out
by me.

They're a nice lot though, if a bit cliquey at first.

But it's not hard to get to know them. When I first started at Prowlaround, I have to say, I was thrown in at the deep end. My first day was spent behind the beaded curtains. I came face to face with Jeff Stryker in a box. This was a bit un-nerving, mainly because I kept thinking, **Well, I'm underprivileged.** I mean, it was huge.

The array of mags and vids were not as hard to stomach as I had first imagined. I didn't think I'd be able to handle it, but I needed a job badly. Like three weeks in arrears badly. I'd been in London for a long time, and I'd worked around, but I'd never been in a sex shop – so I was nervous to say the least. Do you talk to the customers? Is there some sort of code? And every time I wrapped a copy of **BLACK BALLED III,** or a *Tom of Finland* hard back, I had to avoid eye contact. People were offended – the other boys said I was snotty. But, it was honestly just embarrasment.

'Oh, look at her. Thinks she's above it all,' I heard more than once.

Usually I was saved by someone chipping in, **'Leave him alone, he's just nervous.'**

Now, of course, it's like second nature to offer a tube of lube with every double ender. And even though it's wall to wall, after a while you don't even notice it. **HardcoreSoftcoreBi** all just merge like wall paper. I've even tried out some of the products – with varying results. Smelling Space highs [poppers] is like sniffing glue – avoid it at all costs. Love Lotions, however, are heavy – they really get you in the mood.

Me and the boys get on really well. After my frosty reception I expected them all to be real bitches.

Especially when it came to explaining that I was different, I worry about that a lot. Still haven't got around to telling them. Don't know how they'll react.

I'd seen snatches of gay lives on TV, where everyone was fab and glam, but after I had settled in I was amazed to find that they were all pretty normal. These boys in the big city were just the same as me. They aren't a group of pervs hanging outside schools and toilets, lusting after thirteen-year-old boys. Neither are they hedonistic fashion victims, the reality is somewhere in between. The only other gay man I'd met before was a friend of my brother's from art college. It was okay for him because everyone thought it was cool, but the boys here have faced a different crowd. I mean, if one of the lads ran into one of the boys there's little chance they'd be discussing Dali.

I kept my job a secret from my mates for as long as I could. It was made worse by the fact that I look gay. Everyone tells me so, and eveyone expects (or suspects) that I am. I'm shortish, with close-cropped hair – the style that gay boys have because they think it makes them look hard. Girls always say I'm stylish, the lads say I dress like a fairy, I've always just liked to look good. When it all came out about my new job the lads ribbed me mercilessly.

'Don't get too comfortable Jon. That's when they'll pounce!'

'That's if you don't pounce first eh! I mean this isn't your way of telling us you're one is it?'

'Ha-ha,' I laughed nervously. **'No, no. Course not.'**

'Fuckin' good news mate!'

And they all laughed and clanked bottles together. I did feel more at home with the boys at Prowlaround, though. Not that I was going to let the lads know.

The most unexpected thing I found in the store was how they all grouped themselves into types: **Camp** Chicken **Trendy** **LEATHER** SHABBY-ABBIES

All defined by age and dress.

The SHABBY-ABBIES are pitied. They just look normal to me though, normal rather than a mess. Just going about their lives without worrying about the gym rituals, or the need to be dressed to impress simply to buy porn. I say they group themselves, in reality they are labelled. On boring days we stand around compiling scorecharts to see how many of each type come in. Usually we get a majority of **Trendy**, closely followed by **LEATHER**. I think it's because we're so near Soho, and that's like Trumpton. A walk along Old Compton Street after dark is like stumbling into a big pink parallel carnival universe. At first the diversity makes you think, **'Who couldn't fit in here?'** Then you realise it can be quite hard to.

For each customer we ask, **'Would you dog it?'** With most ticks going in the Chicken box. The lads reckon my type is **Trendy**, but they're missing the mark. Loads of the other types – especially Chickens – use the store as a cruising ground. Hanging around the greetings cards, glancing over the racks of HOT ELBOW GREASE at each other.

It's blatant, but we don't want to get in the way of a bit of random man love, so we let them just get on with it. They're usually too shy or too young or too self-concious to go into a bar, so they stick with a shop. If the worst comes to the worst they can dash out exclaiming they never knew it was one of *those* shops.

None of it shocks me – sex really is everywhere. It isn't suprising, when you think that all the boys are grouped together by sexual preferance. I mean brandy afficinados get pretty wasted at their monthly meets, so it follows that man sex lovers will get truly fucked when brought together. And sex is a stronger pull than booze – well usually.

The clubs are so much freer, there's no messing about. It's just off with your t-shirt and on to the dance floor. You see it, you want it, you fuck it. No asking friends to do the talking, or obligatory slow dancing. It's so different to what I'm used to, in a way it's liberating.

And on Sunday you can watch T4 (which I really do like) and admit it, with no one going, **'That Dermot O'Leary's a fuckin'puff.'**

It's cool, but you can get trapped in it, trapped in a GAY LIFESTYLE TM. I mean, we all work in a gay superstore selling fag magazines, fag clothes, even fag food. We drink in gay bars, eat at gay restaurants, dance in gay clubs, know the hot labels and only have friends who are gay or girls (but not lesbians). Women are still no more respected in this little limited world, everything is superficial, and it all seems so contrived, like gay men are some new super race who believe their own hype. Or this is segregation.

I worry that I don't fit in, that I'm not quite what I should be. I mean I do look the part but I'm not the part – if you understand. When a coupla gay boys come in, with fag hag in tow, everyone's eyes turn to the roughish blond one. Except mine. Mine linger elsewhere, poring over softer curves and leering smoother flesh. Because me and all the boys get on so well I kinda feel bad, like I'm lying to them, and honesty is important in friendships. But, when I want to tell them the truth about me – that I'm not what I've maybe led them to believe – I freeze. I can't do it. I don't want to be different, for that part of me to be my introduction, my master status, **'Oh, *that* Jon.'** So, I cop out.

There's been loads of chances to say it, like when we've discussed who has the biggest cock we've ever seen – I could have said it then. Or when I had a drunken two-second snog with Chris and they wanted to know all the ins and outs. As it stands, I spend a lot of my time juggling two sets of friends – not quite telling the truth to either – hoping that one of the lads doesn't run into one of the boys. This tension is the worst aspect of the job. Worse than having to explain the no refunds policy on Studded Brace Jocks, worse than the hi-nrg remixes of Kylie and Britney, and worse than posing for a million photographs a day with Dutch tourists.

'Hey Chris.'

Chris is back from lunch. Fiaz springs up from behind the till to say, **'Hey'**, too. He's been tucked away, discreetly eating salt and vinegar crisps while we've been quiet. He's about to spout some mad nonsense until he sees that Chris is looking a bit nervy, that his face is all twisted up – it's cute. When I ask Chris why, he says his Mum and Dad are coming to visit him next weekend. *And?* You might think. *So?*

The parent's don't know Chris is gay, he's gonna

have to tell them when they arrive. Not that they couldn't guess, as I said before, *not* a very convincing act. They're apparently very conservative – not at all happy with his move to London in the first place. Chris doesn't want to be disowned by them, especially as his first boyfriend just dumped him. He says that when they were together it was like a big **OK!** to him being gay, a feeling of this – is – so – right – how – could – it – be – wrong? And now that they've finished, **'It's like all that stuff you read about queers just having sex, not love, is true.'**

How anybody could leave Chris alone is beyond me, he's sweet and naïve and hard-faced and wide-eyed. A cool boy to work with, and a really nice kid. But, he looks particularly distresssed right now – like his twisted up face is gonna un-twist sharply in tears. I want to tell him NOW. **'Don't worry about them Chris, I've got something to tell.'** But I can't, because I worry he'll only get more confused and twist up his face in a new direction.

We all gather about to calm him down. At times like this you really need your second family around. We all talk through our coming out stories. Most are really funny. James told his Mum on the day of his wedding (shortly before fleeing the service). Steve found his Dad at it with the neighbour, Mr Johnston, and simply said, **'Well Dad, that makes two of us!'** His Mum went off the rails for a while, he said. But she's in store now at least once a week, handing out scones and syphilis awareness fliers.

Brendan says he's always known. **'The only time I ever fancied a girl was on this mad weekend to Blackpool, we were in this massive** bar, an' I was *sooo* drunk. I was saying to my friend Suzanne, "Suzanne! Suzanne I think I'm goin' straight, I really fancy her!" An' I was wavin' an' pointin' at this woman. An' Suzanne was like, "Her? The DJ? *Her? She's* a fuckin' bloke love! We're in a fuckin' drag bar!" '

Then they all look at me. Eyes all glistening with nostalgia and laughter.

'**So then Jon. How did you come out?**'

A warmth like Christmas is radiating off them, and I don't want to be Boxing Day.

But, I wonder if I should be. As I think of how to put it, some little bastard cues up *I'm Coming Out* on the sequencer!

I panic and blush, they cheer and laugh. Could I do it?

'**Come on!**' says Chris with a shake of my shoulder, '**Tell us.**'

I can feel his breath behind me, warm with laughter and nerves on my cheek. It smells of sharp, sugar free minty chewing gum masking over a stale layer of cigarettes. His aftershave is cast over it all, and the three scents are interspersed with a hint of sweat. He's fully dimensional and I remember our kiss.

'**Come on,**' he repeats.

So, more to help Chris than anything else, I bite the bullet and say, '**I haven't. I haven't come out yet.**'

All the boys look on in shock, like the chorus in a musical. They are all open-mouthed and crinkle-browed. Brendan even starts to do the fake talking with Fiaz who's standing next to him. I gulp a breath and steady myself. This is my big Roxie Hart moment.

'Cos, I'm not even gay.'

Gasping, swivelling of heads, comedy double takes, the chorus reaches a crescendo, I wonder if I'll lose my job. I'm sure they'll come to terms with it, I mean we're still friends. And I suppose now my shag rating will go up. That's another thing, why *do* they all want to fuck straight men?

CATHY BOLTON

Denial

Mal walked out on me in the early hours of Christmas Day. Bitch.

We were about to celebrate our woollen anniversary – the one with the itch. None of my friends, gay or straight, had made it to paper. They were concerned, curious. Performed the usual caring acts: numerous cups of tea. Large brandies. Told me how they'd never really trusted Mal, how I deserved better. Then, trying to pretend they weren't sitting on the hottest gossip in months, they ever so casually asked, 'What went wrong, Megan? Was there another woman?'

'Worse,' I told them.

'Not a man!' they gasped. This was going to be the scoop of the decade.

'*The* Man.'

They looked puzzled.

I spelt it out for them. 'Jesus Christ, the son of God.'

'You split up over *God*?'

*

They were bemused. They all knew I hadn't stepped foot inside a church since my cousin's wedding in 1989 and was politically opposed to all forms of organised religion. Mal, who was raised by nuns, couldn't have so much as an after dinner conversation about religion without bursting a blood vessel. Even Buddhists managed to raise her hackles with their smug 'how much ego have you lost this month?' routine.

Of course, I had to tell them the whole story.

*

It was a Sunday afternoon and I had that solitary confinement sensation I used to get as a kid. I was trying to prepare my presentation on Best Value for Monday's board meeting. Mal was out playing five-a-side with the gang. I'd tried out for the East Manchester Ladies myself when I was a young proselyte of the Sisterhood, but was soon told I had two left feet and given the number of the local netball team.

In the early days of our romance, I used to go along to cheer 'Our Ladies', hang around the changing room trying not to feel like a perv, while they wandered around naked comparing bruises and muscle tone. Later, I took to meeting them in the pub, listening to endless replays of 'top pass' and 'no way was that off-side'. More recently, I'd waited for Mal's phone call. Gone to pick her up from the pub, when they'd started to bore even themselves with the post-game analysis, collecting a pre-ordered take-away en-route.

Like my friends, you're probably wandering what me and Mal had in common. Well it doesn't take much to cement a relationship: good sex, joint mortgage, fear of being single. It's not till after you've hit the big iceberg that you realise you've been coursing the ocean in a death trap.

*

So there I was making pretty pie charts out of last years customer service records when the door bell rang. I wondered who on earth could be calling round on Sunday afternoon. Maybe the match had been cancelled, Mal had caught the bus home and discovered, as she often did, that she had no keys. I went to the door, already thinking about consolatory cocoa in bed. I could wing the presentation – no one would notice if I recommended we axe the entire cleansing department.

I opened the door and there, standing on the patch of weed-cracked concrete that served as our garden path, was an immaculately dressed black woman. Early sixties I'd say, large blue handbag and stack of magazines tucked under her arm. I knew immediately what her game was.

'Good afternoon,' she enthused with a practised smile. 'Hope I haven't disturbed you.'

I just couldn't bring myself to say, 'Well actually you have, dear.'

'Are you concerned about the level of violence in the world today?'

The sales lady leaned into the open door a little. I gave her my you're-talking-in-a-foreign-language look. Wanted her to get quickly to the God part so I could politely but firmly say I'm not interested – I don't believe and close the door on her pitying face.

'Of course you are. A nice young woman like yourself.'

Too nice for my own good according to Mal. Couldn't she see she was wasting her time with me. Where are the nasty lezzie-goading boys on bicycles when you need them?

She pushed one of her magazines into my hands.

'You might think there's nothing we can do about all the hatred in the world, but you're wrong. There's a lot we can do. *The Word* tells...'

'Sorry, I'm not interested.' I let go of my corner of the glossy mag.

'Oh, not to worry,' she said, quite resigned to rejection. She started to back down the path but kind of stumbled, reaching out for next door's fence to stop herself from falling. A chunky, fresh-faced man in a cream linen suit appeared from nowhere.

'You all right, Marlene?' He put a steadying hand under her elbow. 'I shouldn't have let you come out today.'

He turned to me. 'She's just had an operation. She should be in bed.'

'I can't rest when there's Lord's work to be done.' She sighed a little, brushing her forehead. 'I don't suppose you could spare me a glass of water?' I felt like I was being drawn into a well-rehearsed vaudeville act.

'And perhaps a sit down. Just for a few minutes if you don't mind,' the man pleaded.

Have you ever tried to refuse a sick old lady a glass of water? Well it's not possible. She and her side-kick, Saul, were soon ensconced in our front room drinking tea and eating shortbread – at least I'd finally managed to off-load next door's cat-sitting present.

I offered to drive Marlene home, anything to get her out of the house before Mal rang. 'Oh, no thank you dear, I'll be fine in a few minutes, I don't want to put you to any more trouble.'

'It's no trouble, really,' I grimaced.

'She's right. You should go home. I'll soon get rid of these.' Saul leaned down to pick up Marlene's stack of *The Word*. 'We can't go back to headquarters till we've sold the lot,' he smiled, rather coyly in my direction. Clever, but he wasn't exactly the charismatic Adonis you'd expect to be in charge of inner-city soul recruitment. His hair was mousy not golden. His eyes were not electric blue, more seal grey, and even lacked the courage to meet mine. I almost felt sorry for him.

'How much do they cost?' I knew I wasn't going to get rid of them till I'd parted with some money.

'There's no cover price, we just ask for a small donation. Whatever you can afford. It all goes to a good cause.'

'I bet,' I muttered to myself, disappearing upstairs to fetch my purse. Predictably the only cash I had was a ten pound note. Still it was worth it to be rid of them.

'Oh, you *have* given me strength,' Marlene exclaimed when I brandished the crisp brown note. She gripped my hand, eyes brimming with tears. 'I knew you had a good heart.' It was like I was living proof that there really was a God.

They soon left once Saul had my bribe safely stashed in his back pocket. I quickly flicked through *The Word*, to see what I'd got for my ten pounds: a few articles on missionary projects in Africa, the diary of a New York youth worker and, to my horror, a piece headlined by a photo of Saul himself, about how homosexuals can be cured through prayer. I threw the magazine straight into the recycle bag.

*

I had intended to tell Mal about my guests that evening, I thought she'd have a good laugh about how gullible I'd been, but she was so full of beer and their quarter-final slaughter of the Didsbury Belles that I just never got round to it. I guess I forgot all about Saul and Marlene in the preparations for the festive season.

In a special effort to please Mal, I finally plucked up the courage to tell my mother that I wouldn't be coming home for Christmas. I didn't want to endure another of Mal's winter long sulks: when was I going to own up to our relationship? If she could come out to her bully of a father then surely I could risk the quiet disapproval of my mother. She was right, my mother had stood by a teenage abortion and two counts of breach of the peace without disowning me – she'd survive turkey dinner for one.

Mal, however, was surprisingly unenthused when I told her the good news. She'd already arranged to have dinner with mid-field belter, Jackie – it had become a bit of a tradition. Another tradition was the Christmas Eve bar crawl. I'd pictured a cosy night in front of the gas fire, sipping snowballs and watching a remastered version of *It's a Wonderful Life.* I compromised.

The plan was to start at The Union, share some nostalgic memories of first snogs and embarrassing karaoke debuts, before moving on to the glitzier new bars. We'd wind up, as usual, at Vanilla. At least there'd be no big screen sports, just pounding music that negated the need to make conversation. By that point in the evening all efforts to communicate would be reduced to nodding gestures and leers. Those without partners would make one last ditch attempt to catch the eye of the token straight girl, dancing in a trance next to the bar.

*

The Village was unusually quiet for a Saturday night – I guess most folk were home wrapping novelty dildos and Calvin Cline undies. By the time we'd done Metz, I was feeling a little queasy. Too much beer, not enough crisps. Jackie suggested a McTuckey burger would sort me out.

There was a bit of a scene going down on Chorlton Street. Some pissed-up queen shrieking, 'fuck-off back to hell, yuh Nazi cock-suckers.'

'What's happenin'?' Mal asked, marching into the action backed by two defenders and a goalie.

'This lot reckon we're a disease!' The queen gestured towards a group of clones in maroon puffa-jackets and matching baseball-caps.

'It's a fucking God squad, innit?' Jackie spat, her face contorted with someone slipped me a Babycham syndrome.

'We're just giving out free lunch invitations to the homeless,' one of the brothers explained, pushing a leaflet into Mal's hand. 'Christmas is a time for sharing.'

He had a sickeningly familiar face.

'Megan. It's you,' he bawled, like I was his long lost sister.

No, it's not I tried to convince my puzzled companions, contorting my face into an expression of *never clapped eyes on the nutter in my life.*

'This is the young lady who helped Marlene,' Saul explained to his friends.

'What's he talking about?' Mal demanded.

'Dunno.'

'It's me, Saul. You invited us in for tea, bought one of our magazines, remember?'

'I don't know what he's talking about, let's get out of here.' I started to walk back to the canal.

'Don't worry Megan, I understand. Peter also denied our Lord.' Saul's smug voice trailed after me.

Of course I had to own up to my Good Samaritan act. Most of the girls thought it was hilarious but Mal was furious. How could I have been so stupid? What was I thinking, letting those evil-minded bastards into her home? No wonder we couldn't afford to go on holiday if I donated all our hard-earned savings to a queer-bashing campaign.

She'd finished ranting by the time we got into the taxi. Back home, the silence was only broken by the emergency flat-lining of the burglar alarm. Mal struggled to recall the date of our anniversary, eventually punched in 1301 and stomped straight up to the spare room. I cried myself to sleep, dreaming of my mother's nativity scene.

*

I woke early, feeling surprisingly clear-headed. Thought I'd try a peace offering: French toast and milky coffee. I knocked gingerly on the door, 'Mal, you awake yet?' No answer. I gently opened the door. The bed was empty. So was the rest of the house. The car was gone. And there was a big hole in the pile of presents under the tree.

She'll be back soon, I told myself. Midday there was still no sign. I started to ring round her friends. It didn't take long to track her down. Jackie's. It turned out I wasn't the only one with a secret.

*

Mal had stuck Saul's leaflet on the fridge – a snide dig to start the day. Every time I went to make a cup of tea those bold letters urged, *CELEBRATE!* I didn't feel like I had much to celebrate: my girl friend had left me, my mother wasn't speaking to me and my mates were all having a good time some place else. If I hadn't been feeling so sorry for myself I might have phoned one of them up, invited myself round for a little nut roast and sympathy, but I didn't want to spoil anyone's party with my humbug mood. Well, maybe there was one party I could risk pooping.

I wrestled my mountain bike out from the under-stairs DIY and broken appliances cup-board. Gave it a basic service, then cycled through red brick avenues of flashing fairy lights, searching for The Mission.

It was a large Victorian place. Looked more like a doss house than a place of worship. There were a couple of rusty old vans parked on the flagged front garden. A sodden mattress leaning against the privet.

I stood on the step knocking for a good few minutes before I saw a shadow at the glass. Saul opened the door. A look of confusion and then delight as he took me in.

'Megan, wonderful! You're just in time for

dinner.'

'I'm not here for dinner!'

I had to shove my hands in my pockets to stop myself from slapping his oh so righteous face.

'Well come in anyway. You look upset. You all right?'

'No, I'm not all right, thanks to you.'

'Me? I don't understand.' He talked as if he had a slab of non-spreadable Lurpack in his gob.

'She's left me.'

My jaw jellied. I couldn't control myself any longer. I started to sob. I let him take me into the dark hallway and lead me to an office, where he sat me down on a tan leather couch and put his arm round me.

'It's okay,' he mumbled through my blue-aired accusations. Too tired to fight, I let myself be comforted by his shushing mantra.

*

Later, he bundled my bike into one of their vans and drove me home. He invited himself into the house. Made a pot of tea. Told me how he'd been here himself. Sure, he'd been gay. Had spent years searching for Mr Right, hanging round seedy night clubs, going home with anything in leather and a hint of chest hair. Had his poor heart broken a dozen times.

Then he found Jesus. No more heartache. No more desperate nights chasing a mirage. He had found true love.

'Too good to be true,' I told him.

'Too good not to be,' he replied, his hand on mine.

The heat of his fleshy palm gave me a flashback

to my first date. A conversationally-challenged adolescent called Adam. Back row of the cinema. Some slushy film about a kid dying of leukaemia. The stink of longer lasting deodorant for the active man. I felt suddenly nauseous.

'I think it's time you were going.'

I pulled my hand free from Saul's.

'If you're sure you'll be okay.'

'I'm sure.'

'Well you know where I am if you need a friend.'

'You're not my friend.'

I felt a little mean delivering the blunt truth but I didn't want the guy to get the wrong impression. I wasn't about to open my arms to Jesus or any other member of the opposite sex for that matter.

*

Midweek I got a card. A tasteful water-colour landscape. Inside was a prayer, presumably penned by Saul himself. It asked for the burden of grief to be lifted, for my heart to sing again like a bird in spring. Sick.

*

New Year's Day, Mal turned up in a borrowed van to collect some stuff. She'd phoned ahead to warn me, hoping I'd make myself scarce, but I wasn't going to make it easy for her. She deserved to feel uncomfortable.

I spent the morning shoving her clothes into bin bags – no need to prolong the torture. But when I answered the door to her hangdog expression, I felt a sudden masochistic need to detain her as long as possible. I was prepared to argue ownership of CDs I'd never played if it meant she had to stay an extra minute.

'Didn't you buy me that for our week one anniversary?'

'You hate Abba.'

'So?'

She calmly put the box back into the rack.

'Keep the lot.'

'I don't want your crap.'

I started pulling random CDs off the shelf, flinging them on the settee. They were mostly Mal's anyway.

'Who's that from?' She picked up Saul's card before I could tell her to mind her own business.

'Saul? He's that Jesus freak. Been keeping you company has he? Very cosy.'

'Don't be ridiculous.'

'Offered to cure you, 'as he? Free shag for Jesus?'

'Get the fuck out.'

She left empty-handed. I made sure I was out the next time she called.

*

When I got a second card from Saul, I decided it was time to take action. I drove over to the Mission, planning to shove the cards through the letter-box but Saul saw me arrive. Came out to greet me on the step, a huge grin on his face.

'Megan, I was just thinking about you. Come on

in.'

'No thanks. I just came to return these. I want you to stop writing to me.'

'Fine. Why didn't you just post them?

'Huh?'

'Seems like you keep finding reasons to visit me.'

'I do not.'

'You sure about that? I think you're searching for something. Something I may have the answer to.'

'Get fucked.'

'Just admit it Megan, you're unhappy. You've been let down. Women keep letting you down. You deserve better.'

I backed down the path, my hands over my ears so I didn't have to hear any more of his bullshit.

*

The next day a post-card arrived. It simply said, 'He forgives you.' I tore it up. Sent a reply, 'Jesus is dead!' It seemed to do the trick. No more cards for a week. Then I got a plain white envelope containing a crisp tenner, it was clipped to a curt note: 'We only accept donations given in the true spirit of charity.'

I was furious. Jumped two red lights in my urgency to spit expletives in his pompous face.

'At last,' he greeted me, stepping down onto the drive. 'I was beginning to think you weren't coming.'

'Think you're so fucking clever don't you? Well you can fuck off!

'Still at the anger stage I see.'

He sort of bent towards me in that old fashioned policeman kind of way. The temptation was too much.

My hands automatically fisted, the right one jerking into a neat undercut. I caught him smack on the nose. It felt good till I saw the rush of blood.

'Shit, I'm sorry.' I gave him my balled-up gloves to stench the flow.

'I'll get help.' I pushed open the front door, shouted a hysterical 'Hello?' into the dark corridor.

'There's no one in. I'll be okay.'

I felt terrible. I'd never thumped anyone in my life. Saul's face looked a right mess. I wanted to take him to hospital, make sure I hadn't broken anything. He told me to stop fussing. Said he'd asked for it. He'd think twice before offering the other cheek. We both laughed. I felt a sudden sense of relief. Almost joy.

*

I know what you're thinking: betrayed, lonely, vulnerable – easy prey for the likes of Saul. But let me assure you, I was no push over. No amount of brain washing kindness could have healed my cynicism.

No, it was Jesus himself, woke me up one morning with a smile in my heart even I couldn't deny. Now I wake up every day laughing. Want to know how good that feels? Why don't you come along to one of our meetings? Here, take a leaflet. Jesus says there's room for all of us in his Father's house. He understands why you turn your back on him. He forgives you.

SEAN BURN

Edgecity

@ last aa'v got ma hands on the latest gear; *pornstar* long-sleeved tee yr sposed t pay £39.99 import for – its studded, slinkyblack, with *WATCH MORE PORN* writ large these mental colors; ma hipsters hang down, hang loose; iris blue hair; sweet salomon trainers, no 1 hears me comin. yu gotta have somethin t give yu the edge, gotta stand out in the crowd & aa am 1 ov the girls crowdin around, more each & every day, movin in from madchester, middlesbro' & the smoke monster, even southampton.

   sometimes we're entrance t corn exchange, sometimes doorways ov the lower briggate or back ov macdonalds, off sovereign street & the NCP carkparks, other haunts too – our backs t the cctv, keepin an eye out for coppers vans, for cars & taxis slowin, for that footfall, that glance, that chance, dance ov
   yu wantin business love?
   that walk t back ov café rouge, bar 57, ov hash charlies or the potato king. its a thin line from us t sunnyside ov the street – but we're downtown where the sun dont shine, the litters no collected, & bouncers turn their backs, protect their precious customers, wallin us out as another pimp cuts rough or twat in cheap nylon suits so up t speed he's in yr face obsessin, *'go'an* - this is edgecity – the place where yu dont live so very long. specially no now.

   go'an. yu mustov heard on the radio, read the papers, seen it on tv, tuned into the wispers – journos wavin their fat wads around; a few girls tempted –

then sliced & diced as surely as if it wz... that... man, aa suppose. tho most say devil, demon, beast @ least. aa wont take the tabloids 30 pieces ov silver knowin wichever punters doin this – & it is a punter – he's gonna be lookin for those faces that took the ink-fingered cash; he's gonna make it much much harder on em lasses.

another pissin it cold winters night, rain thru ma fringe – can hardly see folks queuein for nightpubsclubs streamline cabs – teeth chatterin as aa 1/2 sing t maself – yu know those songs that speak, that r yu wen yu 1st hear em, searin thru. aa rub ma arms, walk up & down t keep from freezin over, move t the next doorway, hang back in shadow, no showin ma face. always keep ma make-up t a minimum – jes a touch ov kohl – a wee line round ma green eyes, glitterdust bringin up ma cheekbones wen yu get in close – last thing yu wanna do is look a tart; shoot yr mouth off like 1 – that way yr no gonna... survive. aa dont put maself out, they gotta come t me – gotta step right up, look me in the eye, make their pitch – if aa dont like wat they say aa walk, dont like how theyre dressed or how their eyes agitate movin up & down ma sleek muscled thigh aa'll walk. accept their look & aa name ma price –

10 quid a handjob
20 quid a blowjob
anals 40
80 without rubbers & aa'll even piss on yu
– aa dont do owt else

its all about keepin yr looks, & yr locks – locks in place on yr head, yr heart, yr mind, yr... whatever – aa'm definitely no cheap end ov the street. those poor bastards up spencer place – their heroingaze, essexthigh boots – practically walkin the white line down middle ov the road, aa mean we all put ourselves on the line – but theyre stoppin traffic – thats no ma game

yu a bodybuilder? yu work out? tell me wat yu like? like it fast eh honey? christ – look @ the size ov yr head - aa dont mean t be... rude but its mmm mmmm mmmmmm... massive

hopscotchin the cracks ov underland; no 1's gonna scotch those rumors; make mine a glenmorangie – wash it down before aa get back t job in hand or up ma crack; these days hearts a little faster; keep yr eyes a little wider; face away from the wall no into it; if yu gotta – run; theyre no gonna block me in.

been out here year & a 1/2 & 17 now & a pro & theres plenty younger – but wen yu look close yu see theyve aged past me, eyesockets crazed into a crowsfoot mess & yu know these lasses r dyin down the line, throwin caution t our pennine wind, they'll take anythin. aa take it a little easier but aa still take it.

changed ma looks, ma locks 1st enterin edgecity – pullin the wu tang clan beanie down tight t ma skull as aa begged into crushed styrofoam cup. learnt ma lessons. findin this ways easier. home papers said theyd dredged the trent & some local lakes for ma cold corpse, musta been some other body.

'home' never cd take me – always wz walkin hard-on; a walk-in fucksuck fest; the harder they fuck, the harder aa get. always wz the odd 1 out, the 1 coloured sock in yr mix, the tabasco in yer bloody mary, spike in yer homebrew, ladder in yer stockin, tilt-switch in yer mercury, scratch on yer 12 inch, always wz the 1 in yer sisters size 12, messin with her dress & hairset, yr mindset, & the brickbuilt midlandways – their flatlands, gassed beer, warm gear, giant coolin towers, their pallets for sale, lumpy sandpits, mis-stacked breezeblocks, & their bring & buy nobodies buryin the hatchet; oh how they buried the hatchet. never cd live down puttin that dress on wen aa wz 12 – longin for that silk-finish, the bright colors, how they caught the light, felt so tight, right, neat genst ma skin – wore it everytime aa cd. knew wat aa wanted; skipped school – robbed skirts & make-up – hid maself in this world brighter than em dusty redbricks ov the jobless, the hopeless, the brick-in hand *yu must be fokkin jokin wearin a bloody dress for fokks sake* while secretly they give us the eye goin *not bad* – thinkin *looks better than ma sister & she's a right slag,* aye probably cos yu wz shaggin her – aa'm givin head that cdnt be bettered but wen theyd all done me, they did me, beaten, thrown in the trent, near drowned & hounded outta town – yr no son ov mine, ov ours – & still gettin eyed & on the rent – specially wen aa learnt t hide ma dick, bind it in tight – play it coy, get em t buy me toys, if it got too much ma pay-off wz t give the best head – like ever, & for those special men – ma tight, hot, young arse – & me swearin it always wz virgin t em. aa headed up the m1 fast as my 2" spiked-heels cd, hearin the street ov leeds wz paved – least thats somethin. & earnin ma trade, learnin the hard way; & now? everythins gettin close – can feel the storm risin. talk ov the towns how maniacs on the loose, bodies floatin, theres signs, & even tho aa'm keepin eye out for all this aa gotta have ma bread & eat it.

so aa walk ahead – knowin the road – feelin it under ma soles – bout 1/2way down the pavement changes – yu smell the rutted dark where they cant be arsed puttin in lights save those kickin off down sides ov pubs. we calls this place underland; on account ov how we're all but buried anyway. its a howl ov 70's concrete, a cruel blade ov darkness stabbin the heart outta edgecity – intercities in flight overhead on victorian viaducts, their roar descendin down here t us under its arches, keepin our eyes t the next 1 round the block – a winnin ticket or wacko enough t take yu out without eye-in-the-sky even zoomin in. been down here so long its hard t stay outov shadows – & thats wat mostov us r – shadow. no substance t em. the citizens – who want somethin a little harder, a little harsher than *south ov the border*, *dv8* or the rest. aa'v been down here so long margin-walkin streets & canal & waterfront & blondewood bars ov edgecity; that aa'v lost all... wat... self?... control?... whatever.

prefer it up on boar lane, yu'v some chance ov runnin, a stack ov alleys, taxis hangin round – but cops keep edgin us towards river, its like they want us in the aire – its like the cops fuckin want us underwater. right now the margins r shiftin – floodins worse this year – a battle between rain & concrete & the waters winnin – down here the only place t turn, t take yr man is round back all those new apartments – quarter ov a million quid & still they claim they dont have extra tenner

cum yet? look luv – aa'm sorry. yu know aa'm good; but a girl like me – aa gotta work – now if only yu'd got that other tenner – yu'd get a reeeally good time so dark down here – lights r up t no good, & yu know the cars nosin round r for yu – whether theyre gonna pay or pray or prey, yr their sport & they want yu t pay only yu dont know how much. its no easy off neville street, meadow lane doublin back past asda t bridge-end – & still the dark waters ov the aire r lap, lap, lappin... their midnight colors same as the bruisin on wat remained ov that poor lasses flesh. they've pulled out 3 bodies, & claim anothers disappeared – damned if aa'm gonna be next. but aa need the cash t survive. & the bastards from that other place r no gonna take me alive & aa darent do dole cos theyll find wat else aa'm wanted for & cuttin school & havin nothin else, no other skills, no routes t a bit ov gold.

& zeroin t this slow night pissin it down – wz a night like this wen angie – oh angie, angie, angie – yu poor sweet fuck. rainin hard – aire floodin streets down @ the bottom & that wz wen aa last saw her – angie – angel we called her – she wz another like me – walkin along singin t herself – we shared 70p ov chips – she never cd keep much down – jesusfuck poorbastardchrist – fishin her out after river went down – @ 1st they didnt think she wz like the others – aa mean she wz blue & bruised but that wz stuff in the river batterin her t fuck wen she got jammed in hard genst the pier & all those branches – aa remember the sirens goin but they wz way too late – nothin anyone cd do, oh ma poor sweet angel.

press buzzin like flies & plainclothed coppers comin round – *nothin t fear, luv – anythin yu see pass it on, anonymous like. heres ma card.* fuck that – aa'm no stupid – he's watchin, he's lookin, he's givin me the creeps – #1 had a mess ov fishin line tyin her arms up – these engineers found her rammed genst arches on granary wharf – she wz all wound up – & #2 had fishhooks thru her tits, leadshot in her throat, & now poor angie they wont say wat it wz, but theres wispers goin round – its somethin t do with fishin, with fish.

& pissin it now like it wz then & aa'm with no make-up t run but ma jeans clingin right t ma arse so's yu can see ma g string thru – most ov those pullin know who aa am – a few surprised looks but most times nothin heavy – theyre usually too shocked t do anythin; actually its kinda warped-sweet – aa mean these guys they got wives & they all come t me, no the other girls – like if aa'm 1/2 made up as girl then it dont – yu know – challenge anythin – & theyre doin it with eyes 1/2 closed imaginin aa'm girl – pretendin its jes cos ov how their wives wont take anal; or how aa give better head – but deeeep down, aa mean inside – yu knows how its MORE than that.

& aa'm in *hot stuffs* kebabs for some warmth – trades non-existent & that darkness down there ov rents givin me gooseflesh thru worn denim. ... & then it happens: - some bugger steals a chip, aa swing round t see this bastards lopsided winnin grin, wdnt call him pretty, but theres somethin bout him, his eyes, cant help maself... start losin it, aa'm shakin like a girl – aa mean if aa dont snap outov it aa wont be able t get back on top & spin it past him – yu gotta keep it strict: *yu lookin 4 business...?* – nothin changes in his face as aa ask – he jes nods @ door, aa turn t lead way & he swipes another me salt&vinegars, gettin outside he wispers *dont want sex,* aa start t anger – *aa'm workin, aa'm fuckin...* he goes *sssssssshhhhh* – strokes hair from ma eyes – no 1 ever does that – says *its ok, aa got money, aa mean if its that important* – flashin this wad – so subtle like it wz meant only 4 me like no 1 else cd see – like theres magic @ his fingers. repeats he'll pay but he dont want sex. he dont look like 1 ov em dirty buggers who only wanna watch, dont look like 1 ov em saddos either

yu jes wanna talk? its still 40 for the 1/2 hour

smilin t maself knowin aa'v stung him – theres been no trade all night – he kindov makes 40 appear – aa know that sounds tacky – but that huge wad becomes 4 notes – cant work out wats goin on - & in a game like this yu gotta read the signs, read it wrong & yr like those poor bastards floatin past – sick, bloody sick – cant read him – he dont look like 1 ov those who wants t talk – he looks sorted.

& he dont look a christian – christ, that 1 guy, mervyn his name wz – kept comin t me – weeks he wz, gettin down t his huge off-white knickers, he jes wdnt/cdnt do it but sweatin & shakin, false teeth rattlin & rollin, aa'm tryin no t piss maself as he goes quiet like he's jes cum sayin this is genst his god then dressin again, every other night for weeks aa get ma cash on route back t his sadflat jes off tetleys – & every time aa get t no do it indoors, kept warm for 40 quid as he gets off on this godtrip. last aa heard wz how he scrawled *spires point upwards* all round his bedroom, *spires point upwards* painted down the stairwell, *spires point upwards* on his front door – he ran down the street in those oversized markies knickers, stopped @ the parishchurch where somehow he gets in & up, up, up, comin out some 50 feet above the ground shoutin *spires point upwards* @ coppers below, @

wich point he's up & over parapet shoutin *spires point up* & coppers below breakin necks & godmans desperately flappin wings like the cartoons, aimin beyond that coppers gravestone only gravities too much, sucks him to ground, some far-out gargoyle splattered all over the tarmac ov kirkgate, poor fuck.

but this sleight ov hand-man, this widemouthed, gaptoothed, magicman, *pierre* he says wen aa ask his name & wisper mine quiet – they never repeat it back right, keep a little bit ov maself that way – but he repeats ma name perfect, accent & all as we're walkin t alley back ov *arts bar* & small-talkin, & christ, his eyes, its in his eyes, his hypno-eyes wich he keeps flashin @ us; but aa'v his 40 quid & all he wants is talk, we pass *arts* & into the next where he ups & buys me a double rum & coke – freaky, how cd he know its ma favourite drink – that starts t creep me out – but he looks deep in ma eyes, sayin *its alright*, & aa stop thinkin maybe aa shd walk... christ knows its been a slow night, searchin out eyes ov that 1 last punter seekin redemption shag, & least aa'm in the warm on double rum & coke, the cash tight inside ma trainers. pierres wedged us in back ov bar, small table, wee bench genst the wall, safe here, loadsa folks seein wat we're up t. pierre all gentle, hands under ma chin, tippin ma head back t look again into his cat-eyes, a kindov siamese slategrey. he holds ma gaze, opens mouth

aa... aa know how those lasses died

ohsweetjeez. as aa look deep into his soft poolin eyes ma lips work a personalprayer, a loopedline ov some far-off song replayin across mind

WAYNE CLEWS

Eczema in Gothenburg

I'd lied to get here. Lied and thieved but, well, that's how I made my living. Not exactly what I'd imagined after passing my Masters degree, but where did I ever think that would get me?

Although I was here, pale and shivering, the stale taste of early morning gin in my mouth, my luggage was nowhere to be found. Copenhagen they said. Sorry. Be with you later today, where are you staying? I couldn't remember what he'd told me. A hotel, obviously, vaguely recalling he'd said it was by a park, near the university. Did that help? No. They gave me a card, asked me to call when I had some semblance of a mental facility, adding in their toneless, perfect English that I would miss the bus to Gothenburg if I didn't get a move on.

It was April, and cold. Foolishly thinking it would be as spring-like here as Manchester, I was clad in a flimsy piece of Duffer which, needless to say, didn't belong to me. Lit a cigarette to stay warm as I queued to have my non-existent luggage stowed on the coach. It began to snow.

Technically, I was at my grandmother's funeral. Only met her once; there was some row or other about a record player in 1975. Things rather escalated, as they do in my family, and she never spoke to my mother for ten years. Still, what you don't have, you don't miss, do you? Like when Channel 4 wouldn't work on our old telly. You get by. Anyway, she isn't dead, as far as I'm aware. Just a helpful excuse to get off work for the week. No-one ever counts how many grandmother's funerals you go to. Eileen was only being spiteful, anyway, in not giving me the time off from the theatre. We only had a drama on, something that Rosemary Leach had re-mortgaged her house to produce. Just one hundred and fifty in for the opening night in a venue that seated almost two thousand. Shame really. I always liked Rosemary Leach. Remember her on *Jackanory*, reading ghost stories by Helen Cresswell, but I'm like that. Who else would recall such nonsense?

God, I needed a drink. Got funny looks on the plane when I ordered a strong G&T. I know it was only 8am, but this was almost a holiday, wasn't it? That's what he said; our first holiday together. Forgot the fact that he was actually working here, painting some new amusement park. Scenic artist, he called himself, theatre sets, murals, that sort of gubbins.

Really was snowing now. I considered my footwear, the old New Balance trainers with holes in. Perhaps not quite right for a Scandinavian blizzard. Could hardly see a thing, apart from the odd cautionary sign warning of moose. I rubbed my neck, it was still sore, and I shrank with embarrassment and wished I had never come.

Eczema, I would say, you know what it's like. Perhaps the only time I've been thankful for having a skin disease. He wouldn't question it.

Arrived at the bus station. Saw a stand selling hot dogs and felt vaguely nauseous. Be fine after a drink. Think I was supposed to be meeting him in a bar at lunchtime. An Irish pub, he'd said, almost proudly, bragging of his impoverished descent. They get bloody everywhere, I thought, lighting another fag and drawing my jacket tightly around me, feeling a chill sweat lace my skin.

I didn't notice the city then, the boulevards crossing the river, the elegant square, the unusual beauty of a city sunken beneath snow. Didn't get that back home any more. Not in Salford. But then you didn't get much of anything in Salford.

Found the bar, couldn't be more than one Irish bar in Gothenburg, surely. Barely open. Felt the warmth shudder through me as I unnecessarily ordered my drink in stilted Svensk. Needn't have bothered. Bloke behind the bar was from Portadown with one of those nasal Ulster accents. I ignored his attempts to engage me in banter and skulked away to a corner. Another fag, another rub at my neck. Must stop doing that. The cold beer warmed me, began to feel awake rather than the comatose state I'd been in since the cab had arrived, beeping outside my flat at 5am. Almost missed it, what with getting rid of one thing and another. Couldn't really be arsed to tell the truth, but I was expected and had never been to Sweden before. Still, one pub is very much like another. Could be anywhere.

A trip to the loo. As I suspected, it hadn't gone. Eczema, I said to myself, rehearsing, thanks for pointing it out. Wasn't convincing. Not even to me. And I'd always been a good liar. All those times I'd said to Eileen how I really couldn't understand why the bar takings were down. Angelic face, butter wouldn't melt, whilst I had four grand in the bank and was out every night of the week. Ask my liver.

And then I met him. The artist. Hadn't really

planned on it but what with the beer goggles and the cheap pills he had, felt obliged to go through with it. Strange looker, really, as I perceived the next day when I'd woken, blearily drunk on his futon. Had to rifle through his post to remember his name. Somehow ended up seeing him. One of those arrangements you blunder into without much thought at all and then find yourself obliged to go round on a Tuesday and have sex when all you want to do is stay in with a couple of bottles of wine for company and watch *Changing Rooms*. Said I drank too much as well, after three months. I do. I know that but am I really supposed to have sex *sober?* Not sure if I ever have. Well, there was that time... those public toilets in Belle Vue some years back but that was an accident.

All we do is get pissed, he'd said.

And? I thought. Didn't say it. Couldn't tell him I found him boring when he was sober. Couldn't tell him I found everything boring when I was sober. Truth is, that's all we ever have had, really, the drunkenness. He didn't know the half of it. The times I'd lied. 'Visiting my parents' when actually I had caught a dose of crabs from a Dutchman in Wythenshawe Park. Never trust a Dutchman, that's my motto, although he did give me a lift home. Can't recall what I was doing in Wythenshawe Park now. An odd destination at the best of times.

In fact, I'd even had illicit sex whilst out with him one night. In the loos. Salubrious, I know, but he never noticed, even in spite of the speck of jism that I had neglected to wipe from my chin. I don't swallow, never have. All he had observed was that it was my round.

I got another drink. He would be here soon, how nice to see me, offering a fag, buying a pint, asking what I had been up to. I wouldn't tell him. Couldn't, could I? We'd go to the hotel, wherever it was, and I would have a hot shower. Must stink of sex as well as booze. Can't really blame the air hostess for sneering at me. And then, of course, we would have sex. Perfunctory frottage, weary blow jobs, but thankfully, he always comes first.

And then he might say, What have you done to your neck?

I would lie, of course. I wouldn't tell him that I had woken up to find a man twice my age in bed next to me. Brian from Wigan. A bloated, hairy electronic engineer, which he had told me somewhat proudly. Where he came from, besides Wigan I mean, I had no idea. But he had left me a lovely memento. Perhaps the largest, most disgusting bruise of a lovebite that it has ever been my misfortune to wear.

Thankyou, I had said, now fuck off, as he waved his telephone number at me.

I hitched my collar tightly to my neck. He would be here soon, asking if I had brought his pills, buying a drink, like I said, and it would inevitably happen.

What have you done to your neck?

Eczema, I would say soberly, Gothenburg doesn't agree with me.

JULIA DAVIS

The Potter

It started on the first day with the clay. Looking down at the lump of brown on the huge trestle table, I had a sense of contentment. Resolution.

The other women happily kneaded, chiselled, worked their pots. But I was the new girl on the block – they'd all been making jolly spotty teapots, cavernous casserole dishes, neat-lidded jewellery jars for months. In some cases *years*. And then there was me, and my lump of clay.

'Start by just working the shape you think about a lot – don't worry what the end result is,' my patient tutor batted her pale lashes at me encouragingly.

It began – the boat shape – a ship upon water and well, somehow, inside water too. The clay responded to every touch of my fingers – a pinch here, a subtle stroke there and the imprints were left exactly engraved. Soon I discovered how to make the sides of my boat shape move and it became like the inside of two very large lips.

Sandra interrupted my boat-making:

'Interesting shape – keep going now – and if you want real smoothness there's this tool'. She offered me a kidney-shaped green plastic object which fitted perfectly into the palm of my hand, together with a metal shaped kidney, exactly the same size but with a fine serrated edge.

'So, where would you like to start?'

Patiently she tucked her pretty golden bob behind her ears and ran her hands in readiness on her overall – we all wore them. I copied her, smoothed my hands impatiently over my blue striped piny and pointed to the inside of the large lips.

'In there.'

'Okay. Like this.'

She waved the serrated edged kidney in front of my eyes.

'Roughen the surface with this,' her eyes twinkled. Mine did too.

She scraped. Ridges appeared all over the soft brown innards.

'This is very therapeutic... you smooth very slowly.'

She changed the metal kidney for the green, soft, flexible plastic one.

'Take this over the edges and you'll get a perfectly smooth surface.'

I snatched the green kidney off her in anxious anticipation.

'Now, be patient, remember.'

Green kidney in hand, I slowly caressed the serrated insides. I gasped. The soft edges licked the sides and I went around the whole of the inside, deeper and deeper to the bottom of the boat.

The afternoon wore on; the insides became smoother and silkier. She was mine this boat, these lips, this –

'Never mind,' an experienced potter sidled onto the high stool next to mine.

'Never mind what?' I quizzed. Her hair was dyed

blond, she was a busy sort, advising her fellow students of the rights and wrongs of potting. I seethed with anger.

'Well, soon you'll be able to make useful things, once you get the hang of it.'

I cradled my boatlips protectively.

'Oh, no, you don't understand, I want to make this, I don't care if it doesn't, well, get used.'

The next week I found my boat again. Covered in a plastic bag it looked just like the other creations. I carried it to my bench once more and unwrapped it carefully. The shape was set, ready for the next stage. The glazing room.

My fellow potters moved out of my way. Sandra tweaked her bob behind her ear nervously and I plunged boatlips into a huge bucket of transparent glaze. I wanted it to look and feel wet and so checked out with Know-all that I was doing the right thing.

Know-all eyed me suspiciously.

'It'll look transparent rather than wet – but if that's your idea of describing it I suppose...' she trailed off.

Sandra bobbed round the corner again, twirling a couple of small knives in her delicate fingers.

'Everything okay?' she asked, smiling.

I nodded. Know-all shrugged.

The next stage was the firing and I would have to leave my treasure a whole day in the hot fiery recess of the kiln, heating up until the glaze spread all over the innards, sliding over every nook and cranny.

Six months on and the collection has flourished.

Coloured in flaming reds and moody greens, the shapes are all perfectly smooth inside and moulded to give, well, complete satisfaction. My pieces are seriously sought after now, written about, collected and exhibited.

I've become known as that vagina, fanny, pussy woman.

SIMON DE COURCEY

Lick

Mascarpone Ice Cream
Serves 4
Preparation: 20 mins, incl. freezing time
Ingredients:
500g (1lb 2oz) mascarpone
15ml (1 tbsp) lemon juice
125g (4oz) fine icing sugar
4 egg yolks
45ml (3 tbsp) Marsala or Grand Marnier
Ground cinnamon bark as topping
30ml (2 tbsp) secret ingredient particular
to Guiseppe's Ice Cream

He tucked a stick-em note on his father's window wipers, telling him that the van had an oil leak, then climbed back into his own vehicle. Knocking the fluffy bear rear-view mirror toy as he clambered onto the seat, he had to grab it by the crotch to stop it swaying. It was a shit day; the clouds looked like stale candy floss and Guiseppe was in no mood for being busy. Helene had left him some god-awful sandwiches splattered to a plate with cling-film but he just tipped them into the swing bin and lit a fag. He had made good coffee, though. Fresh.

To prepare the ice cream, beat all the ingredients thoroughly in a bowl and preferably with a good metal whisk. The mixture should have a silky smooth consistency.

Guiseppe decided the park was a good bet for a Wednesday afternoon, even though the weather looked temperamental. There would be some old duffs around and their grandchildren. It was, after all, only two weeks to the summer holidays and some kids would be dodging school anyway. He could sell some. Enough to please his father.

'Bloody clutch.' It was always sticking.

The two vans were going to be given to him when he reached thirty. That was two years away. His father had said last Christmas over dinner, drowning out the Queen in a drunken state, that he would sign the business over. That hadn't been spoken about since but it was on the cards. Did Guiseppe want to spend all his life selling fucking ice cream? That was the question. Did he want to let his father down? A catastrophic choice.

As the van left the back of the house, three lads stood around whilst Guiseppe hopped out to padlock the big steel gates. One of them threw him a middle finger as he drew himself back into the driver's seat. He was going to give them a bit of a taste of their own, but he paused. One of them was only nine, maybe ten. He pretended he hadn't seen them but as he drove past, the same lad called out, 'Fucking tosser. We'll have them wheels mate!'

Guiseppe couldn't hold back, and threw a clear two fingers through the side window. He let his fingers linger there a few seconds too long, just for good measure. The pleasure was the same as holding a cigarette.

Place the mixture in a large suitable container and then freeze, beating at regular intervals of approximately an hour and a half, to ensure a smooth result and to stop the formation of ice crystals which impair the taste.

The park was quiet and he kicked off his trainers whilst he waited, switching on his MP3 player and humming to some chill-out piece with his headphones on. He used to lie down in the van but his father once caught him and beat him over the head because the vehicle looked unattended.

At about three twenty-five, he watched countless streams of school uniforms, black blazers with green ties, walk and scream past. He was busy for about fifteen minutes and then nothing. He smiled at the uniforms, it was his old school. He didn't want to go there but Helene insisted. She usually got to make most decisions. Guiseppe knew she was able to work her way into his father's mind. She knew the one and only password: sex.

He had found his father's porn collection once, in a carry-all in the wardrobe. Spent ages peering over the ten or eleven mags, wondering which girls his father longed for, curious which ones made his father change his breathing. Looking to see which magazines looked the most fingered.

'Rocket Shooter? Ninety pence. Cheers, young man.'

Today Guiseppe had his own porn tucked away inside the van, slipped down by the side of the deep freeze. He thought his father had seen it last summer, possibly at a festival where both vans were needed. He thought the atmosphere was artificial that day, as if the old man were travelling some mental distance away from Guiseppe. As if he didn't want to be a father.

Anyway, that was then and tough shit, Guiseppe was twenty-eight – albeit a very young looking twenty-eight – and he didn't care what his father thought or knew. He took out one mag and pushed the others further back into the dark. He looked at the pictures slowly, carefully, not leafing through them, but savouring each one. He stroked himself and used an empty ice cream tub at the end of his thoughts.

Three minutes later.

'Two ninety nines – that'll be one-eighty.' Close call.

Mascarpone ice cream is best served with summer fruit which draws out the subtle flavours and richness of the ice cream.

At about six, he began to make his way from the park. The van stalled twice and at one point he thought he was going to have to use the mobile to ring his father up to come and sort the bloody thing out. Guiseppe decided to take Route Three home tonight. Monday had been One and Tuesdays were always Two, no matter what the weather. And Route Three was good. Lots of council estates, few curtains. He could just park up and wait. Maybe watch.

As he turned past the petrol station at Blackley, he watched a gang of lads spray paint a war memorial. One of the lads kicked another and their attention left the bright pink statue. They ran along a dirt track, laughing. Guiseppe watched them for as far as his eyes would allow along the path.

At Alkrington, he parked on one of the long avenues that faced the large houses. It was nearly eight thirty. The house occupants opposite were having their evening meal late and sat in the front room, plates on their knees, watching something on the box. Pretty typical family. Nice boy, about sixteen, maybe seventeen – moody, spotty, even from a distance. Spotty but cute.

At eight forty, the mother drew the front room curtains quickly. She was trying to shield the television from the sunlight. Something good was on. Guiseppe tried to remember the week's television guide from his head. He was sure it was a movie. A Bond film.

Moving the van to a quiet avenue, he spotted something worth waiting for. A council house with flaky pebble dashing, an upstairs window, light on; a half-drawn curtain and a young lad topless, probably getting changed. Guiseppe sat himself in the back of the van. Nine twenty and going dark slowly. A smooth body. Nice. Yeah, he'd been here before, three weeks before, same lad. Would he perform like last time? Guiseppe got himself all comfy, reaching up for the empty ice cream tub as before, a nearly empty ice cream tub.

Guiseppe's Ice Cream   guarantees extra smoothness.

At ten thirty-eight, Guiseppe hauled himself into the yard and parked the van. The yard lights weren't on, which got him thinking. As he headed into the house, he could hear his father's voice in the hall. There was another voice, one he didn't recognise, a man, probably in his forties. Helene was not to be heard. Guiseppe figured she was maybe in the living room since the telly was on, real quiet behind a closed door.

'So where is he?' The voice was clearly angry.

'He's finishing work. Not that it matters.' His father sounded defiant. Not good.

'Well, he's a bloody perv and if I catch him round our way again, I'll break his fucking legs.'

There was a silence, his father was standing his ground. Maybe thinking.

'No son of mine is a Peeping Tom, mate. You've just got it in for us. I know your type, blame the Italians. Probably compensating for a small dick.'

'Why don't you come closer and say that. Go on, pop a punch and see what happens.'

No noise, the hall clock drawing out time, breaking the silence.

'I'm gonna call the police if he comes round again. Be warned.' The man's voice had slowed a little, perhaps a little calmer.

'What proof you got, eh? You making accusations at my son, my family. What proof?'

'I don't need no proof. I saw him, looking in my son's bedroom window. Watching with them eyes. Disgusting perv.'

'This is probably mistake, you make mistake.'

His father is gritting his teeth; Guiseppe could feel the anger.

'Why don't you have a tub of my ice-cream huh? I got a special tub somewhere. Mascarpone Ice Cream somewhere in freezer down in the cellar. You like, huh? You ever tried it? You ever had our ice cream, huh?

You'll love it!'

'Well, I...'

'Wait here, I'll get you some and then you go and forget the whole thing.'

Hearing his father's steps, Guiseppe stepped into the coat cupboard and waited in total darkness.

He remembered, as a small lad of ten, going down to the freezer room. It was dark and smelled of moss which grew on the cellar walls. He had lost a toy, an action figure, and had gone quietly down the stone steps to look. He remembered seeing his father on his knees with his back to the door, to Guiseppe, shaking, looking down at where you are not supposed to look. Magazines scattered on the floor in front of the man. He remembered an empty ice cream tub on the floor, a nearly empty ice cream tub.

Guiseppe's Ice Cream is made with a recipe that is generations old, a well-kept secret, handed down through the family.

'Here, you take this. You enjoy it and forget the whole thing. You must have been mistaken.'

Guiseppe heard Helene cough in the living room and his father shut the front door. His father muttered something.

'Bloody clumsy son of mine.'

In the darkness, Guiseppe knocked an old toy that was once his, stuffed in the coat cupboard. It was an old action figure, some soldier. He heard his father pass the cupboard. He had to grab the figure by the crotch to stop it falling.

LEWIS GILL

At Fifteen

At fifteen you love money.
At fifteen you love wanking.
At fifteen, if you got the chance to wank for money, you'd go for it.
At fifteen other people are in charge.
At fifteen other people take the blame.
At fifteen you're not old enough to be responsible for your actions, so it's *never* your fault.

*

When Lawrence's parents went on what they called a 'second honeymoon' he was sent to stay with his brother Kristian. At fifteen he wasn't trusted to stay home alone. Lawrence didn't really mind – his brother was loaded.

Kristian had some kind of big media job. Something flashy in TV. He only seemed to be in his office about twice a week, the rest of the time he would spend at home just lolling around.

Lawrence was dropped off on a wet Saturday afternoon. His parents only stayed long enough to say hello, thanks and goodbye. It was obvious to Kristian and Lawrence that their mother couldn't wait to get their father all to herself for a week in the Lake District and now she knew that her youngest was in the capable hands of her eldest, she wasn't going to waste any time hanging around.

As soon as the car was out of sight, Kristian

informed his brother that he was having a few people round that evening. People from work. At first Lawrence's eyes lit up at the thought of a party but then when he found out that it was just an extension of Kristian's office hours he lost interest. He was soon resigned to spending the night in his room with the remote control. Not such a bad thought when he remembered Kristian's array of 'pay per view' channels.

Lawrence usually stayed in the huge games room downstairs that housed a pool table, pinball machine and an enormous Dolby Digital Surround sound TV. Lawrence slung his bag over his shoulder and proceeded to make his way there but Kristian stopped him.

'Not your room anymore mate. You're upstairs now.'

'How come?' Lawrence asked, disappointed.

'I needed it for work stuff, look.'

Kristian opened the door to what used to be the games room and as Lawrence peered in he saw it was full from floor to ceiling with electric equipment. TVs, CDs, DVD players and desks that looked like switchboards were all packed in together.

'It's now my editing suite,' Kristian gloated.

Lawrence was impressed, but was also concerned as to where all the other stuff had gone. Kristian could see this.

'Don't be worried, it's all in the loft now. I got it converted.'

'Show us then!'

They climbed the two flights of stairs. Lawrence was blown away when he saw all the gear. He was left alone to unpack and lay down on the bed to survey his temporary new home. He looked at the wide-screen TV and hoped that Kristian still subscribed to all the porn channels.

*

Around eight o'clock, Kristian's guests started to arrive. Their muffled voices woke Lawrence. As soon as he sat up his stomach rumbled. He realised that he'd slept all afternoon and hadn't eaten anything since breakfast. He ventured downstairs in the direction of the voices. As he pushed the door of the dining room, the smell of cigarette smoke mixed with a heady whiff of sickly after-shaves slowly enveloped him. There were about seven people in the room. He strained his neck to try and make eye contact with Kristian who was talking to someone by the kitchen.

Lawrence was spotted by a man in his twenties wearing a mismatched array of designer sportswear and a heavy silver chain around his neck.

'Kristian, mate, I think this is yours,' the man yelled, putting his arm on Lawrence's shoulder to guide him through the group towards his brother.

Kristian looked up. ' 'Ere everyone, this is my brother Lawrence, I told you all he was coming to stay for the week.'

The man with the silver chain lifted his hands from Lawrence's shoulders and did a mock game show pose, with fingers outstretched, showing him off as the star prize.

'Lawrence this is... well, everyone.'

The group all looked in his direction and either

nodded or greeted him verbally. Some looked a little too long for his liking.

'I was just wanting to get summat to eat, Kris.'

'Oh right,' Kristian fished around in his pocket and produced a twenty pound note.

'Phone and order yourself a pizza or Chinese, whatever.'

'You got one for me, Kris, or is it just brotherly love?' joked another man in a baseball cap.

'You make enough money already, Rudy.'

Everyone sniggered, except Lawrence.

As Lawrence was leaving he thought he heard his name being mentioned. He hesitated behind the half-closed door, curious to know what was being said about him.

'How old *is* he then?'

Lawrence recognised the voice of the guy in the baseball cap.

'Turned fifteen last month...' Kristian answered, but Lawrence didn't wait to hear the rest of the sentence – his stomach wanted food.

*

Forty five minutes later a delivery bike pulled onto the driveway and the doorbell rang.

As Lawrence bundled himself down the stairs he heard a woman's voice ask, 'Someone else come to play?'

'Just pizza for Lawrence,' Kristian replied.

Lawrence exchanged money for pizza at the door then went to get a bottle opener for his beer. The dining room was now packed with Kristian's guests. All except one, were men. Sat on the sofa were two guys in their late teens: one wearing twisted denim the other sporting a bandanna. Stood nearby was a broad-shouldered man in his mid thirties, thick with gold jewellery, which made him appear uncouthly wealthy. He was talking to a younger man who was trying to act older, adopting over the top, masculine mannerisms that only made him appear more boyish. The pair gulped beer from bottles. It seemed to Lawrence that one was subliminally being taught how to act by the other.

Around the table sat the man in the baseball cap and two other younger lads, maybe only nineteen years in age, but all leery and laughing loudly. Stood by them was Kristian, the man in designer sportswear who had brought Lawrence into the room and the only woman amongst the group. The woman was around the same age as the man draped in gold jewellery. She too was well decorated but what caught Lawrence's eye was her low cut dress. He found himself staring at her and trying to make out what she was saying. He was too far away to hear what was being said so he tried to lip-read instead. He thought he saw her mouth the word 'FUCK' and this turned him on immensely. He was envious that she was talking to Kristian and not him. He considered staying in the room but didn't want to feel in the way.

As Lawrence started to climb the stairs, bottle opener in hand, he saw Kristian leading his guests into the living room and caught his eye.

'We're gonna be in the living room from now on mate so if you need anything from the kitchen – its free,' said Kristian.

'Okay.'

'Lawrence...'

'Yeah?'

'Don't disturb us though mate.'

'No, I won't. I'm goin' to bed now. Night.'

'Night mate.'

Lawrence went back up to the loft to feast on the extra large Mexican hot and flick through the stations. His mind began to wander downstairs to Kristian's guests: a bunch of lads, apparently loaded, though none of them looked particularly bright enough to make a decent living. In fact they reminded him of the scally boys he went to school with. They continued to occupy his mind while the film began to blur into the background. Were they discussing work downstairs or was it just an out of hours party? What did they all actually do for a living? Who was the boss? Where did all their money come from? And why only one woman?

Women.

Lawrence remembered the porn channels and quickly fumbled around for the remote. He remembered from last time he stayed that the foreign ones were the only ones that were screened before midnight, because of the time difference, so he looked for those first. He eventually found one and started to get undressed. He turned off the light and when he got under the covers, realised he would be needing some tissue paper. He hopped out of bed and, without even thinking, opened the door and went down the stairs. It was only when he got to the bathroom that he realised he hadn't put any clothes on and that the house was swarming with strangers.

He pulled the cord and the light came on, reflecting all around the room in the tiny mosaic mirrors that covered the walls. His reflection was divided into a thousand little pieces. He studied them proudly. His legs were supple, his thighs firm, above them his cock hung flaccid and his balls loose. His stomach was flat and his chest rounded out a little, starting to take shape. His jet black hair shone crisply in the bright light and his hazel eyes were wide and darting about, taking in all the miniature images of himself. He wanted to pick off just one tile and keep a tiny reflection of that moment to take away with him but all at once the door opened and the image was lost.

'What the fuck!' Lawrence yelped as he leapt behind the door of the shower cubicle.

The woman from downstairs glided in.

'Oh I *am* sorry, I thought there was a lock on this door last time I used it.'

'There is a lock,' Lawrence replied sheepishly.

'Well, I suggest you use it next time. I know a lot of people that wouldn't mind seeing what you've got there, but if you *don't* want them to see, its up to you to stop them. That cubicle door is glass, you know. Doesn't cover a thing.'

Lawrence jumped out from where he stood, grabbed a towel from the rail and wrapped it around his waist.

'My name's Claire.'

She held out her hand.

Lawrence shyly brought his hand to hers.

'Lawrence.'

'I know. Your brother told us.'

'Oh yeah, right.'

'Well I'll leave you to it and come back when you've finished. Okay, Lawrence?'

It sounded to Lawrence like she was actually *asking* him if he wanted her to stay or not. Part of him did but he replied, 'Okay then. Won't be long.'

*

When Lawrence was back in the loft he pulled the bed up close to the TV. Foreign women writhed across the screen moaning in a language he didn't understand. He was soon entranced by their alluring alien tongue, nodding and gesturing at the screen while wanking. No need to wait until twelve o'clock to be satisfied by the post watershed women.

Later, he lay in bed drifting in and out of sleep while the TV continued to expose itself. He watched hazily, in a subdued gratification. Then he thought he saw a movement out of the corner of his eye. It was too dark to see what it was so he sat up in bed and peered forward. The door was opening.

'Kris?' he whispered

'No. It's Claire.'

The boy's mouth went dry.

'Hi,' Lawrence croaked.

As she moved into the room the flickering light of the TV made her glow in a surreal way. The changing images made her skin appear pale and ghostly one minute, lit with a mass of burning crimson the next.

'I thought you'd still be awake,' she whispered, sitting down on Lawrence's bed. Her thigh pressed against his as she adjusted her position.

'I thought you might have been joining us all downstairs. Why have you been staying up here on your own?'

'Well it's a work thing, isn't it? I don't know anyone and I'd just be in the way. Kris never invited me anyway.'

He tried to avoid staring at Claire's body. He could feel the warmth of her thigh through the duvet and realised that it was only this thin cover that separated his youthful nakedness from her eyes. This made him hard.

'I was having a word with Kristian, actually, and I said he should have invited you to join us, so that's one of the reasons I'm here. After all, he has to follow my orders,' she laughed.

'Does he? Are you his boss?'

'Yes, didn't you know? I pay him all that money to live in this place.'

'Any chance of a job for me then?'

'Do you know what it is exactly that Kris does?'

'Editing for TV or something.'

Claire turned towards the TV that was still colouring the walls.

'It's similar to that kind of stuff actually,' she said, nodding towards the screen.

As she said this she didn't turn back to Lawrence but seemed to become transfixed by what was playing on the screen. Lawrence watched her eyes dart about, taking in all the images.

'What, Kris edits this stuff? Porn?' Lawrence stuttered.

Claire turned her gaze from the TV.

'Yeah, he edits porn for me and the group downstairs. I take it you didn't know?'

Lawrence shook his head, partly in response, partly in disbelief. He was in some kind of dream. There was this gorgeous woman sat on his bed talking to him about wank videos as one played in the background. He felt confused, bewildered, but also excited.

'He's good at it too, you should be proud of him.'

Claire edged her body up the bed closer to Lawrence and leant towards his face, 'I've tried to get him to be *in one* too, but he keeps saying no.'

Lawrence stayed motionless. Claire was just inches from his face.

'Why doesn't he want to be in it?' Lawrence asked quietly.

Claire straightened up and moved back.

'Says he's not into it. Says it doesn't do anything for him. I've offered him more money, too. He's good looking and he's got something that would look good on screen.'

Lawrence's eyes suddenly widened as the facts finally hit home.

'Are you serious?' he blurted. 'Kristian *really* edits porn for you?'

Claire looked taken aback at his sudden abruptness.

'Yes.'

'What kind of porn?'

'Well, not really the kind that you're into,' she gestured towards the TV. 'Shall we say it's for a different type of gentleman.'

Lawrence knew what she meant without her

having to spell it out, yet he still had to say it out loud so he could believe it himself.

'Queer?'

Claire simply nodded.

The image Lawrence had held of his brother was fast being crushed by this woman's words. Before he had time to ask his next question Claire gave him the answer he wanted.

'He's not gay. None of my boys are. That's why he says he doesn't want to be in the films. I've told him he's stupid though, it's just acting and it's a lot of money. The others do it and they're not queer. They get paid. Just acting eh? What do you think?'

Lawrence didn't know how to answer.

'Are you mad with me now?' she asked.

Lawrence was confused.

'Mad?'

'You probably think I got him into it or something don't you? Trying to turn your brother queer?'

'No... I don't know... it's up to him I suppose.'

'I'm glad you think like that. That's good. That's mature. He wanted me to tell you because he thought you'd take it okay from me. I don't think he had anything to worry about did he?'

'I'm shocked!' Lawrence protested.

Claire brought her hand to his face and held his chin.

'I know, I can see why.'

Lawrence felt her warm breath on his face and his skin tingled. She held his chin and his stare.

'I knew you'd understand. That's why me and Kristian had a chat about you.'

Lawrence frowned, but held Claire's stare and

kept silent.

'He was telling me how much you love staying here, with all this stuff. The games and the DVDs and all the other expensive shit.'

'Yeah, so?'

He knew Claire was after something. Knew she could give him things, too. All the stuff that Kristian had, had come from Claire, so Lawrence was going to try for it as well.

'Well, maybe we could help each other out.'

Very slowly Claire moved her hand from where it had been resting on the bed and put it on Lawrence's thigh. She then moved it slowly to his groin and felt his hard-on.

'After I saw *this* in the bathroom, I knew how you could help us out.'

'How?' he asked.

'There are certain films that a lot of my clients would like to get hold off but I can't always make them...'

Lawrence was getting the picture. She was trying to make him feel good about his cock but what she was really interested in was his age. He cut her off.

'You mean films about boys my age?'

'Yes.'

Claire seemed shocked that he had sussed her out so quickly.

'Boys at fifteen?'

'Yeah, that's right. And younger,' she said, trying to shock him and regain her authority.

'What exactly do they want to see?'

'A nice boy your age. Especially a good looking straight boy like you,' she tried flattery first.

Lawrence smiled and *was* slightly flattered, but at the same time knew that Claire was saying these things for effect.

'Okay. What would I have to do?' he asked, fed up with avoiding the issue.

'Well,' she replied, 'lets put it this way – the more you do, the more you get paid.'

'How much for just once?'

'You haven't got me, Lawrence. Not the *amount* of films. It's the more you do in one film that measures how much you get paid. Let's put it this way, if you were just on your own in the film then you would get less. But if there were two of you, or a whole gang, and you let them do stuff to you, then you *would* be rich!'

Lawrence's heart started to beat faster. He couldn't tell whether it was the thought of all that money or because he was imagining what he would have to do to get it. He loved this feeling of excitement, of being in charge.

'I want to be rich!' he told Claire, decidedly.

'Okay,' she said with a big smile. The light from the TV lit up her teeth and made her lips shine wet and full.

Lawrence looked at her and was still hard, although it wasn't her in his head. It was the money. He thought about it in simple terms as he gazed at the delighted expression on Claire's face.

I love money.
I love wanking.
I won't get the blame.
If I get caught SHE IS RESPONSIBLE!

ROBIN GRAHAM

She's Come to Tell

When did they say they'd have breakfast? When do I
have to go downstairs? Soon. Not yet. Then we'll get
the paper. James and me. Find out the news. See
what's happening in the world. Once I've put my face
on. I wish you'd bring me a cup of tea, James, and say
hello. If only I had told you on Friday. I wasted
Saturday. Now Sunday. This is the day. I may not be
able to do it tomorrow. It's now or never. Before I go
back home. I have nothing to be ashamed of.

*

I remember the first time you brought me tea in bed.
You and little Andrew. What a disaster! Your father
was scalded. The sheets were ruined. The mattress
smelt rancid for a week. You cried your eyes out.
Andrew hid under the bed and giggled. Grandma's
teapot was smashed. And all because you wanted to
say thank you. I'd taken you to *Carousel*. James, *you*
were always the one who liked musicals. Your Dad
wouldn't go in case he laughed in public. And we cried
as they sang, *When you walk through a storm, keep
your chin up high*. Where to put my chin now? Up
high? Down low? And eyes up? Or eyes down. Nose
up. Nose down. Head squashed up. Against a window
pane, like that Halloween. You remember? Me and
Andrew. We scared the living daylights out of you. You
remember Andrew? Well, how often do you remember
him? Did you send him a birthday card? Birthdays

were always so important in our family.

*

You know the birthday of yours I think about most? That year we took your friends to see *The Sound of Music* and sat in the expensive seats and spilt popcorn over the balcony. When Julie Andrews came over the brow of the hill, arms wide, eyes wide, smile wide, goodness knows what else wide, singing *The hills are alive with the sound of music*. That's how a family should be. Alive. With the sound of music. Of course, Julie Andrews is over the hill now. And so is your father.

*

Andrew's still with his affair. Has he told you? They're so in love. You should see them together. Maybe one day they'll come to visit you. Would you like that? I'd like you to be closer with your brother. You couldn't be much farther apart. You in New Zealand. Him in Wales. The only thing in common is the sheep. No, I don't believe I thought that.

*

You remember when you first went out with your Lorraine? Andrew was starting A-levels? And acting so coyly. You said maybe he had a girlfriend. I bet you I'd get him to tell me. So I looked in his room. A mother's prying. You want to know what they're up to. Not getting into any sort of trouble. Looked first in his underwear drawer. Then in his bedside cabinet. Found nothing. More or less. Then picked up his washing. Which I hadn't done for a long time. Not that I wanted him to have dirty clothes. But he had to learn sometime. Underneath a mud-stained shirt... goodness knows how he got it that muddy... there was a page torn from a newspaper. And screwed up pieces of paper that he must have scribbled his replies on. *Dear Box... I think you sound very sexy. My name is Andrew. I am good looking, with a nice body, and a...* No! No, no, no! I checked the page from the newspaper to see who this box number was, what they were *into.*

*

It had never even crossed my mind. I can't tell you what a shock it was. I really had no idea. Of course, I said nothing. I wanted him to tell me. So I waited. I'd always brought my children up to know they could come to me. Even if they'd replied to personal ads. But I couldn't say anything or he'd know I'd been in his room. He would never trust me again. And nor would you, James, if you'd thought I'd been prying. You always thought I didn't know about those car calendars. Goodness knows what they had to do with cars. Or the hand-embroidered silk boxers that girl at school gave you, and those lovely poems you wrote to her and she gave you back. I couldn't have any of you not trust me. We are a family. We can be honest with each other. So I put the dirty washing back. Threw it on the floor like he did. And waited for my moment.

Andrew caught me looking at him, on several occasions, and looked away quickly. Then one day, the postman brought the large brown envelope. Andrew was at the door to greet him, then disappeared upstairs via the underwear drawer, and off to school. He had two replies. The first was just embarrassing. Sexual perversions: ice cubes, candles, fromage frais, chocolate sauce and dried apple rings. The other letter was from a lovely young man with red hair and freckles. He'd sent a picture taken on holiday. His mum, his dad, his younger sister. Having a wonderful time. All sipping Sangria in the sun. He was Andrew's age. And ever so sensible. That night, Andrew came home as usual.

'Andrew?' I said. My chin was held a little higher than usual. My eyes looking down at him.

'You and I have got to talk.'

'Okay,' he said, trying to be cool. I knew he was worried.

'Andrew, are you gay?'

'What?'

'Are you, Andrew?'

'Um...'

'Well?'

'Yes Mum.'

'I see.' Not that I could.

'Mum, how did you find out?'

'I just... guessed. When did you know?'

'When I was five.'

'Five! You've been at it since five!'

'No. I wrote a letter. I'll show you. Wait here.'

All those years of knowing. I felt so sad for him, wiped my eyes. I did put his letters back in the underwear drawer, didn't I? He came back and showed me just one letter. With the picture of the *Sound of Music* family.

'Mum, I replied to some ads.'

'Just one reply?'

'Yes.'

To this day I haven't let on that I saw the other.

'He looks nice. Are you going to write to him?'

'No.'

'Why not?'

'He's ugly.'

'Ugly?'

'Ugly!'

'Oh! I thought he looked nice.'

*

James, we brought you up the same. You and Andrew. Sent you to the same school and cubs. Took you swimming and collecting conkers. Dressed you up for weddings and christenings and Halloween. Made you both sing to Grandma and kiss her. Andrew was the sporty one. The athletic one. You were the one who liked musicals. I had so many tears. Don't ask me where all the water came from. For three months I cried.

*

It wasn't that I had any bad thoughts about homosexuals. I just felt that he was going to have a terrible life, not holding down a job, not having any friends, trouble with neighbours and finding a house. You don't want that for your children. You want the very best for them. The best that they can possibly have. And you hope that one day your son is going to get married and give you grandchildren.

'Andrew,' I said, 'I'm scared for you. Scared you'll have such a terrible life.'

'I've never thought of it like that,' he said.

'Andrew, I'm scared that you'll get AIDS and die.'

'Don't worry. Mum, I'm so glad you know and it's out in the open.'

*

He was such a shy boy. He wasn't going to sleep with anybody. Certainly no-one ugly.

*

I hate secrets. I just wanted to put my arms around him. But until I stopped crying, I couldn't hug him because my hands were so full of tissues. Time heals. And James, you hadn't suspected. I'd thought maybe me, the mother, was blind, and hadn't seen it. You said it was fine. One of your friends was gay. And you would defend your brother to the bitter end if there was trouble of any kind. But you didn't tell your Lorraine. We were over for dinner, your father and I, a few years later, and Lorraine asked if Andrew was courting... if he had a girlfriend. And I remember I looked at you with raised eyebrows, and you, sitting a little way behind her, shrugged, shook your head. Yes, at the beginning, I'd prayed that we'd wake up one day and that Andrew would have decided he wasn't gay any more. But that doesn't happen, does it? It was three years before I actually said to someone, 'I've got a gay son.' Now I can say it without thinking. And if they don't like it, tough.

*

Your father hasn't sent Andrew a birthday card since. And birthdays were always so important in our house. Your father just concentrated on his dinner parties. And golf. Drinks. Golf. Sun bathing. Golf. You'd think a man's best friend was his golf club. Wanted to be a pro. Not steady enough. Always liked a drink, your father. Ice cold eyes. Nerves of steel. Handshake of iron. Hands shaking like blancmange.

*

Do you remember when we went away? Andrew was at University and you were married when we swapped everything for sun and Sangria. Car laden. New home. New start. New beginning. You, Lorraine and Andrew waving as we drove away. Your father was too drunk to drive.

*

He wouldn't let Andrew come to see us. He blamed him for scattering the family. Every year I went to Cardiff. Except once, five years on. Andrew deserved a holiday. And this time your father wasn't going to have his way. Andrew came out for a fortnight. Your father said no more than a phrase each time he saw him. 'Cheers, Andrew!' 'Are you on drugs?' 'Are you an actor?' 'Pass me the whisky.' 'I suppose you drink sweet cider.' 'You're not my son.' 'Keep away from me.' 'Little bastard.'

*

Andrew had grown into quite a man by then. A health worker. For gay men. With an HIV support group. Been with the same partner for three years. Another Andrew. Red hair, but dyed red. And I mean bright. Scarlet. We'd always said you can't catch it by contact. But for years, your father wouldn't have him in the house. 'In case he's got that damned gay plague,' he'd say. Two days Andrew had been with us when they rowed like rottweilers.

*

Life hadn't been that bad in Spain. Apart from your father's drinking. He wasn't at all well. I thought he might have cirrhosis of the liver. I went with him to the doctor. They did the usual tests, but couldn't find what was wrong. And how I nagged, for him to stop drinking. To give his body a chance. Other people used to say we were such a close and happy couple. At the golf club they'd say, 'He talks about you all the time.' One woman actually said she was frightened to death of meeting me because I was 'such a paragon of virtue'. He praised me, bought me presents, told me that he loved me *every* day. And I looked after him when he was ill. I thought he was as contented and happy in the marriage as I was. It was only when I left Spain for three months, and came back to Manchester to put your grandma in a home, that slowly and surely things came to light.

*

I telephoned.

'Jack, I'm coming home on Sunday.'

'Where are you going, Jack?'

'Cadiz! That'll be nice. By the sea. I'll see if Mother wants to go to Morecambe, and we can think about you.'

*

Then I called him again.

'Jack, I'm getting a later flight.'

'Never mind. Jack, Madrid?'

'You said Cadiz when I spoke to you before.'

'But...'

'Don't get angry.'

'I can't wait to see you, Jack.'

'We'll talk then.'

And he slammed down the receiver.

*

Even Andrew said to me, 'You don't really think that there's any body else?'

And I said, 'Oh no,' and I really meant it. But by the time I was on the plane, I wondered. I was home well before your father. When he came in, I went towards him to give him a hug, so glad to see him. And he cried and confessed that he'd been away with some woman. He was so besotted with her, he was talking about leaving. And I was begging him to stay. Then telling him to go, not that I'd know what I'd do if he did. Then he realised that she wouldn't fit in at the golf club. And we came to New Zealand for your Suzy's christening, and sort of put it behind us. Then he became sick, with fairly minor things at first. He tried to cut down on his drinking.

*

It was three years ago that Andrew came out to see us for that fortnight. Just after a particularly harrowing Halloween when your father was the horror show, recalling all the other women he'd met. Some by accident. Some through the personal ads or phone lines. Always was up for a trick or treat, your father. Of course, by now the symptoms were becoming quite clear. If you knew what to look for. But I didn't know. I always went to the doctors with your father, except for the one time after he'd had that row with Andrew. Your father stopped me. That must have been the day. You asked for the test. It wasn't included in a normal blood test. In Spain, you had to pay for it. The awful part was the following week. Andrew was off travelling on his own for a few days. Your father had to go back to the doctors.

'Are you coming, Beryl?' he asked me.
'Am I allowed to this week?'
We just walked into that surgery, with me not

suspecting a thing. We sat there together. Our doctor held a slim folder before him and said, 'Jack, this is the problem, this has been the problem all along.'

And I said, 'What's that?'

'I've had an HIV test. And it's come back as positive,' Jack muttered into the carpet.

The ground just opened up. I was falling into a deep black chasm, couldn't see any daylight, just falling.

The doctor's nurse, who was also his wife, put her arms around me and said in her squeaky little voice, 'Beryl, it isn't so bad, he hasn't got full blown AIDS.'

I remember saying, 'You don't understand. That isn't the problem. Where has he got it from?'

*

He'd betrayed me. The whole world fell apart in that instant. Then there was the suggestion that I should be tested. But I was really well, so I believed it wasn't a problem for me. How could it be? I paid the doctor and he took my blood. Four days later he told me over the telephone. Because I insisted. 'Positivo.' This could not be happening to me. I was healthy. I could not be positive. I rang back the next day. Of course, I got the same result. I really thought I'd be dead in a year, I'd die very quickly and horribly. But three years on I'm here, James. To tell you. The shock, the horror. Nothing will ever be the same again. Life's changed. I never thought I'd be happy again. Time is a great healer. But this has been inflicted on me. Your father has done this. Betrayal. Stupid. I believed in him. That we were good together. Andrew had seen the signs. He recognised them. He'd told your father. That's why they rowed so bitterly. But he was on holiday with us - so, of course, I tried to block it out. Have a nice few days with him before he went home. We were out walking. He'd linked his arm with mine. Neither of us had said anything for a while.

'Mum?'

'Yes.'

'Is Dad...' He stopped.

'Yes?'

'Is Dad HIV positive?'

'Yes. Unfortunately he is.'

'Mum, what about you?'

I had to tell him some time. But right now I was tempted to laugh it off. I wanted so much to change the subject. We walked on.

'I'm sorry Andrew, it's bad news. '

'Mum, I don't know what to say. If anybody was going to come home with this, it was me. Not you.'

*

Oh, how I cried. And cried. Tissues. So many boxes, I collected the tokens and could send away for a plastic toreador. Andrew was wonderful. Once he was back home he sent me literature all about the CD4 and viral load, and letters of encouragement: it wasn't the end, I wasn't going to die there and then. Your father to this day has never read a thing. He keeps his hospital appointments, swallows the tablets they give him. But he doesn't want to know. In his mind he hasn't got it.

*

I came back to Manchester because I didn't like the Spanish hospital. I couldn't understand, and I wanted to understand exactly what was going on. I waited until after Christmas. I couldn't come home and spoil everybody else's celebrations. So I put on a brave face. I went out with your father for New Year. Kept up the appearance that we were all okay, with people asking me about him because he was so ill and me wanting to scream at them, 'He's done this to me!' Nobody knew. People still don't know.

*

I came home in the January with nothing. I lost my marriage, my home, the lifestyle that people envied. They disappeared overnight. And when I said I was coming back to England, your father just shouted, 'Who's going to look after me when you're gone?'

'Jack, who is going to look after me?' I said.

He'd never had any sympathy for me if I wasn't well. But when it came to this, he wanted to know who was going to look after him. Not, 'I'm sorry I've done this terrible thing and I'll take care of you.' I said, 'Jack, we've got to talk.' But he wouldn't. I said, 'Someone you've been with has given you this virus, Jack,' and he turned round to me and said, 'What about you, Beryl?' As if *I'd* infected him. It was like a physical pain. With that sentence he killed everything that I ever felt for him.

*

I'll go down in a minute. I'm changing. Yes, I am changing.

*

The day I left him, he just lay there in a drunken stupor. He knew I was off. He just lay, naked, with the taxi waiting outside for me.

*

When I came to Manchester, and presented myself at the hospital, they said I'd have to be re-tested. My immediate thought was that the Spanish had got it wrong, I'm not positive, he's put me through all this for nothing. The counsellor said, 'You know that the result is most likely to be the same, but we need to have our own results.' In that split second, I prayed that the Spanish were wrong.

*

You can never forget it. Every day, you're reminded. James, you must have wondered what this medication is for. I hate hiding, lying, inventing stories to say why I have to go to the hospital, why some days I'm tired and pretending to feel better than I am. You, waiting for clever answers and me not saying much, because I'd trip myself up.

*

This is why I've come to visit, James. Not to enjoy myself. I'm not guilty of anything. I shouldn't have to do this. But it isn't something I can say over the phone or in a letter. I can imagine you: 'Look, I've got a letter from Mum.' And you reading it aloud to your family. I couldn't do that. I have to be with you. It has to be today. I'll tell you when we go for the papers. You and me. I may not be strong enough again. My spirit is here, but my body is failing me. I am wasting away. Soon I'll go home. And if you don't like it? What do I do then? Will you make me leave now? Should I be ready?

*

I look so dreadful without my face.

*

It's only just hit your father what's happening. Because he's never been in hospital before. When he had to go in, he went back to Manchester. He told no-one. He won't let anyone come to visit. Because of the ward he's in. He was sixty four last month. I didn't send him a card. My new lover can't understand why I don't hate him. But I can't live like that. When I was visiting a friend, through a doorway I saw him. And he saw me. He held out his hand. He was so gaunt and sick. I didn't recognise him. He never said what should have been said. That's the way he coped. They were so unimportant, those little affairs he had that he couldn't possibly have got anything so serious. Or me. I went over to him. He told me that he loved me.

*

So, we'll walk to the newsagent at the brow of the hill. Just you and me, James. I'll say, 'You know, I've not been well recently.'

And you'll say, 'Yes. Do you know what's been the problem?'

I'll say, 'That's why I'm here. To tell you what's happening. That I'm no danger to your family, by hugging or touching or drinking out of the same cup. James? Your Mum is HIV positive. I got it from your father who doesn't know where he got it from. And he's dying of AIDS.'

And you'll tell me that you love me. You'll put your arms around me. Lift me up. Swing me round. We'll cry together. I want Lorraine to know. You'll say, 'I don't care who knows.'

And I'll ask you to come home with me. Just for a day. And at the bedside of your father, we'll be a family once again.

MICHELLE GREEN

Prairie Dyke

The urge to run screaming from that town came slowly. What started out as random yearnings for a new backdrop – the parking lot view from my pad was losing its charm – soon mushroomed into a double-D sized ache. I had been sucked face first into E-town, calling it 'home' in the same tone of voice that rolls its eyes. Everyone I knew there had perfected the same yawn. It was, according to most locals, ground zero hell of hick: a bloated small town mall town with sprawling suburbs and homo-haters as far as the eye could see. A little piece of redneck just east of the Rockies – and what a beautiful piece of redneck it was!

Don't get me wrong: I fell in love with that town over and over again. It could sometimes shoot you a look through long, mascara-clumped lashes that would melt you like a popsicle in August. I certainly caught enough of those sidelong glances to want to stick around, and there's something you just have to admire about a chocolate brown river that manages to still look beautiful, as long as you keep telling yourself that it's the *naturally occurring sediment* and not the factory shit that's clouding the water. For all of its acne scars and nasty odours, that town had life in it.

However, I was on the Hate-The-Hometown bandwagon, spending each weekend guzzling dollar-fifty highballs at the one queer club in town, moaning about the dull scene and bad carpets, staggering home to my basement suite and mumbling to my cat before I passed out, 'Hey Kitty... wanna play the string game?'

My reasons for staying in this self-made rut were few – and as time passed, they dwindled down to one solitary reason that was struggling to keep me convinced.

It's a Thursday night, seven thirty. I'm meeting Leigh in the crowning jewel of the women's scene – the last stop on the bus trip of lesbian lust – our local: Secrets. It's the only women's bar in town and, as such, is straining to accommodate every dyke decorating cliché. Moody black and white photos of models stare pseudo-sexually from every vertical surface. The walls are painted the colour of half-dried blood – creating a menstrual bordello atmosphere. The scent of cheap beer and oestrogen hangs thick in the air as k.d. lang watches over the pool table from her prominent back wall poster. The defining item rests at a forty-five degree angle beside the bar, held in place by a thick chain and a few wooden supports. Front wheel raised two feet off the ground in an Evil Knieval stunt pose, all gleaming chrome and polished leather, the decorative motorbike does one thing: it shamelessly proclaims to the world 'YES! We are pulp-novel lesbian stereotypes and we are *proud!*' Thankfully the world is not here. I am alone at my table, sharing the room with the bartender and a handful of women in plaid wool coats.

As another game of pool begins, the music pauses between songs, changing again from top forty country hit to top forty rock anthem. In that quiet few seconds, as everyone pulls their glass to their lips and the CD's click over in the jukebox, the door swings wide, and in steps Leigh. She scans the room slowly with that deliberately distracted look I've watched her cultivate, and then, when she's satisfied that everyone has noticed, she sees me. I can almost hear the revving as she kicks into butch overdrive. She approaches the table in a few slow, studied strides, a half smirk/half charming smile playing the corner of her lips. I expect her to open with a line containing the word 'doll' or 'darlin', but instead she simply comes out with a husky 'Hey'.

'Hey,' I return, wondering why it is that each time we meet feels like the first scene in a badly written porn. Leigh's feathers are momentarily ruffled when, after a long and uncomfortable dig through her pockets, she turns up only a few coins, a crumpled pack of Marlboros and an expired lottery ticket. It's not easy being a gentleman when you're chronically broke. However, she's a seasoned pro at it now and blushes for only a second when I offer to buy her a drink.

I arrive back at the table a few minutes later with two beers, and Leigh begins to tell me about the new apartment she's looking to rent – spacious one bedroom, underground parking, view of the river. It sounds like a real estate wet dream. I get a sneaking sensation that I'm being pulled into this somehow, but she doesn't come right out and say it. I do remember bitching about my basement palace a few weeks ago; perhaps now I'm supposed to throw myself at her black boots and beg to be rescued from subterranean housing hell. This isn't the first time she's danced around the 'moving in together' issue... or maybe I'm just being paranoid. We've been together long enough now to avoid turning into one of those second-date lesbian U-Haul jokes, right?

I slump back into my chair and jump as it slumps with me. Shit. She's stopped talking. As I clear my throat, ready to revive my end of the conversation with something relevant and witty, she places her bottle carefully on the table and fixes me with a look that says I haven't been listening. Her mouth curls up into a strained smile. She pulls all the stops from her worn leather jacket and flips a cigarette into the corner of her mouth.

'I know the owner. She's just bought another place, but wants to keep this one on as a rental.'

Her eyes move back and forth across my face, waiting.

'She just wants to get someone in there to cover the mortgage. It hasn't been advertised yet – she said she'd hold it until the end of next week if I'm interested. No deposit, half the rent I'm paying now... if... you want...'

She stops and fills the space with her cigarette, self-consciously stuffed into her mouth. Though she still hasn't said it, we both know the question I've been asked.

'Umm – look... I... uhhh.'

She cuts me off.

'Look babe, it's not like this has to be decided right now. We can go over there later and check it out.'

The 'taking care of business' look sets across her face and I realise that's my cue to cream myself and start mentally picking out sofa patterns.

I let her milk it while I take a mouthful of beer.

A moment passes.

She taps her chunky silver ring on the plastic wood-grain tabletop, one – two, like a slow-hand clap.

Her eyes half-shut behind a pair of dark-rimmed Elvis Costello glasses.

One – two.

Smoke shoots down from her nostrils and curls up when it meets the table.

One – two.

Melissa Etheridge blares at the end of the room. One.

A Molson Canadian patio umbrella looms in the corner.

Two.

I reach down for a cancer stick of my own, prop it between my lips, and breathe fire.

The air is full of blue green chemical smoke and, as my teeth grip the edge of the filter, I inhale and slip out a request for more beer before blowing onto the ashtray and turning us into an angst-dyke snowdome. Little burnt up bits of tobacco leap into the air, and before I realise what's happening, I start to laugh – big, 'nice-girls-don't', belly busting, very *uncool* laughs. I can't stop, and I've almost emptied the ashtray before I realise that Elvis is not amused.

I look over at Leigh, now sitting stone still, forearms stretched across the table, head bowed to show the even dusting of ash that covers her dark gelled spikes and reddening ears. It suddenly dawns on me what a major problem cigarette ash must be to someone whose wardrobe consists of black, dark grey, and denim. Her left hand shakes slightly as she reaches to the crook of her elbow and plucks a crushed brown filter from the folds of her sleeve. Without looking up at me, and still in total silence, she raises both hands deliberately to her face, removes her glasses, and sets them down on the table. The pit of my stomach is falling through this cheap wooden chair, and though I've started a thousand sentences in my head in the last five seconds, none of them make it past my lips. I don't think I could actually say sorry without laughing again. So I stay silent.

Leigh rises from her chair, and without a word, a flicker of a smile, or even an unmeasured breath, she turns and walks to the bathroom. There I am, left with two bottles of beer and a look of concern pasted on my face. With Little Miss No Sense of Humour gone for the moment my thoughts have time to percolate. I feel like I'm five again; I'm at day care and I've just upset the teacher by throwing up in the reading area. This whole 'too cool for her own good' thing is really getting tedious. Where did the fun go? At what point in the transition from tomboy to baby dyke to now did the excitement just... evaporate? She still hasn't come back from the toilets, and my patience is wearing thin.

At exactly eight thirty four I've had enough. Cute with no sense of joy just doesn't cut it anymore, and no one says a word when I slip out the front door between songs, a bottle in each hand.

I suppose I should have given her a call at least, or sent a postcard from the Greyhound station to let her know that I was alive, but I honestly forgot. The moment I stepped through that door and stood on the sidewalk, blinking at the sunset, I felt a fog lifting from my head. I had one spectacular moment of clarity – and, two days later, a one-way bus ticket from Prairie Town to the rest of my life.

P-P HARTNETT

CCTV Eyes

Here, area by area around England and Wales, is a recently published collection of statistics reflecting the vast number of child-sex offenders who are on the current paedophile register:

SOUTH WEST
Plymouth: 531; Exeter: 209; Newquay: 50; Torquay: 260; Ilfracombe: 20; Bristol: 842; Weston-super-Mare: 133; Swindon: 380.

WALES
Cardiff: 604; Swansea: 481; Newport: 290; Tenby: 30; Colwyn Bay: 71; Rhyl: 62; Wrexham: 260.

SOUTH OF ENGLAND
Bournemouth: 340; Poole: 304; Christchurch: 100; Southampton: 450; Gosport: 156; Portsmouth: 400; Isle of Wight: 263; Worthing: 206; Brighton: 513; Eastbourne: 190; Hastings: 180; Dover: 230; Margate: 120; Maidstone: 300; Canterbury: 130; Lewes: 180; Crawley: 200; Dartford: 180; Guildford: 270; Woking: 200; Reading: 310; Slough: 230; Watford: 164; Luton: 390; St. Albans: 182; Stevenage: 171; Harlow: 160; Brentwood: 150; Basildon: 340; Southend-on-Sea: 370; Chelmsford: 330.

LONDON
Barnet: 710; Croydon: 714; Ealing: 650; Bromley: 662; Wandsworth: 287; Lambeth: 400; Enfield: 550; Hillingdon: 530; Brent: 531; Lewisham: 400; Redbridge: 490; Southwark: 480; Westminster City: 480; Newham: 480; Havering: 480; Waltham Forest: 460; Haringey: 460; Bexley: 457; Greenwich: 450; Harrow: 440; Hounslow: 430; Hackney: 410; Camden: 400; Merton: 270; Richmond-upon-Thames: 121; Tower Hamlets: 380; Kensington and Chelsea: 124; Sutton: 323; Islington: 201; Hammersmith and Fulham: 330; Barking and Dagenham: 332; Kingston-upon-Thames: 132; City of London: 21.

EAST ANGLIA

Colchester: 331; Ipswich: 236; Norwich: 260; Cambridge: 251; Lincoln: 180; Great Yarmouth: 190; Peterborough: 322.

MIDLANDS

Gloucester: 225; Cheltenham: 230; Owestry: 81; Worcester: 200; Oxford: 300; Milton Keynes: 430; Kettering: 170; Northampton: 411; Corby: 120; Rugby: 128; Coventry: 640; Daventry: 151; Redditch: 160; Birmingham: 2080; Walsall: 550; Wolverhampton: 510; Nottingham: 510; Stafford: 270; Stoke-on-Trent: 530; Derby: 491; Leicester: 630; Chesterfield: 210

NORTH OF ENGLAND

Burnley: 190; Chester: 187; Liverpool: 976; Manchester: 902; Stockport: 280; Rochdale: 201; St. Helen's: 220; Warrington: 401; Salford: 480; Chorley: 210; Sheffield: 1110; Rotherham: 530; Halifax: 200; Bradford: 1013; Leeds: 1420; York: 370; Rochdale: 201; St. Helens: 219; Barrow-in-Furness: 144; Berwick-on-Tweed: 57.

NORTH WEST

Preston: 294; Blackpool: 322; Morecombe: 110; Whitehaven: 79; Carlisle: 220.

NORTH EAST

Skegness: 90; Cleethorpes: 78; Grimsby: 159; Hull: 532; Scarborough: 230; Middlesborough: 310; Durham: 200; Sunderland: 621; Newcastle-upon-Tyne: 588.

07:00

Best time of the day, this. Before the shops open. So quiet. Like church. Everything so clean and still.

07:01

That new chap does a good job on these floors. Sparkling, they are.

07:10

'Morning Si. Y'all right?'

07:14

Bustin' for a piss, I am. Ages till my break.

08:20

Weird, that one. Carolina. Collects Beanie Babies. You'd think she'd have better things to spend her money on. Three jobs in four months: KFC, Spud-U-Like and Top That Pizza. It'll be Singapore Sam next, I bet.

08:22

'Morning.'

08:22

Always chewing, that one. With her mouth open. Wide open. Look at her. The sunbed slapper.

08:23

These trousers are getting tight on me. All those chips. Fish 'n' chips every day, for only one reason.

08:25

'Morning.'

08:27

He was nice enough when he started, soon showed what he was made of. Out slagging his arse up and down Canal Street most nights. He's probably riddled. Dirty sod.

08:35

'Morning Justin, 'ow's it goin' mate?'

08:35

Tosser.

08:45

Okay, I'll give you a nod, Mrs Marum, but that's all.

08:52

She's well odd. Mandy. Friendly enough, but odd. Notquiterightinthehead.com they call 'er. Telling me that her electric toothbrush '...is the best vibrator I've come across!'. She can't be more than seventeen. I'd slap 'er if she were one of mine.

08:53

'Morning Lucy.'

08:54

Now Lucy's nice, not like one of those tarts you get in Smiths or Poundland. She'll be manager of The Body Shop soon enough. I'd place a tenner on it. Always got a smile for me she 'as.

08:58

There goes that woman from Supercuts, cutting it fine again. God knows why she wears those shoes.

09:00

Here we go, opening time. Cold outside, could be a busy one. I hate Thursdays.

09:10

He's nice. Lovely hair.

09:12

He's nice an' all. Doable. definitely doable.

There were certain things about a boy which made that old man's eyes twinkle.
He once decided to knock off a hundred pages about himself on a bashed-up Remington typewriter. This is as far as he got, a single sentence:

My favourorite kind of boys are of an age just old enough to go to the toilet by themselves.

Often, when patrolling the Arndale Centre, he would say to himself just under his breath and with only the smallest movement of his lips so that no one would notice, 'I'm a paedophile. That's what I am.'
It was something he said in a very matter-of-fact kind of way. Occasionally this would have a trailer thought tagged onto it, like those banners sometimes glimpsed from the tail end of small aircraft. 'P-A-E-D-O-P-H-I-L-E. Top of the

shit list. Public Enemy #1. That's me.'

As with the majority of paedophiles, this man – somebody's husband, somebody's grandfather – did not have a prison record. His name was not to be found on any register. The Head had been exceedingly nice about it all, most sympathetic in fact, but, as he said, they really couldn't afford a scandal of that sort. It was with a very quick sayonara that the man had left the little prep school run by a retired colonel and practising sadist plus a succession of defrocked monks to get over the shock/humiliation/ thrill of it all. After all those years of being a school caretaker, his exit had been a rapid one. That, and the move up North. Both back in '79. A long time ago. Bolton, Burnley, then Oldham. As is so common with gay male paedophiles, he married. Had a few kids. Boy and a girl.

09:22

'What's that luv? Argos? Straight on, all the way down.'

09:23

I want to pick my nose, but... no... I can't.

09:24

'The BT Shop? Upper mall, luv. Escalator thata way.'

09:35

Wish that one was a lifter. I'd love to chase after 'im, catch the bugger by the neck, pin 'im down till the cops came.

09:35

Go on, steal something, you know you want to. Your fingers are itching.

09:35

I'm gonna follow you a while. Wherever you go, I'll be right behind you.

Throughout England, Ireland, Scotland and Wales there are whole coachloads of rosy-cheeked boys who had received on the tender skin of their bellies the man's foul discharge. Little rosy-cheeked boys who'd been warned that they'd become little white corpses if they ever told.

11:10

Oh my God, he's a must. Gonna have to keep an eye on 'im a while.

11:11

Nice arse on it.

11:12

Ah, sweet. Look at 'im. Checking out the shaving range. He won't be needing those for a few years yet.

11:13

Unusual that, he's not spraying himself with all those samples. Most boys do. Stink the place out they do on a Saturday.

11:14

Nah, not 'im though. He's just taking a sniff of this one, looking at the side of the bottle. Reading the ingredients.

11:16

Oh, lucky me. Taking a ride on the escalator, are we? Now, if I time this right I'll be...

11:17

Yep, perfect. Right behind him, four steps down. Magical view.

11:17

White denim. Tight, white denim.

11:18

Go on, turn around. Take in the view. Let's have a look at you, see what you've got. What you're made of.

11:18

Oh, very nice. Face away from me again. That's right. Lovely. Love-ly. Marvellously uplifted, good separation. A ten out of ten little arse.

11:18

An' jus' look at that neck. Some barber had fun shapin' that.

11:18

I used to love that, the feel of the clippers buzzing away.

11:18

He smells nice, clean.

11:18

Uh-oh, here we go.

11:19

'Berketex Brides? Certainly, madam. Opposite Rogers The Florist, next to Boots.'

11:19

Damn, lost 'im. Which way did 'e go?

Neil Egan had been his favourite, a boy who the man had always thought of as 'Lovely Little Neil'. Often that man would be reminded of Neil as he stared at the posters of the perfect, computer-enhanced features of the model boys in the windows of Next. So much time was spent remembering.

Small and strong, with a huge head, and pale blue humourous eyes that wrinkled in amusement or opened wide in wonder, Neil was forever young, locked away in the man's head.

Gorgeous, spindly-legged, bright-eyed. Little Mr Egg 'n' Bacon. The man's darling little lover boy, with his fine, curly, very light blond hair that came out in a wave from under the back of his blue cap. That face with the contours of babyhood, that pink and white complexion. A face that had a milky transparency through which the shape of his skull could be seen - skin which didn't freckle in the sun but turned heavy gold.

Neil E. So young. So soft. So partial to chocolate cake.

Neil. A boy especially careful of manners; brown, spongy-soled, long-lasting shoes polished to an amazing shine. Silent soles. Nails clean; socks pulled all the way up - right to the scabbed knees. About school, sport, hobbies - he always answered clearly, precisely, without making silly faces.

Lovely Little Neil: a boy so extremely

proud of his batting averages.

Lovely Little Neil: a perfect living boy.

And those eyes: so blue and so black within the blue and around the blue and through the blue, and so brilliant - twinkling – they'd made that full-grown married man think of rabbits - not of their eyes but of that quivery-shivery business at their noses.

He appeared in a new thick tweed sports coat almost every term - luxurious and original in colour, never gaudy. A boy who exuded a strong, clean, tweedy smell. So angelic in white surplice on the altar; all washed, brushed and on display. Psalms and hymns became mesmeric with that little one in the spotlight, face raised over hymnal. Neil, kneeling: a vision.

Young Egan, a boy with a deep-seated and totally unconscious craving for affection and admiration. Yet a controlling presence, too, again in white, at the nets. The immaculately pressed longs with a white-flannel smell. The soft feel of his dark blue blazer. A ridiculously beautiful creature in fresh open shirt.

Neil, always so careful to arrange the points of his shirt collar outside that blazer.

The fragility, the vulnerability. The potential.

So good at ping-pong. Grinning and blushing.

So tiny-hipped, shiny-lipped.

His tentative and vulnerable quality,

smelling of fresh grass and sunburn.

Naughty Neil, tie always just that little bit askew, top button undone.

Back in those days the man used to chant as he swept, chant as he mopped, chant as he wiped and shined, as he switched off and locked up: He is a boy of eleven years, and I am a man of thirty. It seemed important, a score.

Alas, the beatutiful boy was history, and Chiswick a place so very far away.

Neil had been just one of many favourites. Over the years there had been Agius, Burke, Cassidy, Cookson, Glancey, Harford, Hajduk (the most caned of boys), Ingram, Jewers... so many favourites. Those boys, with lovely, big, first-time eyes. Boys he'd have liked to swallow whole, one after another. In every case he found himself remembering not only a name but a nick-name and at least one cruel fact to which they would be vulnerable: an armoury of pyschological stings - flat feet, a tendency to lisp, stutter, wet the bed. Dead fathers, alcoholic mothers. So many young undeveloped hearts.

In ancient Rome he could have married a boy. He would have liked that.

11:32

This muzak's gettin' to me. Hate the fact that I find myself hummin' this one sometimes. I never liked Paul

McCartney. Smug bastard.

11:33

Soon be time for lunch. Just as well, I'm starvin'. Not long to go before I see Fish 'n' Chip Boy. Noel.

Mind collapsing backwards again through the years, a life landmarked with pornography, he was scanning the casts of Boy, Beautiful Boy, Dream Boy, Sexy Boy, Boy+1, Boys, Best Boy, Boy Wonder, Sexy Boy's Body, Mad About The Boy, Boy Oh Boy, Birthday Boy, Boy Next Door, Action Boys, Aussie Boys, Bohemian Boys, Brilliant Boys, Bubbling Boys, Smiling Boys, Super Boys, Private Boys, Lover Boys, Toy Boys, Golden Boys, New Golden Boys, Bondi Beach Boys, My Three Boys, Boys Wrestling, Secret Boys Club, Bad Boys, Boys Gallery, Boys Boys Boys, Euro Boy (editions #1, #3, #6, #8, #11), Home Made Bad Boys.

Anything with Boy or Boys in the title got a cheque in the post automatically. His wife didn't have a clue. Not an inkling. Every smutty little purchase went to a PO Box, right in the centre of town. The stamps went to a charity.

11:58

I'll miss this place.

Flashes of school ties against starched white shirts and table-tennis bats zapped through the man's head. A school trip many years back, a trip to Studland in Dorset, getting his shoes polished by little Antonio in Malaga - he'd never had such fun for a hundred pesetas. There was that lovely little memory of catching Martin Higgs and Jeremy Armstrong zipped up together in just the one sleeping bag beside a scattering of Beano, Hornet, Hotspur, Hurricane and MAD comics, plus wrappers from Picnic bars, Crunchie bars, Toffee Crisps and Wagon Wheels. Darlings away from home. With his eyes closed he could smell the Tizer combined with salt and vinegar flavoured Golden Wonder crisps. With his eyes closed he could smell that... and... And that smell which is created when one person's body touches another person's body, chemicals under the skin break down and recombine, setting off an electric spark which leaps, neuron to neuron, to the brain. It was all a question of potassium and calcium and... They'd said they were cold. Homesick, too. He'd questioned them both, making them stand naked before him, then insisted they take a long cold shower with plenty of soap. 'We were just kiddin' around,' Martin had said, secure in his status as a useful football player and twenty-a-day smoker. A boy aged ten years, eleven months.

12:09

God only knows how I'm gonna fill me days once I'm retired.

12:11

Time to get another dog. Good excuse to walk the park.

12:12

Maybe time to follow the doctor's good advice as well. Nip down the pool a couple o' times a week. Do a few laps during the school sessions or 'Inflatable Fun'.

Thoughts always returned to Neil - Lovely Little Neil: forever a happy, fresh-faced child who made heads turn, aroused smiles. You could almost smell the bright world of illustrated books off him, the man often thought. The orange trees, the friendly dogs, sandwiches off soft, good quality picnic blankets by the sea. All that sun oil - so evenly spread. Neil, with those perfect seaside subteen limbs which made many a man groan through clenched teeth behind binoculars.

Lovely Little Neil: a boy who seemed to peak aged somewhere between seven years, five months and nine years, ten months.

Lovely Little Neil: the kind of delightful, healthy and lively joy rarely seen in the three-dimensional world. Irresistible beautiful boys like him seemed only to belong to yellowed magazines and scratchy Super 8 films made in the seventies - a marvellous time for paedophiles all over the world, particularly France and Holland and the US of A (1976 - 1978) where the censor's axe missed a few times during the course of the twentieth century, providing material where minors were 1) engaged in sexual activity, including masturbation and sado-masochistic abuse 2) in a state of sexual arousal and 3) posed in such a way that the genitals or anal area of the minor were lewdly/lasciviously exhibited - all three cases intended to appeal to the prurient interests of persons seeking sexual stimulation or gratification.

12:26

I hate America. Them damn Americans. They dreamt up these places. Shopping malls. Hell on Earth.

12:30

Right that's me done. Off for a bit of nosh.

That elderly security guard had a friend, a pal - someone he had first made contact with via the Internet. Gay.com. The 'Youth' message board. They met once a month to 'share'.

The man was somewhat of an expert. When it came to intergenerational sex, age-structured same-sex relationships, something a bit on the dark side, that man knew all there was to know, all the ins and outs. The man-boy insemination rites among the Sambia in New Guinea and the Melanesian islands in the South Pacific and tribes of the Nilotic Sudan, where the culture of the white man has not become the model, was something he was really hot on - paricularly the man-boy relationships among the Marind-Anim. It was deemed vital, among the Etoro, that young boys swallow the semen of their elders to promote physical growth. Among the neighbouring Kaluli it was possible for boys to actually choose their own inseminators.

12:45

Ah, look at 'im, jus' look at 'im. My tiny little bird boy.

117

12:47

I don't come 'ere for the fish, I don't come 'ere for the chips, I don't come 'ere for the tea – which ain't half bad as it goes – I come 'ere for 'im: Noel.

12:49

I hate it when 'e's not 'ere. He's my sunshine boy, that one.

12:50

Noel.

12:51

His brother was cute when he was Noel's age. Not now though. Smokes, got a tattoo the size of a Kit Kat top of both shoulders. Pierced eyebrow. I hate all that, ruins a boy.

12:52

These chips ain't 'ot enough.

12:58

Wipes those tables so well does Noel. Lifts the salt, the pepper, ketchup and vinegar. Good lad.

12:59

Always on task, bless 'im. Soon as a customer's finished the plate's whisked off the table.

13:07

I'm not the only one who puts a fifty pence under the saucer for 'im. He's a popular boy. I'm not 'is only admirer, I know that for a fact. If I had my way, Noel would never wear nothin' but that apron, his yellow baseball cap and those trainers.

13:09

Oh, I wish... just for one full minute I could...

13:10

He'd look lovely in white. Old fashioned PE kit. A vest, not a t-shirt.

13:13

He'll be back at school next week. Monday. End of the summer holidays.

13:14

Better be making tracks, back to work. I'll just spend a penny.

13:16

Oh, I can't believe my luck. Look whose just popped in. And he's...

13:16

Unzipping, right now. Right beside me.

13:16

He could've used the cubicle. Is he...

13:16

Is he lettin' me 'ave a look? Is that it?

13:16

I know I shouldn't do what I'm about to do, but I want to. Want him to see it, what he's doin' to me.

13:17

Uh-oh. That was a big mistake. Never seen a kid zip up 'n' run so fast. Shit. *Shitshitshit.*

13:17

Hope 'e doesn't tell.

13:18

He won't tell, will 'e?

ROBIN IBBESON

www.ihatechriswilliams.co.uk

On the intro page of the website I have dedicated to my hatred of Chris Williams, is a photo I found on his computer one day when he was out of the house. It is a doctored picture he took from the *Boyz* tv guide one week when it had a piece on *SMTV*. The face of Cat Deeley has been replaced by Chris's own, so that he appears in between Ant and Dec. It looks ridiculous, all the more so knowing that for Chris, it will be less of a joke and more of a fantasy.

To enter the site the visitor must click on a gun graphic which shoots and kills the Chris/Deeley hybrid. On the next page, I give a brief history of our relationship. At the end of our second year at university, me and a friend of mine needed a third person to fill up the recently vacated room in our shared house. It seemed like a good idea at the time to advertise in the gay press rather than the usual avenues so that's what we did. A few people came to see the place, the girl we wanted to move in found somewhere else, and eventually the pressures of time, money and our landlord meant that Chris, not really a high on our list, but at the time not seeming so bad either, took the room. One month later and my friend did a runner. Never said goodbye, he's never been in touch since, simply took all his stuff one weekend when I was visiting my folks. I think he just snapped. I can barely blame him, but I resent him, of course, for leaving me behind. The landlord has been surprisingly generous with the rent, although he did tell me that if

I broke *my* contract he'd break my collarbone. I've tried to get other people to move in, but as soon as they meet Chris, his personality a lot less subdued than in our initial meetings, they become strangely disinterested. At first I was frustrated. I went through deep burning anger, depression, until I finally decided to put the HTML course I took last year to good use and provide myself with an outlet for my emotions.

At the side of the intro page is a column of icons that provide links to further explorations of my feelings towards Chris Williams. The first is a picture of Oscar Wilde's head. I animated the graphic so that Oscar's eyes and tongue pop out in horror when you pass the mouse pointer over it. Click on Oscar to be taken to some classic Chris Williams quotes. A lot of these I just wrote down from memory either after being exposed first hand to Chris's enlightened views, or overhearing them. As I became more interested in the quality of material I was putting on the site, I began hiding running tape recorders around the house and sometimes carrying a dictaphone to catch some of Chris's better bon-mot. I induced the 'Get them (immigrants) out!' conversation in our lounge one day and you can download a RealAudio file to listen to his whiny 'whatEVerrrr!' styled voice attempt to put across his obnoxious rant.

Chris on women: Chris is a misogynist in the kind of way old style drag acts hate women. His repertoire is filled with fishy smell japery and jokes about bleeding. He has a particular hatred for Cat Deeley who he sees as being the main block between him and his beloved Ant and Dec. One Saturday morning, I found him talking to the TV while CD UK was on. 'No use for you around here,' he snarled as Cat interviewed some boy band or other. 'Ain't you heard. It's men only around here.' There are many other lines like this in this section devoted to women, and Cat in particular, but this one is my favourite.

Chris on human rights: 'It's gay people who cause a fuss who cause homophobia. The world would be so much more accepting if they stopped complaining all the time.'

Chris on Education: Chris makes many lengthy phone calls to his family. By lengthy, I mean two to three hours. At first this just annoyed me. But when I started really listening to him in disbelief at what he was actually saying, I found my anger quietened by the sheer entertainment factor.

I am not sure why or how Chris made it to degree level. In one phone call he made it explicit to his family that he wasn't eager to learn.

Chris (to his Dad, I think): 'I don't see what university could teach me... maybe... the people who go are stupid... I know everything already... They're stupid... Stupid, stupid, stupid... (sings) STUPID! STUPID! STUPID!... I'm just wasting time before... I'd like to have a career in the fashion industry...'

Chris's parents pay his fees, rent and living allowance. His comments on the 'fashion industry' in mind, perhaps they should have paid for him to go to art college rather than to do a physics degree.

One night when I was busy working on the culture section of the website, it suddenly hit me, I was a culture snob. Who was I to place these judgements on Chris's tastes I asked myself. Then at that precise moment, my walls began vibrating with the theme tune from *Bob the Builder*, and I finally realised I didn't fucking care.

The section starts with a list of Chris's favourite music.

1.   The *Bob the Builder* album. Especially the singles. Especially the theme tune played several times before Chris goes out, when he comes back and in the morning at full blast to wake me up as a joke. I've tried asking Chris not to play it less frequently, but to play it less loud, to no effect. I am a killjoy he tells me. I have no sense of fun. I think Chris has no sense of humanity.

2.   *Reach for the Stars* by S Club 7. This plays when Chris is in a similar mood to above. He has a friend who shall only be named X (I have no beef against X – he seems lonely and shy and rather bullied by Chris into friendship). Often they practice their dance steps to this song on a Friday and Saturday night before heading off to Canal Street. Whenever either of them fucks up the routine, Chris re-starts the song and they have to do it again. I can no longer block out S Club 7's fascistic cheery banality at the weekend and yes, I am brought on a regular basis to the extent of my nascent snobbery. All those years of oppression, deaths, imprisonments, tortures, all the years of fighting against invisibility and hatred and for what? To lessen the stranglehold for such vacuous expressions of invisibility as making choreographed moves to an annoying pop record in an unpleasant pub.

Chris and X dance like camels with splints. I am hoping to get hold of a web cam so I can document their abilities

There are many other boy and girl bands in Chris' CD collection but I don't remember them ever being played. Only S Club 7. Only this song.

3.   The Emperor's New Groove soundtrack. For Chris's more reflective moments.

I don't listen to much chart music. It goes without saying that the bands I like are 'weird'. The films I like are also 'weird', as are all of my friends.

BBC2 is a no go area in our house.

Some of the things Chris has done don't fit neatly into the other categories on the site. There is a miscellaneous section named simply 'The horror!' The navigation button here is Marlon Brando's face. A woman's scream is heard as you make the jump to the next page.

Last November Chris and X had an argument. I never found out what it was about, but I do know a friend of a friend of mine saw X in town the following day and X had a black eye. Suffice to say for quite a while X no longer visited our house. During this period Chris's behaviour and appearance changed drastically to embrace a set of affectations so inappropriate that they need pictures to help describe them. And so I introduce the story with a family snap taken from the frame on Chris's wall. It shows Chris and his parents on the patio of their home in a surburban village in Bedfordshire. Chris is wearing a World Wildlife Organisation T-shirt with a picture of a seal on it. His parents look like models in the gadget catalogues you get in the magazines of Sunday newspapers. You just can't get any more cosily middle class than that particular photo. It just screams of occupational lifetimes spent in the civil service, of years of mornings characterised by *Waking up to Wogan*.

I couldn't find a way to get photographic evidence of the abrupt shift in Chris's life without him smelling a rat, so I simply took a picture of him one afternoon as he slept on the sofa. In the shot, Chris's cap is wonky and his mouth is open giving the portrait that extra touch of Norman Wisdom style stupidity. But even without those bonuses, I think the head to foot sportwear, the *Tasmanian Devil* socks pulled up over the bottoms of the legs of Chris's tracksuit would display the extent of the ridiculously desperate quality of Chris's about-face personality change. All it took was one argument and several trips to JD Sports for Chris to transform himself into a born again Scally. It didn't stop at the clothes, either. During this time, Chris attempted to swagger, listened to happy hardcore and began leaving car magazines on the coffee table in our lounge. He brought one of my friends to tears of laughter one night trying to intersperse his conversation with as many swear words as possible in a voice that would be much better suited to such phrases as 'Mummy's at the golf club' or 'I really like Kent'.

I think he had decided to pass himself off as rough trade, but the relative absence of one night stands in his life at that time may have meant that the illusion didn't quite work.

Chris and X made up after a few weeks, at which point Chris's black shiny tops made a notable return.

For my birthday in March, I threw a party. Not a

massive thing. You know, just a gathering of a few friends and acquaintances, loud music, six cans of Stella each. Although of course, I'd not really wanted to, I invited Chris, seeing as he did actually inhabit the house at which the party would be located. I caught him in one of his more amiable moments when I asked him if he'd like to attend. He just laughed in mock horror at me, and declared he was *sure* he could think of something better to do than hang around a bunch of manic depressives listening to miserable music. He didn't seem to consider for a second I might actually be relieved that he wouldn't be making a show. But I was. Incredibly so.

Chris's plans for something better to do turned out just to be the same thing he does every Saturday night and *Reach for the Stars* was playing at an obtrusive volume as the first of my friends arrived for the evening. Not wanting to let a chance to snub me go by however, Chris stuck to his word and went out for the night, but not until after he'd given my guests a pitying goodbye smirk.

The party went well. People got wasted, someone was sick outside in the street, a lot of time was spent in the kitchen. I was chatting in the hallway around two when the front door sprang open. Chris stumbled in, possessed by one of his forced, caterwauled laughs, as if to announce to all around who exactly was home. He wasn't alone. Behind him, his quarry stood nervously on the step looking rather out-of-place. On seeing me in the vicinity, Chris dragged in the man and began wrapping himself around him. His small grunts were audible even at a distance, punctuated now and then by porn quotes of the 'ooh baby you turn me on' type.

My entire body cringed at the sight.

I was about to sneak off to, say another continent or something, when Chris collared me with a sing-songed 'Lu-uke', asking me if I wanted to be introduced to his 'new man'. I didn't but at the same time I knew I really didn't have much of a choice.

Frank's skin was an orangey brown colour of the kind that can only be produced by over-use of cheap fake tanning cream. He wore many large items of gold jewellery. His face had the texture of silly putty, and its crags deepened as he bared his false teeth in a smile. He was pleased to meet me, he told me as his sausage like fingers clasped my hands for a length of time that creeped over from 'friendly introduction' to 'hinting at sordid pleasure'.

Frank's voice had a million B & H stubbed out in it. I swear his wig slipped a little as he winked at me.

Chris grabbed hold of Frank once more. He mumbled something to me about jealousy and that there should be no stealing between friends, before telling Frank that it was 'high time for bed time'.

Chris gave Frank's arse a hefty whack as they climbed the stairs. He paused halfway up to fill me (and all who stood around) with one final detail.

'And he's married!' he whispered at me, delighted, before continuing on up.

I only thank God that the party was in its final throes and that many people had left already when Chris came back downstairs. He entered the lounge wearing only his underwear, his neck decorated with several fresh love bites. Finding me immediately, he took the chance to interrupt the conversation I was having, and positioned himself on the arm of the chair I sat in.

I'd just like to stress here that by this point in the academic year, me and Chris were not exactly best buddies. He had never previously seen me as a confidante, never felt the need to share the details of his private life with me. There are only two reasons I can think of why at that moment he decided to loudly reveal to me just exactly what he and Frank had been up to for the past forty minutes. They are a) to gain attention in what he must have seen as a suitably shockable audience and b) TO WIND ME UP.

I tried humouring him for a while, even at one point stressing how little I was interested in his sex life, but it was to no avail. I was force-fed every little detail, right down to vein-ridden anatomical descriptions and a precise body hair atlas.

Chris had not showered after sleeping with Frank. He smelt like sex. Anal sex. With someone who has irritable bowel syndrome.

I put up with Chris for about twenty minutes, after which I made it clear how ill I felt, then escaped upstairs with a couple of friends.

My bedroom door has a lock on it.

I lit incense sticks for the remainder of the night, but my nostrils seemed to have captured the bad air, and my stomach turned repeatedly until I fell asleep.

There are new additions to 'The Horror!' almost weekly. Visitors to the site can opt-in for e-mail notification of any updates, and many do.

It's nearly the end of summer term now, and soon me and Chris will finally part our ways. I shall not miss him at all, but I shall miss the support of the people who regularly post on the site's message board, and the stories they tell of the Chris Williams that feature in their own lives. Of course, I also get mails attacking me for the very concept of www.ihatechriswilliams.co.uk, and for spending so much time on being so cruel. But they're missing the point. It's not just about hatred. It's about survival. And you've got to understand that means Chris's as much as my own.

MAISIE LANGRIDGE

The Butcher's Shop

Sally wants to be a butcher. Kindly teachers, friends and neighbours, smiley, chatty people in the street politely say, 'And what will you be when you grow up?' And Sally will reply, 'A butcher – I want to be a butcher.'

Sally sits in a room with the other children. She is listening to the day's story. It is nearly hometime. A Monday. Sally's mother will be waiting at the gate. Sally can put on her own coat now and tie her shoes. She is very proud of this and often wants people to watch. Daddy will watch her unbutton her coat, one, two, when Sally gets home. He will praise her for it. Sally knows he likes her to be a good girl.

Sally runs, hop, skip, into the arms of her waiting mother. Kiss and squeeze and miss you eyes make Sally feel warm. Sally loves her mother. Sally's mother loves Sally. Hand in hand they walk, chatting, to the car. Sally tells of her day. Sally's mother listens, tells of hers. In the car – going home – time for home. Time to see Daddy, see Daddy!

*

Sally's teachers tell her mother, 'Sally says she wants to be a butcher.'

'I know she does,' says Sally's mother. Sally's mother says, 'I know.'

*

Sally and her mother drive to the shops, 'What shall we get for Daddy's tea?' Sally and her mother park the car. Sally and her mother are in the local butcher's shop. They are standing patiently at the counter. Sally's mother holds Sally's hand. Sally holds hers. Sally loves the stains and sawdust on the floor. She moves the sawdust with her feet and wants to bend and touch the stains but knows she mustn't. Sally mustn't touch the stains. Daddy doesn't like that. Sally loves the shiny butcher trays. She smells the metally smell of the blood. She sees the slabs of meat all red and brown and grainy. Sally loves the neatness of the rows. Sally's hand is slippy and moves around inside her mother's. A woman behind the counter asks Sally's mother what she wants. Sally's mother says, 'Breast of lamb, please.' They like lamb. Daddy likes lamb.

The woman serves Sally's mother, shows the cut, asks if she'd like more – 'Just over a pound. That enough, madam?' Sally's mother nods and asks for bacon. Sally can hear the men in the back of the shop laughing. She listens to the backroom clink of knives, the chatter, the thud of cleaver hitting bone and wood.

*

When Sally is older and has a butcher's shop of her very own, she will love her work. But Sally will not serve like the woman in her childhood butcher's shop. Sally will be in the backroom with the laughter and the crunch and splinter-thudding cleaver hitting bone and wood. Her heart will beat and rush whenever she smells the sticky blood. She will crack open the ribs of once bleating lambs and find herself with every carcass asking for forgiveness, but she will never know who of or why. She will be comforted by the crunch and splinter of bone and sticky marrow on the blade.

*

Sally's teachers tell her mother, 'Sally is drawing pictures at school – your Sally likes drawing pictures.' 'That's nice,' says Sally's mother, 'that's nice.'

*

When Sally is in her last year of school her friends will say, 'God! Sal – I mean *God* why do you want to be a *butcher*? It's yukky!' When Sally is not there they will say 'God! Sal's *weird* isn't she? I mean, don't you think it's *weird* her wanting to be a *butcher*?' But still they will be Sally's friends. Some of them will come and bring their children to her shop to buy their meat when they are older.

Lots of boys at school like Sally. They think she's 'attractive'. They like her smell. They like the way she moves. They think she's sexy. 'Sal's a good laugh – one of the lads – only you wouldn't want to fuck one of the lads!' – this always makes the boys laugh. Sally laughs too. Sally likes the boys liking her. Sally is very affectionate. Sally is very touchy-touchy. She likes to touch. When Sally is a butcher she will like to touch her meat.

Greg Stevens is in Sally's year. Greg Stevens wants to be a butcher. He is already working evenings and weekends. Sally's friends think it must be great to have as much money as Greg Stevens even if his part-time job isn't 'very nice'. But Sally knows that she who holds the cleaver does the chopping and Sally wants to be a butcher and she will.

*

'Will that be all, madam?' The woman behind the counter gives the meat to Sally's mother. It is 4 o'clock. The shop is filling up with hometime mothers. The mothers crowd the counter, each one looking for some tea.

A backroom butcher comes to help the woman serve. 'Now ladies; can I help you?' He has a smiley face and big hands and walks like Daddy does when he has something important to do. The butcher wears a big white apron stained with blood. He wipes his hands on his apron ready to serve a mother at the counter. Daddy wipes his hands too, just like the butcher. Daddy wipes them on towels. Daddy puts the towels in the washer. Then mummy comes back. Bits of meat and blood are sticky-shining-new on his stained apron and Sally sees the blood between the fingers of his hands.

*

When Sally is a butcher she will love her work. Meat will arrive from the slaughter house and she will silently bless each carcass. She will be astonished every time at the perfect smoothness of the dead muscle lightly sheathed in fat. She will love the selfless giving of the carcass, the headless, organless, bulks of meat

136

and Sally will transform these into thousands of sustaining dinners, keep-you-going lunches, sandwich snacks, that are the foundation of the nation. Sally knows that to be a butcher is important. She knows the power of the cleaver.

*

Sally and her mother leave the shop. Sally carries the meat for her mother. Sally feels funny carrying the meat. The weight is very even in her hands. Sally is comforted that the meat is familiar. She is shocked that the meat is strange. Sally is holding the meat for Daddy. Daddy likes lamb and bacon. Tea and breakfast. Tea and breakfast. Tea and breakfast. Sally and her mother climb into the car.

*

Sally's teachers tell her mother, 'Sally draws at school you know. Sally draws her family,' they say.

'Sally is very small in her pictures,' Sally's teachers say to Sally's mother.

'How sweet,' says Sally's mother. 'How selfless, like a girl,' she says. 'How giving,' says Sally's mother, '... giving.'

*

When Sally is ten years old she will have a friend called Suzie Watkins. Sally will tell Suzie she wants to be a butcher and show her her books with pictures of cows cut up as joints of meat. Suzie wants to be a nurse.

Suzie likes Sally – thinks she's clever.

'She knows all the names of stuff, mummy – topside, rump steak, silverside, and the names of lots of sheep and cows. Pigs, too.'

Sally and Suzie play in Sally's bedroom. Sally has some nice new coloured felt pens. Sally and Suzie play a new game. Suzie takes her clothes off and is a cow. Sally draws on her body the lines of joints of meat. She draws a blue line round Suzie's shoulder, a red line round her buttocks and hips. She draws other lines over the front and back of Suzie's body, her legs and neck. Sally's felt pens are indelible – they do not wash off with water. Sally writes the name of each joint inside Suzie's lines. Sally and Suzie look at Suzie in the mirror. Sally and Suzie like this game.

Sally says to Suzie, 'now you're my meat and I can chop you up!' Sally and Suzie laugh.

Suzie's mother will, when Sally is ten years old, complain to Sally's mother. She will tell Suzie to stop playing with Sally – but Suzie won't.

*

Sally sits in the back of the car. The meat is next to her on the seat and jiggle-jiggles when her mother turns a corner. Sally will be home soon – home soon. Soon she will see Daddy. Home to see Daddy. Monday nights with Daddy. At home Sally's mother will cook a Monday tea. Sally's mother will go to her Monday evening class. Sally will stay in with Daddy. Daddy will lock the door. Daddy always locks the door on Mondays – to protect them while mummy is away.

Daddy will unlock the door later. Then mummy

will come home. Sally will sit on Daddy's lap. Little girls must please their daddies. This is their secret night. No need to tell mummy that Daddy gets all hot. She'd only worry and it's cruel, very cruel to make a mummy worry. Daddy isn't poorly. Being hot means a Daddy is very well. Sometimes on Mondays, when Daddy is hot, Daddy calls Sally by a boy's name. Sally screws her face up.

*

When Sally is older with a butcher's shop all of her very own, Monday will remain a special day. She will go to the shop very early. She will be ready for the slaughter house delivery. Sally likes to sell fresh, not frozen, meat. Sally likes a quick process from slaughter house to table. On Monday mornings, much before Sally's first customer, much before Sally opens the shop, Sally will be chop-chopping through the animal flesh. She is a priest at the altar. She is a rainmaker. She is in a trance. Her face is statue set. Sally is silent and tears fall as she brings the cleaver down. Sally sweats and wipes her brow with a bloody hand. Sally's face mingles sweat and blood and tears. Sally knows that really Daddy wanted Sally to be Sammy and she brings the cleaver down upon the backbone of a pig. The pig splits. Tiny shards of bone pearl the air.

Later, the part-time boy will sweep them into the yard. Rats and sparrows will scavenge off the tiny tiny bits of marrow. In the yard, unknowing butcher feet will grind them into dust.

Sally makes short work of the day's delivery. She takes her butcher's knife and slip-slices through the silent muscles of unsuspecting lambs, once sturdy cattle, recently stunned pigs. Sally doesn't notice her blood-pinking hands. Sally's hands often get butcher raw but still she loves her work. Sally loves to part the sticky reluctant sinews with her butcher's knife. In their striated splendour, in the even-in-death tenacious strength of the sticky sinews, Sally sees her God. Sally brings down her cleaver on Mondays. Mondays begin the butchering week. On Mondays, Sally and her cleaver are one.

*

Sally's teachers tell her mother, 'Sally says she wants to be a butcher.'

'I know she does,' says Sally's mother.

But Sally's teachers know her mother does not, cannot, even as she says, 'I know – I know,' they know that Sally's mother doesn't know.

*

Sally's mother parks the car. Sally squishes the meat with her fingers. Sally pokes the dead flesh. Sally prods the gradually decaying meat. Sally watches as the still wanting-to-live muscle pushes back its plastic shroud. Sally waits for her mother to unlock the car door. Sally runs up the path. Daddy will be home soon – home soon. Home. Daddy. Sally is at the back door. Sally's fingers are slipping on the big shiny brass handle. Sally's fingers are sweaty. Sally's mother says, 'I'll do it dear,' and opens the big back door. Sally and her mother are inside the kitchen. 'Why don't you play darling, 'till Daddy gets home?'

Sally has a toy box in the living room. It lives under the table in the converted dining area. Sally is rummaging-scrummaging in her toy box. Sally is hot but she will keep her coat on. She will keep her coat on to show Daddy when he comes home. Sally's mother is in the kitchen. To braise? To boil? To roast? To grill? Lamb or... O God – lamb's too hard. Bacon. It is Monday and for a quiet life Sally's mother will grill the bacon. This is quicker and the lamb will do for Tuesday. Or Wednesday. Sally and her mother and her Daddy are an eat-it-while-it's-fresh family. Breakfast will have to be cereal. Sally's mother puts the lamb into the fridge. The fridge begins to chill the blood swollen cells. The lamb is cool dead muscle in the fridge. The lamb doesn't move.

Sally is playing with her plasticine. Sally likes plasticine. She can make it, mould it, squidge it and fold it into anything she wants. Unbelievably, Sally's plasticine is still different colours and is rolled up into pink balls, blue balls, brown balls, green balls. Sally's plasticine is neat like Sally's butcher's shop will be.

Sally's mother lines the strips of bacon on the grill. Strikes a match. Lights the gas. Sally is making a plasticine farmyard full of animals. Sally uses an old blunt butter knife to cut her plasticine. She uses it to help make her animals. Sally makes cows and sheep and pigs and goats. Sally makes chickens and ducks and geese and hens. Sally's little brow and lips are pursed with concentration.

The bacon fat is warming. Cook it well. Daddy likes crispy bacon. Crispieee – bacon! Sally can hear the fat spit. Daddy will be home soon.

Sally's mother hums in the kitchen – turns the

bacon slices in the pan. Sally is taking some farmyard animals to the slaughter house. She is cutting the throats of sheep and cows with her butter knife. Sally is lining the carcasses up. Daddy. Daddy will be home soon.

Sally is chopping the stumpy legs off plasticine cows. Sally hears the back door, hellos and kisses in the kitchen. Sally stops what she is doing. The house is full of the smell of meaty bacon.

'Where's my little girl?' Daddy is standing in the living room. Sally hears the bacon spitting in the grill. Sally is turning round and Daddy watches her unbutton her coat, one, two. He praises her for it.

Sally is a good girl and Daddy is home.

MARY LOWE

Skating

Outside the caff, Ray's on the mobile, shouting, 'Aye man, Aye man, Aye.' I waited painfully, as my guts were minced. I'd been up most of the night, wondering whether I was brave enough to go it alone.

Ray barked, 'Bye man,' slapped the phone shut, slid it onto the clasp that dangled from his hip and paused as if weighing up what to say. He had that look about him, the Dad look I call it, even though he's not my Dad, when he'd take me aside to talk 'man to man', dispensing advice like soft toilet paper. He's well-meaning, a lovely geezer but Ray thinks he knows me and he doesn't.

'Had a good night of it, by tha looks of things,' he said.

'Right, Ray.'

'Been clubbin, ha ya?'

'Right.'

'I can tell by the look in yer eyes,' he said, pursing his mouth into a tight round 'O'. He kept looking at me. The round brown eyes, the stubble on the chin, turned towards me full-tilt.

'What?' I said. He got on my wick sometimes. His affection prickled under my skin.

'Oof I danna,' he said. There was a long pause as he unlocked the metal shutter, straightening his back, after bending down over four sets of locks and keys. 'So, next Thursday night, you're still on for the gym?'

'Tttt,' I slapped my forehead. 'Shit. Damn. Sorry, Ray. Not this week. Something's cropped up.'

'Ah,' he said, head down, busying himself with the key.

'I can't get out of it either, it's a favour I said I'd do for a mate.'

He sniffed.

'He's not well,' I lied, 'I'm going to run some errands for him.'

The truth was I had an appointment at the hospital which I couldn't miss. I turned away. Whether he was hurt or angry, I didn't want to know. I imagined his face crumpled like a piece of litter, feelings strangled like crossed wires. He muttered something under his breath.

'Maybe next week, eh?' I said.

'For Chrissake sake,' he said. 'Open this door for me will you?'

Thursday was Our Night, down the Triple Gold gym to help him with his repetitions. It was one-ah, two-ah, come on Ray, you can do it, pull that muscle up through your layers of meat, your pastry forearms, get that gravy shunting through your veins again. I was his trainer, shouting encouragement and ignoring the curses. I carried his bag when his back couldn't hack it. The old man was training his way back to health after a dodgy time with the angina. I went along for the company mostly, it was the nearest I'd ever get to exercise. Thursday nights had been a chance to relax, to mix with a crowd of blokey blokes who accepted me purely because I was a friend of Ray's. Hey Jezzer, howayer – they'd shout – Champion, I'd say, never better.

There was the familiar shout of metal as he

heaved the roll upwards. He made a meal of it every time. Keys and mobile dangled from his plastic belt. Ego on a key fob. Six months ago, my first day in the job, he said, 'Son you're in charge of tables, service, hygiene – *Ahm the one* with the keys and *I* cash up at the end of the day. Gottit?' Two months later, he made me his Assistant Manager and Maureen, who's been working in the caff since the invention of eggs, became the Assistant to the Assistant.

The greasy gloom hit me when we stepped inside. Ray snapped on the lights but still the smell of yesterday's chips hung in the air, so tangible I could almost see them; dripping girders of pale potato, suspended from the ceiling like oily windchimes. I wanted to retch but placed my hand on my stomach and visualised cool sheets and a damp flannel. I reached for the room freshener, varnished the air with magnolia and within minutes I felt okay. Maureen would be here soon, wittering on about her son's veruccas or her husband's piles, and we'd settle into our routine. Maureen in the kitchen, Ray on the till, me, bowing and scraping.

Ray limped his way to the counter, his bags of change ready for the Saturday rush. 'What do yer fancy for brekkie, lad? Bacon sarnie?'

My stomach churned.

'No Ray, not this morning.'

His eyebrows knitted together so hard the line at the bridge of his nose folded his forehead in two. Poor sweet Ray. He was struggling but I couldn't help him.

'C'mon lad. Best meal of the day. Fried egg, toast?'

I shook my head, grease didn't sit well with my medication.

'I'm fine Ray, honest.'

He started taking the bags of buns from the bread tray, piling them up by the toaster in the back. 'The missus has been asking after you again. It's weeks since you've been round. She's doing your favourite on Sunday. We'd love it son if...'

I pictured Shirley, the missus, with her untrained fluff of hair and the wedding ring standing out like a carbuncle on her finger. 'Sounds great,' I said. 'I might be out tomorrow, I'm not sure. Can I phone you first thing?'

Ray looked puzzled. His brown eyes widened. He was staring at me so hard I thought fuck, he's rumbled me. The thing is Ray...

'When are you going to settle doon lad? Hey? You're nae spring chicken any more.'

That one again.

'What's that got to do with anything?' I said, 'I'll let you know, okay?'

'Me and the missus worry about you yer know. It's not right, a man of your age, to have no...' he paused and lowered his voice, *love* in your life. You're thirty two and forever acting like a teenager.'

That phrase again. Me and the missus. It rolled off his tongue as smooth as a Rizla. There was a long sigh from long-suffering Ray. 'There's nothing wrong son, is there?' He looked so old, his face was grey and haunted.

Leave it Ray.

Drop it.

Maureen burst through the door, shouting fuck, fuck, fuck with an imaginary rabid dog at her heels. She picked up her shoes, first one, then the other, studying the soles. New stilettos by the looks of things, and judging by the shade of orange that was daubed across her face, she'd be going out with the lasses straight from work, down the town for Bacardi Breezers.

'That's lucky that,' I said.

'What?' she snapped. Whether it be her husband who drank, her cousin with the bulimia, her mother who'd shacked up with a supergrass and was under 24 hour police protection, something was up, which meant that me and Ray would spend the day like two minnows circling a piranha fish.

'If it's dogs, it means bad luck. Cows means money in the family,' I said.

'And when was the last time you saw a cow on the Shields Road?' she snapped.

I moved out of the way to let her into the kitchen. She eased herself out of her new, malodorous shoes and wiped them clean with a floor cloth before slipping her feet into a pair of old slippers. I wondered about mentioning health and safety but thought better of it.

'What's up with you then?' she barked and peered up a moment from her shoes. She softened a little. 'Look like you've seen a ghost, you're that pale. Alright are we?' As if you care, I thought and nodded, making a mental note to keep out of her way.

Fat cars buzzed outside; Audis, Volvos and the lorries from the docks. The door swung open and in breezed Love's Young Dream, a couple in their early twenties. On closer inspection, the older one could have been any age, his moisturised face having fared well against the North wind. The younger one was a cute version of Prince Charles; all ears and cravat. I made the move, offered them the menu, tossed them my winning smile but it was wasted. They only had eyes for each other. Their tanned hands touched fingertips and the menu passed between them like a sacrament. I shuffled back to Ray at the till, who was counting the notes, a large tongue poking from his mouth like a curled fiver. He was pulling a face but trying to hide it.

'Friends of yours?' he asked stiffly.

'Never seen them before in my life,' I snapped. So he was back to his old self; the macho meat eater, the Toon supporter with the big bollocks. He didn't complain when the pink pounds piled up in his till, the hypocrite.

The clientele was changing and I was responsible for that – gay couples, quaint old ladies from the right side of town, customers with big disposables, in for their cappuccinos or their Death by Chocolate - few labour costs and a big return. I don't know why Maureen carped on about it so much, most of the orders these days required only a dab hand at packet opening. The days of your hotplate are numbered I'd told her.

It was time for a wager. 'Ray, man,' I said, 'Next customers. Two fat ladies?'

'Eighty eight.' He said quick as a ferret, 'Your full o' yourself this morning. How much?'

'Pound.'

'Go on then. It's good for starters.'

We waited for what seemed an age before the door teetered open and sure enough the pound was mine. Minnie and her sister Kate, two retired teachers, chirruped Good Morning before settling their big old bodies down by the radiator. I sidled over.

'Lovely to see you again,' I smiled and they returned the compliment by turning their big old faces towards me simultaneously, smiling like a couple of crinkled moons.

'I div'na how you do it, sometimes. I don't really,' said Ray, smiling as he handed me the money.

On a good day, Ray reckoned himself to be a local business tycoon. Raymond Diamond he called himself: had a lucky gem sewn inside the hem of his coat or so he said. Hadn't brought him much luck so far. When heading for a downer, he reverted to his other name, Ray of Snotshine. Months ago, he'd wept like a baby on a cold, snowy night down by the quay, in a deserted carpark, after too many beers. It was one of the rare occasions we'd gone drinking. He'd wanted to show me the town in its nocturnal glory, to have a night on the tiles dodging the puddles of puke and the screeching girls in their short skirts. After a skinful, a curry and a medley of Neil Sedaka songs, he told me about his only son, killed on black ice years ago as he was crossing the road, by a driver on his way home from the pub. 'He was just like you, Jezzer, blond hair, smallish.' Tears slid down his cheeks. 'And he was...' he paused, searching for a word that didn't materialise, '...And now he's gone. And there's just me and the missus. He was all we had.'

He said it quietly in a deep daddy gruff voice, patting me on the back, so very gently, as if he were afraid I'd turn to dust.

I was sifting the lumps out of the sugar bowls. Hoying

gobs of crystallised brown onto the table – customers, wet teaspoons – it's a lethal combination. Maureen was lording it in the kitchen, letting rip on the Julie Andrew's Songbook, shrieking her head off and making me feel tense. Any moment now, Ray would explode and two minor earth tremors would jostle for precedence.

'What's that awful racket? For Chissake!' Ray shoved the till tray hard. 'How many times have I told you?'

'Aw, C'mon you used to love a bit of a sing-song.' Maureens's head peered out from the kitchen, 'How about this one?' She started to croak, 'Edelweiss. Edelweiss, every morning you greeeeeet meeeee.'

'Can't you see the lad's got a bad head?'

He gestured towards me and I noticed a tight line appearing along Maureen's mouth.

'You used to love that one. We used to sing it all the time,' she said.

Ray levered up from his perch, manoeuvred himself behind the counter and bundled her back to the spitting hot plate. 'Not any more,' I heard him say. 'We've got customers for God's sake.'

Then Maureen's voice pinned up a few octaves. 'Customers?' she shrieked. 'They used to be our friends, yer great pillock. Used to like a bit of life about the place. And now look at it. Like a bleeding Harrod's picnic basket.'

I heard the crash of a pan as it hit the floor. Twenty chewing faces turned in the direction of the kitchen. I smiled like a pillock and did something strange with my hands. There was a moment of silence, then the back door to the lane slammed shut.

By the time Maureen returned half an hour later, the customers had thinned out and I'd been burger flipping and cake cutting to the point of exhaustion. She sloped in, red-eyed, carrying a packet of chocolate buttons and the *Daily Mirror* for Ray and the two of them grappled with each other in some kind of clumsy hug in the kitchen. I looked in the opposite direction, my mouth tasting bitter. Maureen in the kitchen, Ray on the till, me, bowing and scraping.

I was leaning over the counter wondering what the hell I was going to do when Maureen elbowed me gently in the stomach, 'What's your stars, Jezzer?'

'Leo.' I said flatly, holding on to the formica to steady myself. My brain was jumping. I clapped my hand to my forehead and held it there. Maureen gave me one of her slanty looks, head on one side, as if she had the measure of me, as if she was weighing me up. She looked down at the paper.

'Leo,' she repeated slowly, keeping her puffy eyes glued to my face, 'You alright?'

'Yes.'

A questioning eyebrow shot up. She read, 'The heavens are about to shift on their axis as a piece of news wakes up those around you...'

Ray looked up from his till. 'Well then...' he said. I knew what was coming, 'What do yer think?' We looked out at the curls of paper blown into a ballet of plastic bags and beyond to the clear blue sky.

Maureen jumped in with, 'Hey man. I'm in the middle of something here.' Her mouth fell open in outrage. Ray hadn't heard her and I was indifferent. Neither of us believed in horoscopes. 'For fock's sake,'

Maureen hissed, glancing darkly at the two of us, 'You two, like a couple of kids. You've got nae idea.' She slapped back to her den, gathering an armful of paper as she went.

'What's the matter with her?' said Ray.

'Time of the month?' I rolled my eyes.

'Women eh?' he said. We settled down. Three hours of opening time and only one wager between us. We were way behind.

'Okay then, bonny lad, I'll bet you a fiver it rains before dinner time.'

'Dinner time, Raymond. What time do you call that? Be specific, now.'

He scratched his head. 'Well now, son. Let me see. Twelve o'clock. How about it?'

'A fiver you say. I'll take my break now and let you know.'

'Okay son, see you later.'

I slipped past a scowling Maureen and opened the door to the cool fresh air.

I was what they called an RD, a 'Recent Diagnosis'. We met at the hospital once a week, a handful of us, sinking into the incontinence chairs, sulking. They treated us to a series of talks, videos, interactive CDs. Welcome to the wonderful world of HIV. I'd only been to a couple of sessions. At the last one, we were given sticky labels to jiggle around on a piece of sugar paper. Feelings, thoughts, emotions were written in different coloured felt pens by nurses with neat handwriting. We could take the opportunity to express ourselves, they said. Thanks but no thanks, I said and walked home through an evening of stinging rain.

Ray looked up all smiles as I came back in. 'What do ya say, then?' he said rubbing his hands in expectation.

'You're on,' I said.

There was a flurry of customers as the sky clouded over and the temperature dipped. Twelve o'clock came and the rain held off, which meant I was six quid ahead. My lucky day, I thought. I was non-stop busy, taking orders, hovering like a vulture while the college boys ate away their hangovers with all-day breakfasts. It was scoop and pass, scoop and pass. I handed the orders to Maureen who sulked in her greasy pit. She snatched them from me, spiked them on the skewer, banged down the saucepans, clashed the oven door. We were working hard and my head was thumping.

I remembered there were painkillers in my bag. I squeezed through the kitchen, past the bread buns and the sacks of tomatoes, to find Maureen clawing at the coats by the back door. She spun round fast and eyed me suspiciously. I heard the rattle of pills as she moved my bag.

'What are you doing?' I squawked.

'Looking for something. What do you think I'm doing. Pinching?'

I tutted. Whatever I thought of Maureen, she wasn't a thief.

'I don't like you touching my stuff okay?' I tried to keep my voice level.

'Why?' she said. 'Something precious inside? What you got in there, diamonds?' She shook the rattling bag and her hand delved inside.

'What the...' I reached out to grab her but she was a strong woman and held me off with one hand as she emptied the contents of my bag on the floor, scattering pill bottles in all directions.

'Bloody hell. You've got some stuff here.' She scrutinised my face and I stared back at her, willing some logical explanation to spring out and silence her but none came.

'So?' I screamed. My head was hammering, my life depended on those pills and here she was, holding them up to the light, practising her reading.

'Retro... retrovir,' she stuttered. 'What's that for...?'

I snatched the bottle from her. Her lipsticked mouth shuddered like an evacuation from a baboon's bottom.

'Whatever you've got, lad, I wouldn't want it,' she said. Then softly, 'What is it then?'

For a second I wondered about telling her. It would be over, at least. Out in the open. But another glance at the reddened neck and the cold eyes and I was shaking my head.

'No,' I said. 'No.'

Something stirred in her silted-up brain. She paused and her fish-eyes blinked.

'I get it,' she murmured. 'You and your mincing friends.'

I waited.

'Filling the place with... AIDS,' she said.

'What?' I tried to look outraged, tore my mouth open to a look of disgust but it was a poor imitation.

She went on, 'And working in a caff as well, handling food... tut, tut.' A mouth opening and closing, spitting words like chewed gristle.

'For fuck's sake,' I almost shouted. I wanted to

reach out and grab her, shake her until the mouth stopped moving.

'He'll give you a reference if you're lucky, he's good like that,' she said with a little sneer.

'You know nothing,' I said.

'The way you twist that daft bugger round your little finger. Wait till I...' She didn't finish as I struck her on the side of the mouth. She fell, landed on a box. Crash.

I stood over her. I wanted to kill the bitch. She waited for the moment of death and we eyed each other, surprise scrawled across our faces. It was funny really. The blood thundered in my ears and I noticed a hole in her tights, a patch of white skin lit up by the flourescent. She looked like an upturned beetle, wearing holey tights.

Who knows how long we stood like that, me the potential murderer and her, the upturned beetle.

And there was Ray standing between us, bulky as a punch bag, looking from me to her, searching for a clue, hands on hips like a benevolent parent.

'What the...?' Ray's eyes danced with fear. 'Christ. Jez.'

He held out his hand to Maureen and hoisted her to standing. She stood shaking, tears running down her face in dusty channels.

'This is serious stuff,' he said. 'The pair of you... I'm going to have to have a think about this one. Maureen get your coat, you're going home.' She gathered her belongings. I walked out to the front and waited for the two remaining customers to go. As soon as the door closed behind them, I flipped over the closed sign and locked it. A while later she emerged, a tiny cut on the side of her mouth, issuing threats of police and solicitors and how I should be afraid to go out at night.

I was silent as Ray closed the door behind her. 'Well,' he said, 'Some day eh?'

We would talk, there would be tears. We'd decide what to do.

'Ray.'

He settled his eyes on me for a flickering moment. I studied him. The kind brown eyes, the stubble on his chin, the full soft mouth. I remembered everything from that night. I always do. The ice on the inside of the car window. The darkness outside. The smell of his shirt. The feel of his shoulder blades.

Ray padded through to the kitchen. I heard the sound of tea being poured.

'She's a bloody trial sometimes, that woman,' he shouted back to me. 'I'll bet you a pound she'll be back tomorrow, though.' He reappeared carrying two mugs.

'Ray, man,' I whispered as he slapped his arms down on the counter, hands glued together as if in prayer.

'Maureen's a silly cow at the best of times. To tell you the truth I divvent blame you.'

'But Ray...'

He took a mouthful of tea and gulped it down. He looked out to the street. It was raining outside, grey, slanting and cold. We sat side by side at the counter, hands cupped around our mugs.

'I'll get my coat,' I croaked.

When I left, he was counting change into bags for the bank. He was humming a tune I could not catch.

As I walked past him, bent over the silver ten pences, the bronze bolts of pound coins, I wondered whether he'd nod or say goodbye.

ROSIE LUGOSI

file>>corrupted

Annie wakes up talking.

'He looked like Woody Allen, but with a beard.'

'Oh god.' I push back the covers, give up on dozing. The moment she opens her mouth I can smell her breath, stale with beer from the night before.

'He was really hitting on me.'

'Gross,' I mutter. 'I hate Woody Allen. I always hated him, even before all that stuff with his daughter.'

'*Adopted* daughter.'

'Yeah, right. Daughter. I had a lover who really had a thing for his films and would quote from them. It was supposed to be, I don't know, affectionate and funny and clever at the same time. I hated it. And her. Made my teeth grind.'

Annie is gazing off to the left, picking plaque off her teeth and wiping it on the sheet. She stopped listening when I wouldn't let her have *adopted* daughter. It makes me want to go on some more: pound her with words. She stops listening so fast.

'I might. You know.'

'What?'

'See him. Meet up with him.'

'What?' This wakes me up for sure. 'Are you nuts?'

I think I spent too many years in Brooklyn. It's salted my speech in some deep briny pickle: when I get agitated I sound like a low-rent Al Pacino with teats. My voice comes out of my nose. It makes me stand out. I hate that. When people watch. Even though we're alone, lying on my bed, on the sixth floor of this grimy tower block with the door locked and the cheap little burglar chain on, I lower my voice. Try to get the blend-in, bland Englishness back into it. I'm suddenly aware we're naked and I want to pull sweatpants up over my hips, a t-shirt over her shoulders. Though no-one can see us. They'd have to be flying past the window for that.

I'm jumpy this morning. I do *not* need Annie going on about some man drooling over her at a party I didn't go to.

'Why?'

'Why what?'

She breathes out petulantly.

'Why am I nuts?'

'What do you honestly think's going to happen?'

She shrugs.

'The usual, at some point.'

'Why him? What's suddenly wrong with picking up some guy off the street?'

'Maybe I'm bored. Maybe I'm curious.'

'Curious about what? In what possible way is he going to be anything but the bloody same as everyone else?'

'He spoke to me. He listened.'

'Oh, right.'

'It was different. Felt weird, like I was prickling all over my back.'

'That should have been warning enough, I would have thought.'

'I kind of liked it. He said I spoke English like a Netherlander.'

'So he can't be English, right? *They* would say you spoke English like someone from Amsterdam. It's

160

the only place they've heard of.'

'I didn't say he was English. He might not have been. He didn't say he was.'

'You do speak like a Netherlander. You'd been there years when I met you.'

I almost say, *found* you. She claims she doesn't know how many years, or where she was before. I don't know if she has forgotten, or won't tell me. I want to ask her when I've got my fingers in her cunt and her eyes roll up and she spreads across the bed and lets go. But I get worried then she won't let me touch her any more, so I keep my mouth shut and wish I could let go like her. Instead of watching her eyes for pleasure. She does have pleasure. It's the way she falls apart.

'Why do you want to make things difficult for yourself when they can be so easy?' I sigh.

She can be stupid sometimes; I feel like she wants me to be her mother. So I can look after her, hold her when she comes back after one of her nights out; nights when I watch the red light of the immersion heater as it warms water for the bath I know she'll want when she returns raging and intoxicated with it all. So she can have someone to fight with, break the rules with, be a little shit with. I'm safe to be stupid with. I'm not going anywhere.

'I want to try something different.'

'Like what?'

'I don't know. Meet up. Go for a meal. Watch him choose things off a menu and talk to the waiter. I don't think I've ever talked to a waiter.'

Her arms are trembling. She rolls closer to me. I stroke her beautiful arching bones. She lets me. I tell myself I am the only person she allows to do this. Her voice is drowsy.

'Listen to him talk some more. Talk about Holland like I really got to know the place, rather than just inhabited it for a while. Go dancing. Wear something that doesn't cover me up.'

She knows her last sentence will knock the air out of me, so she says it softly, as if that will make it less of a shock. The words dangle between us. I try not to do anything which will let on how much I want to shout and break things, but I might as well not bother. She knows.

'Why not?'

'Why not what?'

'Wear what I want?'

'Did I say anything?' I snap.

She really does want a fight this morning. I don't know what's wrong with her.

'What is it with this guy anyway? You think he's going to want to come near you and play happy couples if you're not covered up? If he sees what you look like under those clothes of yours? You know what it's like out there. He'll think you're a freak. If you're really lucky and he's some kind of PC fiend, he'll cough politely and call you *disabled*, whilst heading for the nearest fire exit. Great idea, Annie. What a swell party this is.'

'I'm not a cripple,' she mumbles.

'Shit. I know that. Don't you think I know?'

I grab a handful of my hair and tug at it. It's way too early to be having this conversation. Let her do what she wants. As long as she comes home for me to wash clean. She always does.

'Just tell me where you're going, okay?'

'Okay.'

She tries not to smile too much. Rolls over, fucks me till my last bit of breath is pushed out.

*

Swallowing is an anti-climax. It's what she says. Prefers to hold the stuff in her mouth, roll it round her tongue, tastebuds popping in salt overload. All reflexes begging her *swallow, swallow*, but holding it there, lips clamped together. Seeing how long she can hold out. Mouth full. I have watched her. I watch her now, before the mirror, carefully painting on her lipstick, a dark red, shiny as a scab. She grins at me and her reflection shows its teeth. Makes a play of gnashing them together, growling noises bubbling in the back of her throat.

'I'll not be long. A bit longer than usual. He likes Italian.'

'He would.'

She raises an eyebrow.

'He's suggested a place near the coach station...'

'Cheapskate,' I throw at her. She ignores me, as she should.

'...called Giovanni's, Mario's, something like that. You'll find it. He'll probably want to go to his place.'

'What's wrong with some back alley? There's plenty enough around there.'

'He's different.' She talks slowly, as if I am the stupid one. 'Maybe I'll see him a couple of times. Maybe not even do it.'

That's the one which gets me. Not do it? It makes

163

me cruel.

'Yeah, like there's some other reason, other than the fucking obvious, why he wants to buy you a meal. He doesn't want what's between your ears, Annie. Look at yourself.'

I expect her to look at the mirror, see the harshness of her cheekbones, her bony shoulders and all the rest of it, and hold out her arms to hug me, sob a little. She sets her mouth into a dull scarlet line, smoothes her hair and stands up. Her face is turned away from me.

'We'll see. You know where I am. That's enough.'

*

I give her an hour. She's right, the restaurant is easy to find. I can see the door from the overhang of the coach station opposite, lean against the wall to give the impression of waiting, not watching. The air is damp and I wish I'd worn more than a sweatshirt. Clutches of people trail past dragging squeaky suitcases. Buses arrive, and leave. Men glance at me, one approaches, mutters, 'Well?' and I tell him to get lost. It seems I can't drop the face I've worked years to perfect: my features set permanently in whore.

It starts to drizzle. I count the couples, always bloody couples, in and out of the Italian. Another hour evaporates. How long does she want, for Christ's sake? How interesting can it be to watch this man shovel food, talk about himself?

I tuck my fists into my armpits. A rectangle of light shows briefly as the door to the restaurant opens and there she is, framed in cheap wood. She pauses, looks in my direction. I swear she can scent me, knows exactly where I am. He appears behind her and his voice carries across the street, over the roofs of the passing cars. Her laughter answers and she takes his arm with a coy gesture. She is wearing her long grey coat. I wonder if she removed it in the pizzeria. Or if she's keeping that till later. I could shout, 'You've seen the face; wait till you get a load of the body.' They would hear me.

If she knows I am following, she doesn't let on. Never has done. I expect them to hail a cab, am ready for that, but they head towards one of the fancy warehouse conversions overlooking the canal. So he's loaded. Annie stumbles and presses against his side. He puts his arm round her and she laughs loud enough for me to hear. If she's trying to piss me off she's succeeding. Why doesn't she just get on with it?

They climb the broad steps to the door. I watch his hands as he busies himself with a bunch of keys. Something's not right. As I close the distance between us carefully, I try to work out what it is. It's his hands. Steady. He's not even a little drunk. I look at Annie, teetering on the flagstone next to him. She is. Or she's faking it better than I've ever seen before. The door opens and closes in hydraulic slow motion. I count them down the corridor, calling the lift, up to his floor, unlock the door, cross the carpet and: there she is, like she said she would, at a French window three storeys up. She slides it open and steps onto the tiny balcony bolted to the side of the building. The size of a bedside table – probably added five grand to the price of the place. Her mouth is working; she'll be saying, 'Hey what a great view you've got up here.' Then she turns back, leaving the window open a crack. Maybe she isn't drunk after all. I find a doorway and settle down for another wait.

Two hours later my bones ache. The light is unflickering in the window above. No-one's moving up there. Shit, she could be finishing him off in the bathroom for all I know. Three hours. The light is steady. Jesus. I stretch. I'm leaving her to it. She can run the fucking bath herself. But something is making my fingers twitch. If that bitch is having her brains fucked out by that runty little bastard, I'll kill her.

Getting up to the balcony is no problem, I've climbed steeper. The first thing I see through the glass is his feet, sticking out from behind a chair.

I tumble through the door and see Annie flung across the mattress, her wrists clamped in silver handcuffs. The quilt is shiny with blood. She is lying on her wings which spread out beneath her like a bedcover. They have been stripped, the delicate membrane cut out, leaving a lattice of bones. Annie bled to death, pinned out like a butterfly on a collector's mat.

I turn to where he is sprawled on the floor. He will not have made a lot of noise. She likes that. Liked that. Was careful where she bit the neck, going straight for the vocal chords before she started drinking. The carpet is littered with small neat lumps of maroon jelly, the size of my breasts. She could fit them perfectly in her mouth. The opening in the upper part of his abdomen suggests they may be parts of his liver. The marks of her teeth have tattooed the skin about his navel. That is where it started. I check his hand, her long hairs wrapped round his fingers. I see him snipping at her wings, grabbing her head, pushing it for her to go down on him, and how she bit him.

Strung like bunting around us are photos, pegged out on fishing twine. I pick at one of them. A blurred black-and-white of a man, cloven hooves for feet. Throat cut. The next a woman, her breasts cut off. An extra mouth gapes in her neck, full of sharp teeth. I grab at them like falling leaves: all of them different, like Annie. All of them dead. He must have had a field day with her. Must have smelled her out. I start howling. From below, I hear someone bang on their ceiling.

I kneel on the bed and rock her gently, kiss her eyes closed. Fold up the tatters of her wings and swaddle her in the sheet she's lying on. She seems so insubstantial when I pick her up. I push the window open wide, jump on to the balcony rail and balance there a while, sniffing the air. Then I loosen my jeans, unroll my tail, unsheath my claws, swing down the side of the building and head for home.

SUSANNAH MARSHALL

'Round Midnight

Every time Seymour walked past the yard, the dog barked loudly, and every time Seymour walked past the yard, the woman who owned the dog that barked loudly barked even louder.

'Fuckinsherrupyerbarkinyerfuckinbastarddog.'

Seymour disliked noise intensely. Her escape was to play one of her old 78's on the cabineted stereogram she kept in the box room. Louis Armstrong. Thelonious Monk. Billie Holiday.

*

On her route home she slowed to listen to the violinist who busked in the town centre. On good days, days which were becoming fewer, Seymour would drop some coins into the velveteen innards of the opened instrument case. On the occasion when she passed, and the violinist happened to be playing *Smoke Gets In Your Eyes*, she left a particularly generous donation.

The frantic barking of the dog and the frenetic yelling of the woman meant that Seymour was nearly home, away from the soft focus of the violinist's cry, and back to the terraced reality of her home and what lay inside.

As she neared the back gate, Seymour pulled a large white handkerchief from the inner pocket of her pin-stripe jacket and dabbed anxiously at her brow. She always wore pin-stripe in dark background shades with chalky white stripes cutting through. Right out of the Prohibition era, with muted trumpets crying in clandestine gin-joints. Double-breasted, turned up over Italian leather brogues; the suits seemed strangely cool on the woman who worked her days in the convoluted corridors of the archive library, rarely seeing the public or the light of day, emerging in the dark even in the summer, to make her reluctant way home.

It hadn't always been like that. At first, when she was besotted even with the thought of Marina, she would tear home, leaving the library in a flurry of dust at five thirty pm on the dot. She'd practically run through the pedestrian-strewn streets, knocking pigeons and *Big Issue* sellers from her path. And the barking of the crazy dog was sweet music to her ears as it meant she was but a few back yards from home. Then she'd fly through the door, through the small scullery, the anaglypta hung back-room, up the bannistered stairs and into the Victorian bathroom kept at Mediterranean temperatures by the multitude of spotlights emulating trillions of stars. She'd be so frantically euphoric at reuniting with Marina that she'd scoop her up and hold her so tightly, she wouldn't have to worry about her slipping from a gentle but firm grasp.

These days, it was a different story. Seymour crept home, taking the longest route possible. Past the smoky, velveteen violinist in the town centre. Then through the park. The park with its rhododendrons seemingly flowering all year long and its promenade, bandstand splendour, with a view of the city stretching beyond like the backdrop from some urban opera. A septet of high-rise blocks known to the locals as the

Seven Sisters, though once it'd been two brothers who'd jumped from their balconies to tarmaced deaths. And the turquoise dome of the church near the station, strangely Romanesque in a mill-dominated landscape. Plenty of those standing still; phantoms of King Cotton's era, chimneys losing out to the golden splendour of the minarets of flourishing mosques. Seymour's route through the park, initially a delaying tactic, had been the beginning of a now habitual pastime. Lake gazing.

One creeping walk home, Seymour had stopped by the lake in the park. She had a balled up piece of cling-film in her pocket with the remnants of a chocolate-spread sandwich crumbled within and she cast the crumbs across the surface of the lake, food for the lethargic and over-fed, though still greedy ducks. The lake surface was a dark green, its water oily and thick. Seymour often found her self wondering just how deep the water was. There were iron railings around the perimeter, waist high, which meant she had to lean over to peer into its depths, or shallows. She'd never seen anyone paddling there, though suspected this was more because of the toxic-looking water than the murky depths.

*

'Fuckingsherrupyerbarkinyerfuckinbastarddog.'

Seymour winced, she was nearly home. She decided she'd steal into the house. Through the back door, through the small scullery, the anaglypta hung back-room, up the bannistered stairs and quietly pass the Victorian bathroom, where Marina soaked in tropical bubble-bath, into the box room, where she'd sit until the safe hours of the night when Marina would do nothing but sing and brush her hair and could not be distracted.

'Shit!'

The eighth board on the stairs creaked, as Seymour knew all too well. She stood, stopping in mid-tread.

'Please. Please...' she whispered to some unidentified gods in the hope that they would not wake Marina.

'Seymour?'

'Shit!

'Sea-mooor, honey. Is that yoooooooo?'

Singing, already? Seymour's watch said only six fifty-four. It was usually at least nine before Marina started, particularly in summer when the dusk descended later. Seymour climbed the remaining stairs.

Get it bloody over with.

She took a deep breath and pushed open the bathroom door. The lenses of her glasses, which Seymour wished were horn-rimmed, steamed up.

'Sea-amour. My love, come and kiss me.'

Seymour stumbled blindly to the bathtub, wiping her glasses on the hem of her dress shirt, already becoming a bit limp in the steamy bathroom. She felt the sharp poke of a fingernail just beneath her left eye as she floundered into Marina's outstretched arms. And then a plethora of overly wet kisses, like being slapped repeatedly in the face with seaweed. Seymour spluttered, half-choked by the slippery arms around her neck and half by the odour, which had become a permanent bathroom fixture.

You, my old trout, are smelling particularly fishy today, she thought but would not dare utter to Marina, who would dredge up the most appalling wailing - like a fog warning, serenading a ghost ship.

'Honey. Sailor. Did you get my shopping?'

Marina had slipped back into the bath water, idly flicking drips from the bath tap with her prehensile tail fin.

Seymour didn't bother to answer. Shopping for Marina was a daily routine. She sat on the toilet seat and fished into the Boots carrier bag.

'Bubble-bath, body lo...'

'Matey. Did you get me Matey? You know it's my favourite.'

'Yes. Matey.' Then, in an under-breath mumble, 'Always fucking Matey. The saleswoman thinks I'm a fucking bubble bath pervert.'

It was a shame, too, because Seymour fancied that particular sales assistant. She briefly considered spreading Matey across her breasts.

'Body lotion. Did you get that?'

Marina was into oil of Evening Primrose at the moment. She said it was good for her scales and stopped them from shedding so quickly. Once, Seymour had felt a tender thrill each time she found a discarded scale. She pressed many of them between pages of books, kept there as mercurial petals. She recalled in the first sea-shanty days of their relationship, when they made love in the bathtub, Seymour's backside protruding from the water and her elbows jammed against the sides, she'd emerge flushed and gasping with loose scales frosting her thighs where

Marina's tail had flickered.

Marina was reaching out, beaded trails of bath water dripping from her fingers to the permanently soaked floor.

'I think I might go back to Oil of Ulay you know. I'm getting a bit tired of this Evening Primrose.'

'What about the coconut oil?' Seymour ventured. At least the smell of that, the flavour of several weeks, had persuaded her she was on some desert island and not stuck with a mermaid in a terraced house.

Marina had already hooked her tail over the side of the bath and was scooping handfuls of lotion onto her scales. Each foray into the jar produced a sucking, plughole sound. Seymour pulled her brogue sharply from an encroaching mound of bubbly slop.

'Can you fix me some tea, I'm starving.'

'What would you like?' Seymour played the game, asking though she already knew the answer.

'Sardines on toast will do.'

The kitchen cupboards were full of the tins stacked like silver ingots. As Seymour moved down stairs to retrieve one such tin, she anticipated Marina's faithful cry.

'Seymour?'

'Yeah?'

'Don't bother with the toast.'

*

Seymour sat on the top stair. She could no longer bear to stay in the bathroom while Marina ate. The mermaid sucked the tomatoey tiddlers into her mouth like strands of spaghetti, then plucked the bones from her teeth with taloned fingers. She left the soft skeletons on her plate – a fishy delight for alley cats. Her mouth was smeared with a thick, oily film. Nightly, Seymour tried in vain to run in then out of the bathroom with the retrieved plate without getting a shower of saline kisses, and also, when she was particularly unlucky, a greasy handprint on the lapel of her pin-striped suit.

The routine after that was fairly straightforward. Fetch Marina's mother-of-pearl embossed hairbrush and hand-mirror from the bathroom cabinet, then batten down all hatches and retreat to the box room whilst Marina sang into the small hours, brushing her hair to the rhythm of curious songs, and breaking any thin glass in ear-shot with her rare pitch.

The essential part was that Seymour had to hurry to the box room and crank up her stereogram before Marina's singing took full force. She was inexplicably drawn by those songs. She had been drawn by them those months back, as a dog to a supersonic whistle, down the back streets of the shopping centre, out beneath the railway arches, where rubbery mountains of old tyres were stored by a man who wore an Elvis t-shirt under which a similar stack of rubbery tyres seemed to lodge. Along to the final arch where a grubby sign painted by hand in Aladdin-font letters read JAKO'S PETS, heralding a small shop beneath.

Seymour could see little through the window. Nothing but rows of fish tanks, coloured deep green by the algae which coated their sides. In several, she could make out green tinted stone-effect arches under which green-tinted fish swam in a manner which she perceived to be either confused or lethargic. In another, a once orange plastic diver wore a familiar coat of slime green and blew the occasional bubble up through the thickened water. Then, in a large tank at the very back of the shop, was Marina.

She had long out-grown the space and one green-tinged cheekbone, and awkward parts of her body such as a shoulder and elbow, were pressed against the glass as someone trying to photocopy their face at an office party. Despite her discomfort, she was still singing. It was her songs, she'd told Seymour later, that had kept her alive through the dark days when Jako had fed her on pinches of dry fish food which tasted like paper, and had tried endlessly to grope her. Unsuccessfully, since Marina's teeth were evolutionarily sharpened to bite the heads off fishes, or the fingers of lecherous pet shop proprietors.

Still, after months, though now with less charm, these songs snared Seymour as treacherous hooks attached to fishing lines, to drag her inescapably to the humid bathroom where she feared she'd end up merely another pile of bones sucked clean – dinner for a scraggy cat.

At least with her 78's in full swing, often accompanied by the gravelled strains of the fuckinbastard dog, she could drown out Marina's *Stingray* theme tune voice.

Over the months, the retreat to the box room had become essential to Seymour, her only asylum in the mermaid-dominated household. As she sat there in the gloom, she realised the saline smell of her one-time lover clung even to her own clothes and filmed her hair and skin as a sea-spray, and though her stereogram cranked out her beloved tobacco-throated singers, beneath the bluesy surface, she could still determine the eerie whale-song of Marina.

Huddled in the corner of the box-room, Seymour looked up through the sash-window. The moon was bright and full, plump as a deep kiss. She thought of the lake in the park, wondered what the moon would look like reflected in its surface of molasses. She rose and pulled open the drawer of the bureau from which she took a sheet of ink-stained blotting paper. She tore it into strands and, twisting them up, packed them tightly into her ears. Thelonius Monk was playing *'Round Midnight'* but Seymour could no longer hear its strains, her thoughts spinning with the music at seventy-eight revolutions per minute. She could hear nothing but a constant hum from within her own head.

She stole down the stairs, in her determination, remembering to step over the eighth stair that creaked. She stopped a while outside the bathroom door. She could not hear Marina's song, but knew from the swinging of the lampshade on the landing that the sonic note was sounding. With a snapshot of a water-rippled moon in her thoughts, Seymour burst into the bathroom and ripped the plug from the bath. The chain coiled around her fingers as she fled the house, stopping only in the downstairs hall to flick off the switch in the fuse box and plunge the house into darkness - and silence.

With the blotting paper plugged firmly in her ears, Seymour had no notion whether the dog was quiet for once, though she realised Thelonius Monk must be, the arm of the stereogram having slowed to a halt on the heavy vinyl.

*

Tonight Seymour steps out of her clothes. Her pin-stripe trousers with turn-ups lie folded beneath her pin-stripe jacket with the fish-oiled lapel, which lies folded beneath her slightly limp white dress shirt, folded beneath her pair of Italian leather brogues. She stands naked at the edge of the lake. It is sometime around midnight and the moon is up. Its clean light picks out the surprisingly soft beauty of her nakedness, freed from angular suits. Everything in the night is hushed. Seymour cannot hear the slapping of the water against her legs as her toes are sucked into the muddy bed of the lake.

Somewhere in the night, a mermaid has stopped singing and a violinist counts the coins from his velvet-vaulted case.

MARK MICHALOWSKI

Skin

'Fuckin' horny bastard!'

Lee grins lopsidedly at himself in the mirror, running his hand back over the sharp stubble of his new crop. It shines like cut corn in the bathroom light. *The business.* He smoothes out the crisp, white Fred Perry shirt, checks the belt, the just-too-tight jeans; he wishes he could have afforded the 18-hole DMs, but the dole only goes so far. 10-hole (or is it 12? – he checks) will do. Black, though; not the oxblood ones that look, you know, just a bit *too much*. Maybe he can work up to them. Them and the braces.

And then he's out, out on the streets, cocky, arrogant swagger blowing him up to the size he'd really like to be. The mild breeze of this cool autumn night feels hard and cold on his scalp and he runs his hand up the back of his neck as the streets of Wythenshawe part for him like the Red Sea. It's as if the whole world knows he's the man; even shadows seem to duck into doorways, holding their breath until he's gone past, knowing that there's no messing with him. Not tonight.

A young couple, checking out the prices of starter homes in an estate agent's window, give him a look and he throws it back at them hard, laced with attitude. They look away again, quickly, start talking about appliances and borders and dado rails, rushing back to the safety of their domesticity, wrapping it around themselves like a shield. Lee wants to look back to see if they flinch as he boots a can into the gutter – like he gives a fuck. Three cans of Red Stripe and he's cruising.

Goose-pimples strike up along his thin, pale arms as a gust of winter arrives early. It bounces away, deflected by his invisible, impenetrable shield, and he strides on, heading for the Balti restaurant and its ever-eager attendant taxis. There's no queue, and Lee feels a bit disappointed. No audience for his arrival.

He raps sharply on the window of the taxi, making the driver jump. He jumps again when he sees Lee, his hand reaches down under his seat, but Lee's already pulling open the rear door, swinging his gangly frame into the seat.

'Ducie Street, please,' he says in a voice just too loud, too cocky.

The driver catches his eye in the mirror - dark brown eyes, long lashes, meeting with Lee's pale, watery eyes - and suddenly he feels awkward. Here, in this space not his own, squeezed in with the smell of aftershave and air-freshener, he's not King of the Castle.

'Ducie Street?'

Lee nods and the taxi pulls out into the road, spins around, and he's off.

'Busy?' he asks the driver after a calculated pause in which he works out how long the drive will be, and how soon he should start chatting to avoid that awkward silence that always fills his rides to the canal. He knows the taxi driver knows where he's going. And what for.

'Not so bad, not so bad,' the driver answers. Brown eyes flash in the mirror again, look away. 'Since the World Trade Centre, everyone's been going out more,' he says. 'End of the world, eh?'

He laughs, warm and liquid. Lee grunts back,

shifting in his seat, thinking that September 11th seems a lifetime – and a world – away, irrelevant to tonight's activities, someone else's problem.

He studies the black, oiled hair on the driver's head, swirling across the rich tones of his skin, down into the darkness of his collar. Can't work out quite what the bloke's laughter's about, wonders if he's a Muslim and laughing at what his lot have done.

Lee tries hard not to think about it as the streets slide past; and, like the driver says, the crowds seem busier as they slip into town: more animated, louder, their enjoyment awkwardly forced. From the shelter of the cab, it all looks a bit pathetic.

Lee tries on a sneer, but stops when he thinks the driver might be able to see him.

The cab swings into Ducie Street after a bit of half-hearted chat about the dark nights and the weather being good for business. Lee scrabbles in his pockets for change, catches the driver's eyes as he hands it over. Without thinking, he smiles, but the cabbie doesn't smile back. Miserable git.

The door clunks heavily behind him and Lee stands there, sucking in his stomach, inflating his tits as the cab scrunches away into the night.

Give it a sec, he thinks, posing for anyone who's looking. The air feels cold on his scalp again and he looks around, disappointed at not being watched, not to have yet ignited the fantasies of some sad fucker who won't stand a chance.

The street's lined with cars, but he knows these are mainly clubbers' cars, parked there until they've finished chewing and sweating and gurning. A couple of shadows peel away from the fence on the other side of the road, drift across and vanish down the path to the canal bridge where it all happens nowadays. Since the council have been redeveloping the area for the Commonwealth Games, the queers have been pushed further and further out. Now there's really just this one bit of grass, hugging the crook of the canal, edged with bushes and the dark, sweaty shelter of the tunnels. The sodium lights are still on overhead, bathing the area in unwelcome orange light. But they'll go off later, and then the rats'll come scurrying out.

Lee lights a ciggie and leans on the wall, looking down on the arena below, wondering who tonight's gladiators'll be. It looks quiet. Normally there'd be the half-dozen early birds, skulking from bush to tunnel, tunnel to towpath. Bare arms jutting from disco tops, folded prissily as their owners mince up and down. But tonight just a few dark shapes, huddling in clots. He spots the green glow of a mobile phone and pulls his shoulders back. Tonight, he's the man.

It takes him a minute to get down to where the short, stumpy bollards line the canal, and he flicks the tab of his ciggie masterfully into the water, flinching as two bats wheel and dip to the surface and are gone again.

He checks his watch. 00.15. He looks around. Fuckin' taxi driver, building his hopes up. Slim pickings tonight. He pulls back his shoulders, smoothes down the shirt again, and starts his rounds, listening to the scrunch of his DMs on the gritty ground. Good sound, he thinks. Hard sound.

Two mouthy queens come flapping past, spiky hair stinking of gel, shrieking about some sad old fucker that tried it on with one of them. Nasty cunts.

One push, thinks Lee, grinning that grin to himself, one push and they'd be in the canal. He doubts anyone would go to their rescue.

They glance at him as they pass and he throws them the look. Their eyes slip away from him, unable to get a purchase. He relishes the look on their faces, knows what they're thinking. He wants to glance back at them, but that wouldn't be cool. He can feel them behind him, heading back up the slope to the road, suddenly breaking into animated, girly chatter, collapsing in on each other with the weight of their spite. Fuck 'em. Nasty, superficial little cunts.

Half an hour later, and he's done nothing but smoke and walk. And a bit of standing, posing, back against the wall, one foot up, knee out, stretching the pale denim. He's had a few looks, but nothing he fancies. Too old, too queeny, too fuckin' weird. Always attracts 'em, he thinks. It's the look. The hardboy look. They all love it, want it.

Not tonight lads. Maybe he'll let someone cop a feel later if it doesn't get any better. *Charity fuck.*

Lee spots another figure, shorter, treading warily down the slope, keeping to the shelter of the bushes. It slips round to the funny sticky-out bit of the canal bank where the ducks sit, watching the queers do their stuff. Not bad, he thinks. Not a mincing Mary, at any rate.

He lights up another ciggie and sets off, checking his posture and gait, sending out the Right Signals.

As he steps into the patch of shadow cast by the bridge above him, he sees the bloke – and for a second he wonders if it's the taxi driver. Paki, definitely, but smaller than the driver, shorter hair. He's wearing jeans (a bit baggy, not much of a packet) and a big dark jacket over a white T-shirt – very straight, very unselfconscious. Not bad. Bit swarthy, unshaven. Smooth, brown skin punctured by sharp bristle. But still a Paki. Nothing against them, he tells himself, feeling generous, beneficent. But he wouldn't shag one. Different culture and all that. Never been keen on curry.

Lee slips past him, making no eye contact. The Paki looks away, nervous, then has a nosey around the corner, but there's no one there yet. Just the distant lights from the car park on the other side of the road, thrown back from the almost still surface of the water.

Lee turns, reaching into his pocket for his ciggies, intending to ask the bloke for a light, see what he's like close up – just curious, just curious. But the bloke's gone, off across the grass.

Fuck off then.

Lee pushes the cig packet back into his jeans, wriggles a bit until he's got it comfortable – and then sees them: two figures, moonlight gleaming off their heads, bouncing down the slope. Something gives a little twist inside him as he recognizes the posture, the gait. *Fuckin' horny bastards!*

The two skinheads – about his height, bigger built – pause, standing like sentinels surveying the cruising ground like killer robots from the future, come back to change history. He watches them, feeling his pulse quicken, knowing that his won't be the only eyes on 'em. Like anyone else stands a fucking chance! He puffs out his tits again and steps out of the shadow into the sour orange light, fingers in pockets. Assuming the position. They catch sight of him, look at him, then at each other, then back at him. Threesome!

Suddenly there's movement from the road and the sound of a screeching car as headlamps flare painfully down the slope, illuminating all three of them. Fucking police. Lee backs into the shadows as the two skinhead bootboys move slowly away towards the cop car and onto the street. He glances up to see if he can catch a glimpse of them on the road above, but the angle's all wrong. While he's looking, darkness suddenly descends as the police decide they've done their job for the night and piss off. Bit of excitement for the night, thinks Lee. Scared the skins off, though. He lights another ciggie, patient in the darkness. They'll be back.

Another fifteen minutes. Shagging like rabbits, someone had said at *Poptastic* last weekend; the world's gonna end with a bang and everyone wanted a bit of it. Not down here they don't. Maybe the police had been round earlier, put the fear of God into everyone. Cunts.

He decides to take a walk back up onto the road, maybe try the bit of waste ground on the other side of the water, in the shadow of the new flats they've built. Lee expects they'll be snapped up by old queens, easy access to the canal. He wonders if any of them are up there now, night-sight binoculars at the ready, one hand down their pants, desperately pulling on themselves.

After the darkness of the canal, the street lights are too bright, too revealing. Lee pauses, looks back down onto the grass – perfect timing: the lamps down there all wink out together and he can't see a thing. A minute later and he's heading down the wide, cobbled path to the other bit of the cruising area. He sees pale shapes move, just catching them with his peripheral vision. He hears a grunt, animal noises, feels a stirring in his groin, slips into the shadows to join them.

It takes a moment for him to realise that there's no role-play going on here, no fantasy fuck talk.

'Paki bastard,' says one voice, thick with hate and phlegm.

There's a grunt and a low sigh. Lee stops, feels his stomach tighten up. He knows what he should do, knows what has to happen. But he can't. He *can't*. It's nothing to do with him, he tells himself. Just walk away. You can't help. You'll only get yourself hurt. Make things worse. Not your problem.

Another grunt; the sound of a fist laying into a stomach or a chest or a groin. Lee doesn't know. He's only ever seen stuff like this on telly, on films, sound effects dubbed on, sharp and punchy like whip cracks. This is all slow and muddy, amateurish in its ugliness.

'Fuckin' Paki cunt. Your fuckin' mates happy, are they?'

Beat.

'Are they?'

Beat.

'Well fuckin' *are they*?'

Just a low groan and the sound of retching blurred by the wind and the distance.

'Fuckin' murdering bastards. Fuckin' murderers.'

The face of the taxi driver strobes in front of him, black and white, cartoony. And then the Paki from earlier on. They flicker together, blurring and morphing into each other until he can't tell the difference between them. Just brown skin, white teeth.

186

Another grunt and a low, dark laugh.

So what now? What now? He could run and get help. He could run and find someone, anyone. Someone would come, someone would. They wouldn't just ignore it, no one'd just ignore it.

'Oi!'

Oh fuck. Oh fuckfuckfuckfuckfuck

'Oi mate! You want a bit?'

Thick, nasty laughter. The two skinheads step aside, the doubled-up figure of the Paki on his knees between them, hands outstretched on the damp ground. Lee feels sick. He squints into the shadows, sees the faces of the leering skins, twisted, eyes bright and hungry, inviting him in silently, opening up to let him join in their fun – like attracting like.

All he can see are the shaved heads, the Fred Perry shirts, the bleached denims, the DMs (fuckin' oxblood, fuckin'oxblood spattered with fuckin' Paki blood) and the look. They've got the look. The hardboy look. And they're inviting him in. They've seen something in him, something that they connect with. He feels sick and opens his mouth to say something, his mind running a million miles an hour, a train thundering through everything he knew, everything he believes, carrying his words away with it.

'Come on mate,' hisses one of the skins – although Lee can't tell which one. And in the end it doesn't matter which one, does it, 'cos they're both the same, both identical, both just fists and blood and spit and hate.

'Have a go. He won't say nuthin', will yer?'

The skins look down at the Paki, bowed, unmoving, like an animal cornered, afraid that the slightest movement will bring another kick or another punch. And Lee's willing him to stay down, to stay quiet. *Don't fight back*, he's thinking. *Don't give 'em any reason to have another go. Don't make things worse for yourself.*

For a moment, he feels a stab of anger towards the stupid Paki, coming out here after what his lot have done. Fuckin' asking for it. What did he expect?

One of them spits on the bloke's head but he doesn't flinch. He's learning – relearning. Hundreds of years of keeping his head down, not making any trouble. Yes sir. No sir.

He has to do something, anything. Otherwise, he knows, he'll relive this moment in his head for the rest of his life. A burden he never wanted, thrust on him 'cos the Paki was too stupid to stay at home.

'There's cops,' says Lee – well, his mouth says the words, but it feels like someone else is pushing the words from his lips. 'Cops, back there.'

The skins look at each other, back at the man on his knees, back at the road.

One last kick for good measure and the skins are heading towards him, all puffed up with hate and adrenaline, a good night's work done. They grin at Lee, look back at the man on the ground, head still down like some kind of supplicant, afraid to lift his eyes to his God. And then they're gone, patting Lee on the arm, on the shoulder as they pass, spitting noisily into the bushes. Rough fingers squeeze his arm. Skin on skin. Lee tries not to flinch as he waits for them to pass. He wonders why the touch of the horny bastards – *horny bastards!* – makes him feel so dirty.

And then he's standing over the man, reaching

down a tentative hand, scared to touch.

'It's okay mate,' he says. 'They've gone.'

The bloke doesn't move, still kneeling. He gives a start as Lee's hand connects with his shoulder, a half-hearted attempt to pull away. Then he looks up, his face bruised, blood across his nose and mouth, one eye closed – and pulls back with a little yelp.

'Please,' he says through bubbling blood and a split lip. 'Please, no more.'

''S'okay,' says Lee. 'They've gone. It's all over.'

'No,' mutters the man, shaking his head, something dead in his eyes. 'No it's not *all over.*'

And then he leans forward and pukes up blood all over Lee's tight and oh-so-perfect Levi's. He's right, thinks Lee, feeling the contents of his stomach, three cans of Red Stripe, struggle to join the Paki's vomit on the flattened grass.

It's only just begun.

KEITH MUNRO

Gutted

July, 1991

I'm on the last family holiday I'll ever have to endure, stuck in a caravan with my parents and my little brother on a campsite in Devon. I'm fourteen, and would rather be anywhere else in the world. Every chance I get I make a run for it, wandering off on my own, going down to the river or sitting in the park, sullenly counting the minutes until the long drive back to Scotland. I'm not a particularly endearing fourteen-year-old.

On one of my various recces into town I clamber up the hill to the ruined castle. Tourists drift about with guide books and cameras. I notice a boy my age sitting with his back against an old stone wall, eating a bag of crisps. He must be a local, because his bike is carelessly discarded on the grass beside him. Like a drug working its way through my bloodstream, I slowly realise he's the most beautiful boy I've ever seen. I awkwardly edge past, staring at him out of the corner of my eye, trying to record every detail of his face, the way his fringe falls over his eyes, the way his hand lifts the food to his mouth and pushes it in. I'm so engrossed that I trip over his bike and land face first on the grass.

'Jesus!' he cries. 'Are you alright?'

'Yeah,' I say, my tattered dignity falling about my feet as he helps me up. 'I wasn't looking where I was going.'

'I know you weren't,' he says, laughing. 'You were looking at me.'

The profound mortification flooding my face only makes him laugh some more. I notice through my embarrassment that he has a devastating smile.

'I'm Lucien,' he says, as if he's been sitting here waiting for me all this time. 'You on holiday?'

'Yeah,' I mutter, trying to place his accent - or rather account for the lack of it.

'Where you from?'

'Just outside Edinburgh.'

'You bored?'

'Yeah.'

'Why don't you come back to mine? It's only ten minutes away. My mum always says I should be nicer to the tourists. She'll go wild if I bring one home with me.'

He winks, picks up his bike and sets off across the grass, only stopping to look over his shoulder when he notices I'm not following.

'Coming then?'

And, much to my amazement, I do.

*

Lucien. Luc for short. The first boy I ever truly fell in

love with.

Luc of the golden hair, brown skin and wide, dark eyes. Nine months my senior. Product of a mother from Yorkshire and a father from Spain (divorced). Possibly the coolest, friendliest kid I had ever met. He spent most of the year in Barcelona and the holidays in Totnes, and could converse flawlessly in English, Spanish, Italian and French. Everything he did seemed effortless. Nothing bothered him, everything delighted him. He managed to seduce me without even trying, without me even realising he was doing it. His smile wreaked havoc wherever it went. I fell head over heels for him.

Luc transformed that fortnight into the most significant of my life. He altered everything. He changed me beyond all recognition. He made me what I am today.

He took me home to meet his mother, who turned out to be one of those cheery, wholesome mums who always has a fresh batch of scones in the oven or a newly-baked cake on the kitchen table. They lived in a small cottage with a huge garden up a narrow backstreet. Within days I was having all my meals with them. By the end of the week I was sleeping there as well, in Luc's bedroom (in Luc's bed). She hadn't a clue what we were up to. I doubt if she had any idea what Luc was really like, or the sort of life her precocious city-boy son was leading back in Barcelona. At the time, of course, neither did I.

For two weeks he gave himself to me. He took me under his wing. He took me to Torquay, Paignton, Dartmouth, whisking me round the sights of the English Riviera. He opened up his life to me, befriending me totally, unreservedly. He gave me what I hadn't even dared dream about.

That first afternoon he stripped right in front of me, skipping about his bedroom in his underwear and taking an unnecessarily long time to get dressed again. I couldn't believe my eyes. That night, walking me back to the campsite, he kissed me, gently pushing his tongue into my mouth. The next day his hand found its way into my trousers, and mine into his. The day after that it was his naked body pressed against mine, his chest against mine, his legs rubbing against mine. Then the blowjobs started – electrifying, mind-blowing blowjobs that left us both thrilled and exhausted, panting in each other's arms. With every day that passed I fell deeper and deeper in love with him.

We kept the best for last. I lost my virginity with Luc the night before I went back to Scotland. I fucked him, then he fucked me. The actual sex wasn't the best we'd ever had, but the whole thing felt monumental, momentous.

Luc assured me it was his first time as well. I had no reason to doubt that it wasn't. Condoms never even crossed my mind. Not once.

*

Of course, we vowed to keep in touch. I left Totnes with every imaginable means of contacting him written out on a piece of paper. Over the next few months, I tried them all. I wrote letters, sent postcards. I even tried phoning his father in Barcelona. No response, no reply. Nothing. I went from fretting, to weeping, to cursing him for his silence. In the end I gave up. It was like he'd disappeared off the face of the earth. I gave up the idea of meeting him next summer. I gave up the idea of ever seeing or hearing from him again. I gave up on the most profound love of my life. It wasn't easy, and it certainly wasn't pretty. It didn't make me a better person – it turned me into an absolute fucking nightmare: spiteful, unhelpful, morose. Even my friends got pissed off and stopped coming round. That suited me just fine. I didn't want anything to interfere with my despair at losing Luc.

*

Here's the last communication I ever sent him, a Christmas card with a comedy Santa on the front. I posted it on Saturday 14th December 1991, my fifteenth birthday. By then I was consumed with bitterness of an almost pathological intensity. Below the sickly message:

Wishing you a Merry Christmas and a Happy New Year!

I simply added:

FUCK YOU THEN

I was not expecting a reply. I was not surprised when I didn't receive one. Fuck him then. Fuck him.
Fuck him.
Fuck him.
I stole an exercise book from school and spent

the Christmas holidays covering the pages with *FUCK HIM*. Fuckhimfuckhimfuckhim, over and over again. Perhaps I went slightly insane, but it worked. By the time school started in the New Year, I was cured.

By which I mean I could say the words 'fuck him' and sound like I actually meant it.

*

That jotter lay hidden at the bottom of a drawer for years. I came across it a while back when I was moving all my stuff down to Crewe. It went in the black bin bag along with my school books and adolescent poetry. There are some things it's just not healthy to keep.

*

On the last morning of the holiday, Luc's mum takes a photograph of the two of us in their back garden. Luc has his arms round my neck, his mouth only an inch from my ear. I can feel his breath on my cheek as his mum struggles to operate the camera. She promises to send me a copy once the film is developed. I make Luc promise to remind her.

I cry on the journey home, silently, staring out of the window as we drive up the M6. Every passing minute takes me a mile further away from him. No one else in the car seems to notice.

The photograph never arrives.

January, 2003

'Very nice. Very moving,' says Simon, tapping the pages on the table a few times, newsreader style, to straighten their edges before handing them back. 'Something we can all relate to. What gave you the idea?'

'What do you mean, what gave me the idea? It's true!'

'Oh?' Simon reaches out and plucks the pages from my hand. 'It's true?' he asks, scanning the first paragraph.

'Yes.'

'I assumed you were having a laugh.'

'A laugh? Why would I be having a laugh?'

'Ahem. *Like a drug working its way through my bloodstream, I slowly realise he's the most beautiful boy I've ever seen... Luc of the golden hair, brown skin and wide, dark eyes... Why don't you come back to mine? It's only ten minutes away...* For fuck's sake, Keith! You've used every cliché under the sun.'

'So it's not the best piece of writing I've ever produced. That doesn't make it *not* true.'

'You've spent too much time in those Internet porn story archives if you ask me. And as for meeting him on *holiday* – that's the oldest one in the book! It's the greatest golden gay cliché of them all.'

'You don't believe me?'

'I don't think *anyone* in their right mind would believe you. The only people who would *believe* a story like that are screaming old queens looking to relive their youth and sexual inadequates who can only dream about what it's like in the real world. The rest of us aren't so easily fooled.'

I snatch the pages back off him.

'Don't get all huffy. I'm not saying it never happened. I'm just suggesting that the passage of time may have clouded your memory, made it all seem more wonderful than it probably was.'

'More wonderful than it was? This is my *virginity* we're talking about.'

'All the more reason to take everything you say about it with a pinch of salt. We're all prone to exaggeration when it comes to things like that. Christ, I lost mine with some Jonathan King look-alike - picked me up in a club I shouldn't have been in and shagged me in the back of his Merc. Every time I tell the story the poor guy becomes more and more of a sweaty fuckin' degenerate, but he was actually quite sweet, and much more terrified of me than I was of him. One of the advantages of being jailbait.'

Simon reaches over the table and retrieves the pages from my grasp.

'Let's face it, you knew this boy for, what? Ten days, max? And that was over ten *years* ago. This story is fine as a *story*, as an entertaining *impression* of what happened. But as a record of historical fact it probably leaves a lot to be desired.'

'Well you would know,' I mutter.

'For God's sake stop pouting. Even if it *is* true, why should anyone else give two shits about you and your lost virginity? That'll teach you to dabble in autobiography. Now shut up and let me read it again.'

I sit studying the froth on my coffee, trying to second-guess which of the tiny bubbles on the surface will burst next. He does have a point – why *should* anyone else care? Why should it mean as much to anyone else as it does to me?

'Hang on, what does this bit mean?'

'Which bit?'

'This bit here. *I doubt if she had any idea what Luc was really like, or the sort of life her precocious city-boy son was leading back in Barcelona. At the time, of course, neither did I.*'

I stiffen defensively.

'And there's another clanger further on. Here: *Luc assured me it was his first time as well. I had no reason to doubt that it wasn't...* Wasn't? Is there something you're not telling us?'

I gaze into my coffee and say nothing.

'You agree it's a trifle enigmatic? *Condoms never even crossed my mind...*'

The last of the tiny bubbles burst, leaving only a small island of brown foam in the middle of the blackness. It slowly spirals away into nothing.

'You are alright, aren't you?' Simon whispers, leaning forward, genuinely concerned all of a sudden.

I sigh heavily, reaching into the pocket of my coat, pausing, undecided. 'I just wanted to tell it the way I remembered it – to put *my* side of the story.'

From my coat pocket I produce a photograph, which I place on the table between us. It's a photo of two teenaged boys in a sunny garden, one with his arms around the neck of the other.

'This is how I want to remember him,' I say, pointing to the boy with the wide, dark eyes. The one who isn't me. 'This is the Luc I knew.'

Simon gazes at the photo. 'Jesus. You're right.

He *was* beautiful.'

'Yes,' I murmur. 'He was.'

November, 2002

That photograph dropped though my door on a wet November morning along with several bills and an invitation to apply for a platinum credit card I don't earn enough to qualify for. It had been sent to my parents' address in Scotland, and they'd forwarded it to me in Crewe. I nearly choked when I opened the envelope.

This was the photograph. *The* photograph.

It could only have been sent by Luc or his mother. There was no other explanation. On the back was simply written *Remember me?* and a phone number. A Manchester phone number. I was aware of my hand shaking as I dialled. It was picked up almost immediately.

'Hello?'

A voice I forced myself to recognise.

'Luc?'

A long pause.

'Keith?'

'Yeah.'

'Oh my God!'

'How did you know it was me?'

'Because no one calls me Luc anymore.'

(That struck me later as a rather strange thing to say, but at the time I was too busy being hyper to pick up on it.)

'I'm living in Manchester now,' Luc explained.

'I only moved in a few weeks ago. I'm still going through all these boxes of stuff that have been in storage. I found the photo and it got me thinking of you. I didn't realise you'd still be at the same address.'

'I'm not, but my parents are. I live in Crewe.'

'Crewe? That's not far from here, is it? My British geography's fucked. I've been in Spain for years.'

'Really? What about your mum? How is she?'

'She's dead.'

'Dead?'

'Yeah. Car crash. Not recently. In fact it would have been just after... Christ, there's a lot you don't know.'

'I'm sorry.'

'I know. Listen, I'd love to see you. When can you come up?'

'How about today?'

'Today? Don't you have work to go to?'

'I'm a writer now. I work whenever I want.'

'No shit? I'm a writer too. Well, sort of. Okay. Get yourself on a train, and I'll come meet you.'

'Okay. I'll phone you when I get there.'

'Cool. Great to hear from you.'

'You too.'

'I got your Christmas card, by the way.'

'What Christmas card?'

'*That* Christmas card.'

That Christmas card? He'd got it after all?

'There's a lot we need to talk about. Can you stay overnight?'

'Uh, sure.'

'Good. I could do with talking to someone.'

'Is everything alright?'

'It is now, I suppose. Sort of. Well. We can talk later. I'll see you this afternoon.'

*

It wasn't until I was sitting in Manchester Piccadilly with the photo in one hand and a coffee in the other that it dawned on me I had no means of identifying him. Ten years is a long time. I had visions of us wandering past each other, repeatedly failing to recognise our grown-up selves.

As it turned out, I needn't have worried. Apart from growing a foot taller, Luc hadn't changed a bit. In fact, as I saw him coming towards me, I was slightly unsettled by just how *little* he'd changed – same hair, same eyes, same disarming smile. I glanced down at the photo in my hand. It was a bit like looking back through time. Scary.

'Hi,' he said.

'Hi.'

He leant forward and kissed me on the cheek in true continental fashion. 'I've missed you.'

'Have you? I mean, yeah – I've missed you too.'

'Come on. I'll take you home.'

It was as easy as that, as if the last ten years simply hadn't happened. As we walked across the station concourse I noticed no fewer than three guys clocking Luc. *Yes*, I wanted to tell them, *I know he is. And he's mine.*

*

Home turned out to be East Didsbury. I was led

202

through the drizzle into a baffling labyrinth of backstreets and cul-de-sacs, past row after row of semi-detached mansions with 4-wheel drives and Volvo estates parked outside. It felt good to be walking beside him again.

As we went, Luc filled me in on the basics: how his mother had died in a car crash not long after I went back to Scotland; how this had precipitated his return to Barcelona on a permanent basis; how his father, who had always disliked his mother's family, had taken the opportunity to sever all ties with Luc's relatives in Britain; how they had moved to a new apartment on the other side of the city, far away from his friends and his old school; how a step-mother had then been introduced into the equation...

'My father was determined I would have nothing more to do with England. If a letter arrived with a British stamp on it, he'd tear it up and leave the pieces for me to find. It was pure chance your Christmas card ever got to me – although it took me a while to work out who it was from.'

The strange thing was, if Luc felt bitter about any of this - as I assumed he must - it certainly didn't show in his voice, which remained oddly detached and emotionless. He recounted it all as if it had happened to someone else.

'This is it,' he said, taking a sudden left and marching up the drive of a large, decrepit, apparently derelict house. The garden was deep with rotting leaves and the paint was peeling from the window frames. Inside the place stank of abandonment.

'Make yourself at home,' Luc instructed, ushering me into the sitting room. I was taken aback by how little furniture there was – only an old settee, a television sat on a rickety dining chair and a table by the window, taken up by a large, humming computer. Cartoon fish swam about the screen, occasionally bumping into one another. Nothing on the walls except uniform magnolia over antique textured wallpaper. A collection of cardboard boxes was stacked in one corner, sealed with brown tape.

'A mate of mine owns it,' Luc shouted from the kitchen at the very moment I was about to ask how the trajectory of his life had brought him here of all places. 'He's letting me have it cheap.'

'Ah.' I could hear a kettle boiling. 'Coffee please. Black, no sugar.'

I wandered over to the window and peered out through the dirty net curtains. There was a large pile of papers sitting by the computer. A polaroid lay on top of the pile – a headshot of a balding, middle-aged man with hairy shoulders. Below was a sheet of what looked like vital statistics – height, weight, age, eye colour, hair colour – a whole page of detailed measurements and descriptions. Thickness of body hair. Colour of nipples. *Girth of penis?* This sheet was paper-clipped to another, on which the information given was more rudimentary. There were also two more polaroids, blurred and oddly angled as if taken surreptitiously. In both these photographs there was a red ring drawn around a tall youth with short fair hair. The youth was wearing what might have been a suit, or might have been a school blazer. It was difficult to tell.

'Your coffee's ready.' Luc stood in the doorway with a mug in his hand. I took a guilty step away from the table, but couldn't stop myself glancing over his shoulder at the polaroid as he handed me my coffee.

'So,' he said. 'You're a writer?'

'It's what I call myself. I've had a few things published. It's not how I earn my living, put it like that.'

'Ah.' He sprawled on the settee, watching me.

'I couldn't help noticing this,' I stammered, gesturing towards the table and its contents. 'What exactly is it you do? You said you're a writer as well.'

'Not like you. It *is* how I earn my living.'

'What kind of stuff do you write?'

'Porn,' he said bluntly. 'Snuff.'

'Pardon?'

'I do requests. Commissions. People write to me. Usually they've got someone they're obsessed about, someone they can't have for one reason or another. I write them a story in which they act out their fantasies. I do a lot of S&M. You can get away with so much more on paper than you can in real life. You probably know that. I specialise in snuff. You'd be amazed how many people want me to mutilate the object of their desires. It must have some sort of cathartic effect. I advertise in magazines. Not the ones you read, I'll bet. It's good money. I charge £500 a story. I get requests from all over the world. Most of them are pretty formulaic. There's a limit to the number of ways you can kill someone.'

He was waiting for a response, but I didn't know what to say. It was too unexpected, almost too bizarre to take in.

'I'll let you read some, if you want. Then you can see just how fucked up I really am.'

'I don't think you're fucked up,' I blurted.

'Wait until you've read them, then tell me you don't think I'm fucked up.' There was a slight edge to his voice which made me uncomfortable. In the dying afternoon light I saw all the familiar humour and warmth suddenly draining from his eyes. For a moment, he looked like a different person.

*

We talked late into the night, mostly – I noticed – about me. Luc produced some tonic water and a bottle of Blavod from the freezer which we proceeded to drink, gradually slithering from the settee onto the floor. It seemed there was no question that we would be sleeping together, so I set about trying to establish, as best I could in my increasingly inebriated state, what exactly had gone on in Barcelona after his mother's death.

The more I probed, however, the less communicative Luc became. As the evening wore on he grew cagey, then reticent, then downright evasive. I began to wonder if I'd had as much of the story as I was going to get, if the explanation of how he'd ended up here, in a Manchester suburb, writing nasty porn for dirty old men, wasn't one he was intending to give. There was something he was holding back, something I felt would provide the link between the Luc I'd known as a boy and the one I was now drunkenly slumped beside, laughing as he produced a second bottle of vodka from the freezer. As much as I wanted to believe they were the same person, the longer I spent with this grown up Luc, the more I feared something about him had changed – something below the surface.

There was an absence about him, an emptiness, a hollowness. There was something missing. He was different, but I couldn't quite pinpoint how.

It was like some vital part of the boy had been ripped out.

In the early hours he suddenly decided it was time for bed. We stumbled upstairs, taking the vodka with us, into a room which was empty except for a double mattress in the middle of the floor. For the next hour we had disastrous, drunken sex, both so plastered that we could keep nothing up for long. I remember trying to shove my limp dick up his arse, falling off him and landing on the floor, giggling helplessly, knocking over a candle, as Luc collapsed on the mattress in hysterics. Eventually we passed out, exhausted and pissed as farts. The last thing I can recall is the smell of his hot breath on my face, sour with vodka and sweat.

I remember trying to pull away.

*

I awoke alone, my head feeling like it had been sawn open during the night. I shuffled about the house, peering into rooms filled with nothing but cardboard boxes. I tracked down the toilet and had a long, 40% proof piss.

In the kitchen there was a bottle of aspirin next to a note:

Sorry - things to do
Help yourself to anything you find
Snuff by the computer for you to read

I did a double-take on the last line – yes, that *was* what it said.

I heaped three spoonfuls of Nescafé into a mug of hot water and headed for the sitting room. Placed very obviously on the table by the window was a pile of stories, ten in total, each one secured with a paperclip. I sank into the settee and began skimming through the one at the top of the pile, feeling duty-bound rather than curious. It appeared to be about the manager of a supermarket molesting a young shelf-filler in the stockroom. The whole thing was written in pornspeak, all glistening meat and twitching love chutes. I frankly didn't find it very arousing.

The next few ran along similar lines. Story #2 matched a wealthy business man with his brawny window cleaner. In Story #3 a police officer abducted a *Big Issue* vendor. Story #4 featured a man tying up and torturing his own father. I began to suspect the stories had been placed in some sort of order, as the level of unwillingness on the part of the victim and violence on the part of the tormentor seemed to be increasing. I couldn't believe there was a market for this stuff, or that Luc was fulfilling it.

Things took a significant turn for the worse in Story #5, which detailed the rape and mutilation of a young Thai boy by two elderly English sex tourists.

Suddenly this wasn't funny any more. It was actually quite sick.

Story #6 featured the first murder, the strangulation of Canadian teen heart-throb Kevin Zegers by a New York taxi driver. Story #7 recounted the dismemberment of some gym-pumped beefcake by his weedy next door neighbour. The chains were getting heavier, the dildos thicker, the knives sharper, the screams louder. What the hell was I supposed to make of all this? Was Luc trying to shatter my opinion of him completely? What the fuck had *happened* to him in Barcelona that his mind was now filled with such carnage?

I glanced at the pile of cardboard boxes over in the corner, all sealed with tape, and wondered for a moment what might be in them.

I was pretty sure the balding man and the blond schoolboy in Story #8 were the ones I'd seen in the photographs yesterday. The balding man quite literally fucked the blond schoolboy to death. The most horrific by far was Story #9, in which a young man nailed his twin brother to the floor and let loose a pack of starving rats. I actually had trouble keeping my eyes on the page I was flinching so much. How could *anyone* be turned on by this?

Which left Story #10, the last in the pile. Perhaps Luc had assumed I'd never get this far, that I'd have quit long ago. I can't think of any reason why the Luc I knew would have *wanted* me to read it.

Story #10 is about two teenaged boys. One is Scottish, the other Spanish. The Scottish one is on holiday, the Spanish one spends a few months each year in England. They are called Keith and Lucien.

My mouth fell open.

The Spanish boy sets about seducing the Scottish one. The Scottish one seems very willing to reciprocate. Before long they are kissing with tongues and wanking each other off. The Spanish one teaches the Scottish one how to suck cock. The

Scottish one is a quick learner. He asks the Spanish one where he picked up such skills. The Spanish one replies that he learned them from his uncle.

I felt my entire body go cold.

The holiday progresses. On their last night together, they decide to fuck each other. The Scottish one goes first, then it's the turn of the Spanish one. He pumps away while the Scottish one groans and wriggles beneath him.

There's sweat running down my face. Sweat and tears.

Luc could feel the cum surging up inside him. He thrust deeper and deeper into Keith's tight hole, his hips pounding harder and harder. Keith wailed each time Luc's throbbing prick slammed into him. Just before he came Luc thrust his hand under a pillow and dug out the knife that was hidden there. As his cock exploded inside Keith's ass, he pushed the knife into Keith's stomach, right up to the handle. Keith froze in shock. Luc was still pumping, wave after wave of hot cum spurting from his dick as he pulled the knife sideways with all his might. A strangled gasp escaped Keith's throat as a torrent of blood and guts spilled onto the sheets beneath him. Luc pumped out the last few spasms of his orgasm as Keith collapsed onto the bed, blood flooding out of the six inch rip

in his belly.
    'Yes!' said Luc.

                *

For a long time I was unable to move, unable to think, unable to stop myself shaking. I was suddenly very aware of the blood pumping round my body. I got up slowly, put on my coat, and slipped out of the house into the maze of streets, into the pouring rain. Blindly trying to find my way back to the station.

JOHN MYATT

Strip

They met and within two minutes Eddie and Vin were married. It was something-or-other at first sight – tackling hearts and pupils dilating, stuff of the punch-drunk stomach, shivers down the thighs. And yes, there were strange expectations and years of boredom that were suddenly undressed and forgotten, there were rash promises and flashbulb smiles. There were all of these things in abundance because this was, after all, the beginning of a fairy tale.

So, once upon a time, two men met in the public house they still call Via Fossa, on a thoroughfare they call Canal Street, in the old, small city of Manchester. They met beneath a pile of glued-up prayer books and a reclaimed hymn-board, just to the right of the fag machine. They met - and were married – while Eddie's bridesmaids shrieked at the bar and Vin's best man gushed an afternoon's lager in the toilets. It was a Saturday night ceremony, no confetti. The music was provided by ABBA, Kylie, Geri Halliwell. The vows were not spoken because there were two pairs of hands to slide down the back of pants and fulfil all the commitments that tradition required.

Eddie was twenty-seven. He shopped at J-D Sports, USC on Market Street, and Ath Leisure in the Arndale. He wore La Coste jeans, Henri Lloyd jackets and Rockport shoes – just like his heroes, who were generally younger, hung around in bus shelters smoking B&H cigarettes, half insane on hormones. He worked in a warehouse, which was the most manual job he could find without offending his university education. He went home to a basic flat and tried to want for basic pleasures: clothes, fags, beer, shags. He hated opera, Judy Garland, face creams.

Eddie was straight acting, straight living, straight to the back of the bachelor queue. All this, so any casual observer could reliably imagine that Eddie was a typical sort of bloke. And whether that honour was reality or lived-out eroticism was a matter for the years yet to come.

Vin was a typical sort of bloke. His efforts, however, were minimal. Blessed with a face made from a few bold strokes of a creator's fist, Vin could divert whole rooms of jaded lovers with one lazy flick of his shaved head. He sported a selection of tattoos that declared his passions in simple sea-blue ink. He walked without grace and never stood still. Kitted-out in standard scally uniform of trackie bottoms and a footie top, he also had the frequent honour of being the most heterosexual homosexual in the room.

Eddie and Vin were made for each other. And they knew it. They made the blood run wild in each other's body. They made their hearts as mad as a whippet in *Watership Down*. They were folklore.

When Vin thrust down the last of his pint, Eddie introduced himself.

'Yer fancy another?'

'Eh?' said Vin.

''nother pint,' confirmed Eddie.

'Eh?'

'So wha' jer fink of Edghill's goal?'

'Eh?'

'Edghill in the match. Jammy or wha'?'

Eddie nodded towards Vin's Man City football shirt, as if the nod would explain it. Edghill: one of Man City's golden boys, who had rammed home an amazing goal three minutes into the first half.

Vin leaned forward, showing an ear and a gold hoop earring.

'Soz, mate, you'll 'ave ter shou'. Speaker's righ' over me 'ead.'

'Edghill's goal. Maine Road. 'bout four hours' ago. Bit jammy!'

Eddie grinned. There was something deeply masculine about being a man and bellowing slowly into the face of another man.

'Yeh,' said Vin. 'Jammy.'

At last, contact. Eddie's grin spread east and west.

'Dead jammy. But 'e fuckin' earned it, yeh. Fuckin' top.'

Eddie had been working on his straightboy image for over a year now – the majority of work revolving around football and lager. He had progressed steadily from erotic gawping at the odd telly match to a full blown, hard-on obsession with Manchester City FC. It was all he could do to feel sexy in this confusing, boundary-blurring world. And finding a man like Vin was Jackpot time.

Vin shook his head and leaned further down, ready to blast into Eddie's left ear.

'Name's Vin. What's yours?'

'Eddie.'

Eddie nodded his head towards Vin's top again. 'New strip.'

Eddie knew that Vin already knew his top was new strip, but saying it, talking about it, somehow turned up the magic. It was about moving matters from illusion to the real thing, Paul Daniels to Merlin.

Vin leaned forward again.

'You a true blue?'

'Disciple, more like. Cut me an' it's blue.'

It was the kind of line Eddie had imagined on countless nights, stroking himself into oblivion, and now it was out there. And the other half of this conversation was clearly impressed. Here was Eddie, talking football, with a fellow of the same species, with a true blue supporter of men on men action. This was the communion of men, two lions roaring at the waterhole, the kind of simple exchange that rendered disco extinct.

'Never thought I'd meet a bloke like you in 'ere.'

'Yeh.'

There was a pause, as something like electricity pushed switches inside the men. Then six seconds later they were leaving – just like Edghill, goal in the first few minutes.

Speeding home in the taxi, Eddie's cock twitched painfully in his new jeans as he played his fingers, all coy and early Madonna, over Vin's lively crotch. Because of the cab driver, because of the closeness of the Nissan's woolly backseat, or because of a more raw sort of fear, Eddie did not look at his husband directly. Instead, he watched Vin's face in the window, watched it flick alongside his own, Jekyll and Hyde, between the orange buzz of streetlights. The honeymoon couple said nothing. Instead they let the taxi driver's Hindi radio station do all the talking for them. And around them, Manchester flashed romantically past.

The bridal chamber was beautiful because it was

dark and because Vin had given it the once over before heading into town. He'd deliberately missed the empty can of Tennants in the corner and left the butt-full ashtray by the bed. Not that Eddie even noticed the deliberate lack of candles and rose petals. The taxi, front door and stairs were all a distant memory by the time they were wrestling open the sheets and grabbing for the lube.

Vin tugged the wrapping from Eddie's arse.

'Aw, fuck,' Eddie spat, pushing back into the groom.

When Vin got down to his own shorts, Eddie felt silky nylon brushing his bare arse and realised that Vin was in full footie kit underneath his trackies.

'Jesus, fuck. Yer got yer footie shorts on. Fuckin' 'orny bastard.'

'Yer like that, eh? Like a bloke in 'is kit?'

Eddie swung his head down in one big nod. Vin roared.

And it wasn't long before they had finished and the sheets were as gamey as team laundry after a punishing two-side battle.

Then it was sunshine. Suddenly, Eddie was awake and Vin was dodging around the room. Eddie hoisted himself out of the bedfunk and stared at his new and wonderful husband, dreading for a moment that the dream was at its end.

'Be back in a couple of 'ours,' Vin said, jamming a badly rolled towel into a sports bag. 'Got practice with the lads. Sunday quickie. You stay 'ere. Make yerself comfy. I'll be home in a bi' t' fuck yer.'

Practice with the lads. Then home to fuck his totty. Vin, it seemed, was the real thing.

'Don't shower, eh?' Eddie asked, staring up at the thick wall of man who had hitched the bag over his shoulder and was staring back at him.

'Yeh. Keep meself nice an' sweaty for yer.'

Vin leaned down and delivered a groin-aching bang on the lips.

'Just one thing, mate,' he said, after the explosion in Eddie's face was over.

'Yeh?'

'Make yerself comfy. Get some brekkie. Sniff me dirty keks. Aint got no secrets. But keep yer mitts off me blue box. Yeh?'

Eddie was thinking of sweaty footballers' thighs rubbing together so he nodded. If anything, he was in shock. Surely this man wasn't going to leave him alone in his flat.

Yes he was. Vin was going to footie practise, and he was going to leave Eddie alone, to wander around his small Hulme castle. And yes, Vin was going to return and they were going to live like mad bachelors and life was going to continue being wonderful, wonderful, oh most wonderful, and yet again wonderful.

Ten minutes' later, it was already too late.

Curiosity reproduces at an alarming rate. Once aroused, it is never truly fed. So when Eddie danced out of bed, padded into the kitchen and began to investigate the cupboards containing Sugar Puffs and Super Noodles, it was already too late. Because some part of him had been nervous about opening those cupboards. Some part of him hadn't known what he would find. Some part of him had feared it was going to be olive oils and fancy jars for Mediterranean cooking. And so, some part of Eddie hadn't wanted to open those cupboards, despite his husband's invitations. And once there was reluctance, there was also curiosity.

After battling back the fears, Eddie had opened a few of the kitchen cupboards and had flung together a good, sugary breakfast. Not long after, the hanker for spouse information returned and Eddie found himself back in the bedroom. He pulled open a few drawers and found, once again, that those backburner fears had been useless. All he discovered were socks and undies, old footie kits, jeans, T-shirts, Coq Sportif and Reebok, the odd thinning pair of Kappa keks. All clean, nothing to get a spunk stain over.

Then came the bathroom.

First, the cabinet. Eddie had seen some queeny show on the telly - few years back - and there'd been this moment when the guy goes to the bathroom after his hot shag and opens the medicine cabinet and realises that his chisel-chinned hero is a screaming queen from hell. The guy opens the mirrored door and discovers row upon row of pre-wash toners, scuffing solutions and moisturisers. But times had changed. If Eddie opened the cabinet and discovered the whole girlie Body Shop kaboodle, he wasn't going to run screaming. This was the twenty-first century, this was Manchester.

As it was, the cabinet contained a ravaged tube of Savlon cream, some old shaving foam and a Kouros gift set from another decade. Little there to scream about. Relieved but not surprised, Eddie took a piss.

Then he remembered the laundry basket.

What would he find? Ladies panties? Some nice

tight Farahs? Chinos and Y-fronts? Or worse, sickly Moschino tops and D&G hipsters? He lifted the wicker lid and sniffed. Then put in an eager hand, came back with a pair of oily jeans and some boxer shorts. Another hand revealed some T-shirts, more boxers, mucky socks and a lilac work-shirt with sweat circles. Nothing to light up a spread in *Attitude*. Then again, nothing for a bloke like Vin to be ashamed of. All part of the healthy costume for the straight young fella, circa 2002. Eddie threw the lot back, hanging on to a pair of ripe boxers for some fun later on.

 Eddie checked his watch. How long had Vin been gone? An hour and a half? Would he really be straight home after the game, ripe from a good ball-kicking with his mates? Or would Vin have the duty of downing a few swift pints?

Eddie dived into the back room.

It was almost bare. There was a computer on a plastic-topped MDF table. Beneath the computer was a small cabinet, three drawers. A scattering of porn mags served as a carpet. Just as Eddie expected.

He flicked through one of the mags then checked through the cabinet. There was nothing to discover except bills, letters, and the odd dirty postcard from Gran Canaria. He considered booting up the hard drive and scouting for porn but then Eddie realised his mind was already on something else. In fact, his mind had only ever been on that one 'something else'. And that one 'something else' was all that mattered.

It was the blue box. Only the blue box mattered.

So where else could he look? If the blue box existed, it could only be in the bedroom. Unless Vin had really hidden the thing, under the floorboards or behind a loose brick. Unless this really was a treasure hunt, where things had to be methodically unearthed and the mind turned over for clues and leads. If Eddie was Vin, where would he hide a terrible secret?

Eddie returned to the bedroom.

The choices were obvious: bed, left-hand bedside cabinet, and wardobe. Looking under the bed, Eddie discovered a box of dildos and straps – nothing to faze a modern gay lad, no matter how straight-laced. Plus they would go well with the boxers for some future fun.

The bedside cabinet contained some tissues, an old Safer Sex Pack, a battered copy of Stephen King's *Cujo* and two old bottles of poppers. No blue box. Which left the wardrobe.

Was there still time? If Vin was going to leave his gang early, there'd be excuses to be made, some story made up. Was Vin the sort who could lie to his mates? Straight-faced queers made a habit of bare-faced fibbing. But would Vin be the exception?

Eddie's head was nearly off his neck with adrenaline. Vin the king could be home any minute. He could return to his castle just as the blue box tumbled from the wardrobe and the contents spilled out. He could catch his new bride with her hand in the secret chamber. He could destroy Eddie's head with just a few quick strokes.

Eddie opened the wardrobe.

The box was on the top shelf, unhidden, bright and obvious. For a moment, all Eddie could do was stare. Was it really that simple? Or was he on camera?

Outside, a car pulled up. A door opened and slammed. Eddie closed the wardrobe and went to the window. A lad in a Man United Jacket was making his way towards the block. Eddie's blood slowed but still seemed to chant in his ears.

He went back to the wardrobe and took down the box. It was plastic, with a lid that slotted into place to cover the contents. The kind you buy at B&Q, three for fifteen quid. Noticeably, there was no lock. Eddie lifted the lid.

Another car door. Eddie went to the window.

Some woman with a kid, drifting towards the next block of flats.

Back to the box.

Eddie looked inside.

There were papers mainly. Sheets of paper, covered in tidy blue handwriting. There was also a stack of Man City match programmes and the odd photograph. One of the photographs, some City player from the seventies, was signed with a big blue felt tip that had faded to purple. Was that it then? Everything that Vin wanted to keep secret? Nothing more disturbing than a stack of memorabilia?

The top sheet of paper was the whitest, the rest had yellowed and greyed accordingly, since some went back twenty or so years. Eddie could tell their age from the dates at the top of each page. How old was Vin? Too old? Eddie felt a knock inside.

The writing on each page must have been Vin's. At the top of each sheet, beside the date was Vin's full name: Vincent Eddington. Below the name and date were rows of other numbers, other names: players from the 80s, players from last week, match dates, goal scores, score times, pitch conditions. All neatly inked out in tight lines of light blue letters.

It was the same on every page.

A terrible image formed in Eddie's mind and the cold knock inside set up a regular beat. He could see Vin crouching over his desk, carefully recording the facts behind the team glories, the maths behind the scoredraws and miseries. Information that Eddie could never hope to learn or pretend to enjoy.

Vin was clearly a man who could undress Eddie in a flash. And even if Vin could forgive a passion more diluted than his own, or even one worn like a coat, Eddie knew his married life had come to an end. He saw the future if he stayed. Vin standing over him, always blocking his way, blocking his light, repeating those endless statistics while stroking his cock. The deliberate repetition of the heterosexual male. Death was in those tidy lines and match reports. Death, as sure as on the end of any axe or between the teeth of any large predator.

And then the front door opened and Vin walked in.

'You still 'ere?' Vin bellowed down the hall.

Eddie almost screamed. He jammed the papers back in the box and raced to the wardrobe.

Vin staggered into the room just as Eddie was returning to the bed.

'Found anything you fancy?' asked Vin.

'Found these,' said Eddie, holding up the boxers, trying to forget those perfect facts and figures.

'Dirty fucker,' said Vin, dropping his bag and moving in for the kill. He grabbed the shorts and shoved them in Vin's face.

Eddie's erection was instant but his heart wasn't in it. Thoughts occurred like mortuary snapshots: the cold blue columns of match results, the tiny veins of footnotes, the slab of each table anchoring every page.

Eddie stood rigid.

Vin pulled away, taking the dirty shorts with him. He stared at Eddie for a moment. Eddie stared back, holding onto his smile, hoping it was inviting and innocent.

Eddie closed his eyes. Opened them.

And then it was over. Vin grinned and began to strip.

A few seconds later, they were back on the bed.

And even while the groom illustrated his love for Eddie using several different positions and a variety of offensive names, the curious bride knew that the blue box had won. Even in ecstasy, headless on the bed, Eddie knew that faced with such nakedness – such bare blue facts about a man – there could be no denying the honeymoon was over.

JENNY ROBERTS

Five Day Blues

As I wake, the all too-familiar hollowness in my belly re-asserts itself. I screw up my eyes and fumble for the clock. It's not yet six and I've had another miserable night.

I push down with my hands, trying to lift my body far enough off the bed so that I can rearrange myself and ease the cramps in my lower back. But, of course, it's futile and I have to make do with hauling myself further up the bed so that I'm semi-recumbent. I'm not allowed to sit up or turn over but, even if I were, the tubes in my arm and lower body would make it impossible. I groan and fantasise about the luxury of curling up, turning over and falling into a blissful, unfettered sleep.

It's been five days now and I'm worn-out, almost beaten. Exhausted by the effort of staying still, doing nothing, going nowhere. Nobody, but *nobody* would do this unless they had to.

My belly growls and I stretch out for the water on the trolley by the bed, sipping the whole glassful in an effort to quell the peppery bile that is burning up into my chest. Five days without food. How could I resist the offer of Oxo drinks yesterday? The weak gravy tasted like nectar after so long drinking only water, but the salts and spices in it have been irritating my empty stomach ever since.

Sausage and mash, pie and chips. Lashings of dark salty gravy. Lasagne with a crisp green side salad... I push away the images that keep on tormenting me and try and concentrate on something else. What day is it? My last meal was on Tuesday morning, just before I checked in. I had the operation early Wednesday. If I don't get to eat this morning, I'll be into the sixth day without food... so Tuesday, Wednesday, Thursday, Friday, Saturday. Sunday, it must be Sunday.

Maybe it will end today... or maybe not. I was sure that yesterday would be *the day*. I was counting on it. I don't know how I'll cope if it goes on much longer. I can't begin to describe what it feels like. The first three days weren't so bad. I was just plain hungry on Tuesday. Wednesday and Thursday I was out of it with a little button in my hand and a morphine drip in my arm. I could shoot some pain relief and the high that went with it, whenever I wanted. The dreams were spectacular, Cecil B DeMille right there in the middle of my brain. But the last two days... I feel weak. I feel ill. My mouth is furry, unpleasant. I'm sure my breath stinks. And there is a dull aching sickness deep in my gut that won't leave me alone.

I lean over and fill the glass from the jug and take another mouthful. That's another thing – I am so fucking tired of drinking water. I feel like I'm awash, afloat in my own juices. I swallow it down at one end and it re-appears in the bag under the bed a few hours later. I've even taken to checking the levels hourly. It's all I have to do. And I'm supposed to down at least five jugs each day. I think I'll go crazy if it's not today. Seriously. I mean it.

I always knew that this would be the worst part and I've been dreading it for months. I know you can't make an omelette etc, etc, but surely this will be the last morning I have to wake up like this? Every time I ask the nurse she tells me that it's up to the specialist, and when I ask him – which I did yesterday, and the day before – he just smiles curiously, nods his distinguished bald head and tells me, 'We'll have to see Sandra, won't we?' Um, well that's okay then, Mr Fothergill, we'll just sit here and fucking wait.

I shouldn't swear now, I suppose. Not even under extreme provocation. Elaine kept telling me that ladies don't swear.

'You'll have to behave differently after they've sorted you out,' she'd warned. It was more a threat than genuine advice. 'You're going to be a second-class citizen, you might as well get used to it.'

'A second-class citizen.' Like I was about to become a sewage collector or something in the slums of Bombay.

A trolley rattles past in the corridor outside and I glance longingly at the door, hoping that this morning the authorities will relent and bring me a nice hot, sweet cup of tea or, better still, a massive mug of strong coffee. Two sugars, only a little milk.

Stop it, Sandra, stop it.

I suppose in many ways I've been lucky. I guess that, if life had been easy, I wouldn't be the person that I am now. Over the last thirty-nine years I've had to cope. To make do. I've done well in my career. Well, *did* well. That's over now, too. Perhaps in my new life I'm supposed to forget all that. Learn to become a lady. Like Elaine, maybe. Learn to be soft and vulnerable. Second-class. Mm, maybe she's right. Maybe that's the way it has to be. Still, I don't think anyone should regard themselves like that. I was shocked when I realised that she did. I always thought we were equal. She'd always said we were.

Before we parted, she started to be more confident and self-reliant. I was pleased and I said so. She said she'd always been like that when I wasn't around. It was just that, with me, she'd been happy to take second place, because that's how it should be in a marriage.

Twelve years together. I thought I knew her.

Then again, I suppose she imagined she knew me too.

I wriggle in the clamminess of the bed, pulling at my nightdress to try and get rid of the creases under me. I get out of breath again and short on patience. Oh to be able to sit up! I am so tired of laying here in this bed. Please God, make it today. Make it Bacon and Eggs with fried bread and tomatoes on the side. Make it hot strong coffee and toast and marmalade. Please, have some fucking compassion. Let me at least get out of bed and have a bath.

I pull myself up short, realising that I'm actually frightened by the prospect of getting out of bed: of seeing myself naked. My stomach begins to churn and, even as I confront my feelings, a small part of my brain wonders how it is possible to feel sick when I've nothing left inside me. I sigh heavily and remind myself that I'm doing this because there is no other way. Then I remember how it has been all my life. And I begin to feel angry.

I don't have to *become* second-class. I've already been that - all through my life. Maybe not in the way that Elaine meant. But second-class all the same. And I'm here because I couldn't go on living like that. With the deception. With the lies. With the pretence. With a life that felt so different on the inside, to the one on the outside. I used to have self-respect when I was young, but little by little, as the years passed, the deceit began to take its toll and I came to despise the person I was pretending to be. The person that Elaine wanted me to be. The person she thought I was.

Can you imagine how much that tears you apart? To be seen as one thing and to feel the absolute opposite. To have to live and breathe as someone you are not. To be desperate and helpless in your soul, yet unable to tell anyone about it. Because they wouldn't understand.

Because, dammit, I didn't understand.

I still don't. I tried not to think about it. To distract myself with work, sport, reading, holidays – anything I could think of. But, whatever I did, whatever I tried, I still felt worse with every day that passed. Two years ago I felt like I was going to explode with unhappiness and all I wanted was for it to end, for me to die in the night and be out of that space. I would have killed myself if I hadn't worried about what it might do to Elaine. But in the end my mood affected her as well, and we began to argue incessantly. 'What's the point?' I thought. So I told her.

She was devastated. Wouldn't you be? She thought she'd been living with a man all those years. She accused me of deceiving her. She was right. I had, from the moment I met her. But only because I thought I could beat it. Because I didn't want our love affair to end. And because I didn't know how to explain it.

I still don't.

My eyes fill up and I think how much I still love

her. I don't blame her for feeling bitter. It is all my fault, and I willingly take the blame. Why should she wish me well? I deceived her. I let her think that everything was fine. For twelve years. I didn't mean to lie. I was frightened. I still am.

I did try, didn't I? I promised that I'd get treatment. It was my suggestion, not hers. And she agreed, of course. Neither of us wanted it to end, so we did the rounds together, for over a year, looking for a solution.

I went to see our family doctor, who didn't know what to say, let alone what to do. A 'gender' psychiatrist who prescribed me the same aversion tablets they give to child molesters, and nearly drove me insane in the process. The hypnotherapist who was convinced that I was simply gay and, if I admitted it, then everything would be fine. After a while it became clear that there weren't any easy answers or compromises. Finally, in desperation, I contacted a support organisation and found a specialist who knew what he was talking about.

And then we both had to come to terms with the inevitable. There was only one treatment, he told me, and that was to be honest with myself. Gender Dysphoria he called it. It wasn't an illness that could be cured. But it was a condition that could be treated. And the treatment was to be myself. To accept myself. To change my life. To become the woman I had always felt I was. Or, to continue coping.

'Well, it's your choice,' Elaine had said, with more than a hint of sourness, when I told her I'd made up my mind. But she was wrong, it wasn't a choice really. If I'd had a choice then I would have kept things as they were. I would have stayed there with her, in our home. I would have kept my friends, my job, my life as it was, and been happy.

I choke on the enormity of all that I am doing and waves of fear and grief swell through me as they have nearly every day for the last year. For all its difficulties my life used to be rich and full. I felt a part of something. I had a rewarding job, a family, an identity. In its way it was safe and comfortable. Busy and noisy. Now the loneliness is sometimes so loud that it frightens me.

I wipe the tears from my eyes and tell myself that I will be alright... and hope, as I've always hoped, that she'll be alright as well.

There's too much time to think in here. I'm tired of staring at the wall and turning these thoughts over hour after hour. Of waking up and crying in the depths of the night. Please God, make it today. I need to get on with my life.

I pull back the sheets and look down at my navel. The big white nappy is still held firmly and uncomfortably around me. Underneath is a secret. Mr Fothergill's handiwork. The new me - waiting to emerge. I lay the sheets back down and begin to worry. I worry a lot these days. About what my new life will really be like. About my deep voice. About the width of my shoulders. My height. About how I'll be treated. Whether I can be happy. I know that it's not going to be easy, but I've coped for the last year in a new home, in a different area. People don't seem to mind. And, in any case, I'm not going to hide. I've done that for too long. From now on, I'm going to be proud of who I am.

Even if who-I-am is a paradox. Almost a nonperson, I suppose. I never fitted in before, but the irony, even after all this, is that I still won't fit. I've never been a man in any true sense, but I can never be a woman either. I can never be like other people. I think sometimes how nice it would be to have been born female and not have to go through this. How nice it would be to bleed, to know that everything was there, in place, whether I needed it or not. This makes me smile, because every woman I know tells me to be pleased, that they would give anything to be free of menstruation. It's hard to explain to them but, for me, the lack of it is just another loss. Something else that will always make me different to real women. Just another experience that I've never shared, never will share.

It's eight o'clock now and people are moving around in the corridor outside. Maybe there'll be some post, a letter maybe... I look over at the bedside table. There are six cards. Messages of support and encouragement from people who still love me come what may. My sister, my best friend Anna, and friends from my new life. But there is nothing from the one person who, more than anyone, I needed to wish me luck.

The door opens and the nurse comes in, the new one from last night. She's young, she can't have been qualified for more than a year or two. But she makes me feel better the minute she walks through the door, and I wonder if I could get her on prescription. She peers at me with her big, dark eyes and purses her lips, trying to weigh up my mood. Then she smiles broadly and puts her head on one side, making little effort to hide her amusement.

'My God Sandra,' she scolds gently, 'What have you been doing in that bed!'

She puts the fresh jug of water on the bedside cabinet and starts to peel back the bedcovers, pulling and straightening and tucking until everything is neat and tidy, tight. I watch her closely. She fascinates me; her fine dark hair tied back neatly with a small clip, her slender neck and a slightly crooked nose that, somehow makes her all the more endearing.

She sees me staring and smiles back, pleasantly, relaxed. Like she's talking to a friend. 'How ya doin'?'

There's just a trace of an accent. Scottish, definitely. Edinburgh maybe.

I smile broadly, in spite of myself, enjoying the warmth that is suddenly filling my belly. She watches me for a few moments, studying me, looking like she really cares. Her eyes flash brightly and I feel like I could fall right into them given the smallest persuasion. The warm feeling dissolves into a swarm of butterflies. For some reason, even the smallest kindness makes me want to cry.

'Oh, I'm okay,' I manage, passing off the emotion and keeping my voice as steady as I can. I'd like to tell her all my fears and be gathered up into the warmth and safety of her arms.

'Och, there's nothing wrong with you that a good meal won't put right.' She smiles wryly and sticks the thermometer in my mouth, then sits down on the bed. 'But you'll be glad to be out of that bed I expect.'

I nod, unable to speak, but my eyes must have said a lot more because she smiles and shakes her head gently.

'Time passes Sandra. You'll soon be looking back

on all this as a distant memory.'

She pulls the thermometer out again and checks it. Then she wraps the rubber tube around my arm, pumps it up and looks at her watch as she releases the pressure. I watch her every movement – her wide soft mouth, the way she uses her hands, the expressive qualities of her face – and a sadness pricks me inside. I know that I can never be attractive in that way. But it doesn't matter, I tell myself, we all have our own special beauty – the trick is to let it show.

'Temperature is normal and blood pressure good.'

She smiles reassuringly, laying a soft hand on my arm and squeezing lightly. 'I know you must be feeling rotten, but I'm sure it will all be worth it.'

I swallow hard and agree.

'I'd go through this ten times over, if I had to,' I say, looking her straight in the eyes. And I mean it too. 'But, all the same, it will be nice when it's over. I suppose it's the bed bath again today?'

I'm fishing, nurse, you know I'm fishing. *Please* tell me that today's the day.

She shakes her head slowly and looks back at me. There's a sparkle in her eyes and something in my belly loops the loop. Then she grins.

'I *think* you might just be allowed out of bed today.' She says it slowly, carefully, watching for my reaction. I breathe in sharply and hold it, my mouth still open in disbelief. She looks at me more seriously now, and nods her head.

'Today should be the day you've been waiting for, love. Mr Fothergill seldom leaves it more than six days – and, in case you hadn't noticed, this is day six.'

I swallow hard and a heady cocktail of excitement and hope floods upwards through my body. She pauses, then smiles broadly again and tips her head towards the wall. 'He's with Joanne, in the next room – you're next. I've just come to make sure that you're respectable.'

Now there's a knot in my belly and a paralysis all over my body. This is it. This is the moment of truth. Suddenly I'm gripped with apprehension. I can't speak. The nurse smiles again, more to herself than to me, and leaves the room. She's seen it all before. We may be a tiny minority but, in here, they see more than a hundred of us every year. For them this is routine. But for me....

This is my catharsis. My renaissance. The moment of my rebirth when my outer body will at last reflect my inner being. Will I like what I see? How will it feel to look at myself and see that the old bits are missing? How will I react? What if I've made some terrible mistake? What then?

I think of all the times Elaine tried to talk me out of it and emotion wells up inside me again. I steady myself and take another sip of water. I didn't think it mattered that we would be the same sex afterwards. We never had a massive sex life anyway – and you don't have to be lesbians to be friends, to continue living together, do you? I still couldn't get my head round her rejection. She said she would always love me. All the time she said it, right up until the day I told her. Even then, she promised that she'd always be my friend. But, for all that, two weeks ago I got a brief message saying that she never wanted to see me again.

I should have guessed long ago, but I suppose I was deluding myself. She was – is – ashamed of me. Deep inside I always knew that. She never said as much, but I could see it in her eyes every time I persuaded her to meet me dressed as Sandra. I tried hard. I spent hours getting ready every time. A dress that made me look good, that disguised my lack of waist and my too-broad shoulders. Make-up – not too much, and tasteful. I kept my hair nice and filed my nails. For the first time in my life I felt good. I wanted her to be proud of me. I wanted her to like me.

But I could see it in her eyes. The distaste. I could see it in the way she drew back from me at the slightest touch. The way she began to have prior engagements when I suggested meeting. I could see her slipping away from me little by little, every day for that last year. Just, I guess, as she saw the man she had married, disappearing as well, right before her eyes.

I reach for a tissue and blow my nose, reflecting on the sadness of it all, but holding on to the hope that I have begun to feel in this last year. The promise that my new life was already offering me. With all the pain, hurt and expense, it's worth it. I'd far rather have nothing, and be me, than take any of it back. And I'd do it all again, every little bit of it – even this last five days – if I had to. Even so, it feels unreal – being here, laying in this bed, swaddled in this huge nappy, a drip coming into my arm and a catheter coming from between my legs. I keep thinking that this is the sort of thing that happens to other people. But it's me, centre stage, about to be unveiled.

Suddenly I don't know how I feel anymore, and I'm scared. I'm wrapped so tight that there is no sensation in my groin. Not even a soreness. Even an itch would be reassuring. My mind drifts and I think about people who have amputations and can still feel the missing limb. Is it the same with this operation? Will I forever be condemned to have a phantom penis? And what will I look like? I'd had no choice but to trust the surgeon. He *promised* to do a good job. Shit, I hope he has. There's no chance of a refund. And it's too late to change my mind.

The door begins to open and I close my eyes tight, trying to get a grip of myself. I'm shaking. I feel ill from lack of food and tiredness. And I'm sick with sudden excitement and fear.

When I open my eyes again, the door is still ajar, his hand curled around its side, holding it open, tantalising me. I can hear his voice on the other side, talking, giving instructions. It seems like an eternity before anything happens.

Finally, he enters the room with a flourish, wearing his Sunday sports jacket and a pale green shirt, looking like he's just popped-in on his way to the golf course.

'Good morning, Sandra,' he says brightly, standing over me, swinging a big torch as if he's about to lift the bonnet of a car and tinker with the engine.

'Today's your big day then.'

He says it as if he's commenting on the weather or the décor in the room and I blink at the lack of drama in his voice. My belly churns. And, through all this, a small part of my brain still has time to wonder if the torch is standard hospital issue.

He takes his jacket off as the nurse removes my sheets and, before I can even think about it, I've spread my legs wide and the torch is shining brightly onto my bandaged groin. I smile to myself at the thought of the spotlight on my new sex. All I need is a fanfare and the occasion will be complete. But that is already swelling up inside me, the grief and fear slipping away, yielding to the excitement that is taking over every molecule of my body.

'Now then m'dear, let's see how you're doing,' he mutters amiably, carefully cutting the bandages, one by one. Stripping them away until all that remains is one dressing, which he removes carefully, bathing the area around it. I can see nothing, but I notice that the pad has blood on it and, quite irrationally, this makes me happy. I concentrate and try to sense my new bits. But, instead of feeling what is there, my mind registers what is not there. And for the first time in my life I feel how I knew I should feel.

There is space between my legs and air around my crotch – and it feels right.

'Good... good...' The man mutters quietly to himself, pausing, reflecting. Like some great sculptor studying his new creation. Then he carefully removes the catheter and takes hold of a pair of forceps, gently tugging at the packing which is holding my new vagina in place.

'This may hurt a little.' He looks up at me, and sees that I don't care if it hurts a lot.

As he tugs, I can feel the stitches pulling. Like sharp, scalding needles threading upwards inside my groin. But the pain feels clean and good. A sacrament to my moment of re-birth.

And, suddenly, it's all over.

'There you are, Sandra.' He stands back and

smiles. This strange midwife in his open-necked shirt.

'The nurse will run your bath, then you can go and take a look at yourself.' He pulls the drip from my arm and waves it in the air. 'You're not going to need this any more. Have a bath, then you can have breakfast. I'll see you again tomorrow.'

I think of Elaine again as I let the night dress fall from my shoulders in the privacy of the bathroom. She was horrified that I was going to take the ultimate step. *Mutilation* she called it, and nothing would convince her otherwise. But now, standing here, looking at myself in the mirror, I feel like I've been healed. I feel beautiful. I feel at peace.

After a few moments, I look away from the mirror and down, at the clear space between my legs. And carefully, gingerly, I examine the folds of my soft new labia. Funny, I expected it to feel odd at first – stitched together – *new*. But it doesn't feel that way at all. It feels like me. Like it's always been there, hiding, just beneath the surface, waiting.

I stand perfectly still for a while, relishing the moment, absorbing the wonder of being myself at last. Then I look up and grin broadly at my image in the mirror, throwing my arms in the air and shouting with pure joy.

You've made it, Sandra. You've fucking well made it.

HELEN SANDLER

The Ride

That blue was a disappointment when I first saw it, too purply. But I got up there and it was a ride, an easy ride, high and fast and smooth as swimming. And now – what, half a lifetime later? – to see that purple-blue glinting between patches of rust, and the handlebars grubby with slug glue.

It's still not My Old Bike, not exactly. I bought it off someone who advertised in the *Withington Reporter* that she was selling a nice bike for thirty pounds. I didn't choose it from a selection that were all laid out in front of me; it came to me through an ad. Is that what it's like to get a girlfriend from an ad? Never quite yours, never quite trust what roads she's ridden down before or why there's that scratch on her seat.

I can't leave this bike in this shed any more than leave those wee kittens in that cardboard box I found them taped up in last week. The sight of it makes me want to get on it, and to make one journey in particular. But first it has to be cleaned up. That is not a one-hour job. That is a job that is going to take all afternoon. My dad is coming to see what I'm doing, too tall and deaf to hear but he concertinas at the knee beside me and takes a look, goes to find more tools, brings out a washing-up bowl when the front tyre won't pump, reminds me how to find the puncture.

Oh, this bike. This bike in this garden. Takes me back. You know that point in your teens when you just can't grasp why you're still in school, in uniform, coming home by ten-thirty and remembering not to swear? That was when this bike came into its own. I used to ride all over, to the shops, to the pub, going swimming, going visiting. I could get to my grandma's house in half an hour, which was less than waiting for the bus. This was when the 157 still ran every twenty minutes to Gatley from West Didsbury terminus – not that it was a terminus by then, but that was what we called it. All the buses were orange and white, and it was worth knowing the timetable because they might come on time.

I can't remember exactly how I got to Grandma's without going up Kingsway. I guess the route would come back to me if I tried it out now, but she wouldn't be there when I arrived, see, so that sort of defeats the purpose, doesn't it? It's almost like she wandered into the dual carriageway, the way the cats did – Timmy, Timmy Two and Timmy Three – though as the years went by she became more convinced that someone had stolen them for their skins. Once, the rabbi reported that he had been driving up Kingsway when our grandma jay-walked in front of him, fearless in her rainhood in poor visibility, a bulging navy-blue shopping bag in each hand.

This bike has been here all this time and I thought it had been given away. It was in the shed, draped in the old lounge curtains, the orange and brown ones that were trendy in the Seventies and would look pretty cool again now if they weren't so ripped. Or at least, they would look cool in certain parts of Hackney, maybe not so much in Withington. I don't know, I don't really have a hold on Withington any more, its spirit has slipped away from me and all I have is what it used to be when I lived here. Every building with its old name. We didn't stop calling the cinema The Scala just because some arse renamed it Cine City and we weren't going to start saying Ale House in a hurry either. And the school. I'm going up to cycle past the school. They can't have changed the name of the school, surely.

You don't get that so much now, people clinging to the old names. To say British Home Stores instead of BHS, for instance, you have to be over eighty or making a point about your own conservatism or Pythonesque humour.

I go inside and get that children's book on how to look after your bike. It's just where I picture it being, in the dark veneer cupboard in the alcove, next to the gas fire that got us through the strikes in the Seventies. It's part bookcase and part cupboard. Like so many things in this house, it came from an auction at the school, before they invented car boot sales. The top part is a bookcase with sliding glass doors with finger notches and a transfer of a butterfly that I regret, that will never come off, the red faded to a watery orange. The bottom is a cupboard with an old-fashioned metal handle, round, made up of many curls. We crammed hundreds more books in there on their backs, you can't see what they are: old annuals, Stanley Gibbons stamp catalogues, magazines that were too thick to be thrown away, too much like books.

I sit and read the whole of *Ride Away* on the pink carpet in my old room. The book has a *Sesame Street* feel, better times, times when children were trusted to learn and to look after themselves. It tells you how to defend yourself from the dog that chases the bike, how to ride after dark, how to respond to aggressive drivers. It doesn't demand that you get off your bike at the lights or wear a helmet. The pictures are mostly of a boy in jeans and pumps but occasionally a tomboy with messy, shoulder-length, dirty blonde hair, like Jodie Foster, rides alongside him in similar gear. You can decorate your bike with coloured sticky tape so everyone knows it's yours.

I take the book back outside and check everything it says to check. Then I get on it. *Woooo-hooooo!* I cry as I ride past my father, who's washing up in the kitchen window. He laughs in delight.

Instead of bending over the handlebars, as I do on my mountain bike in London, I'm sitting nearly upright. My legs grow used to the alignment as I ride around the block a few times, enjoying the way my body knows the streets. Before I got this bike, I had a blue and yellow one, the mudguards were yellow I remember, perhaps only the mudguards. On that bike I learnt to turn sharply and accurately, tight turning-circles that frighten me on an adult bike. I learnt to emergency stop at cycling proficiency classes in the school playground with a policeman. We got a certificate. Do children still get certificates for everything? Swimming fifty lengths in pyjamas, eating in the revolving restaurant at the top of the Post Office Tower, getting fixed by Jim. I met someone recently who works on *Blue Peter*. Apparently grown-ups will do anything to get a *Blue Peter* badge out of her. Anything.

Recite the names: Albemarle Avenue, Abberton Road, Burton Road, Goulden Road, Lapwing Lane and

Barlow Moor, Wilmslow Road and Palatine... places where friends lived, places to go. The street names I grew up with, which seemed to mean chips and gravy in the rain. Strange how some of them now sound so English, southern, formal. But that's the odd thing about Manchester street names. Oxford Street is the top bit of Oxford Road, the bit that's in town proper. You don't think of that, or Piccadilly, as having the same name as a bigger street in London, not till you move away, disloyal, and come back, guilty.

I try to shoo away these thoughts on my ride. I try to be the kid who had so many uplifting moments on her bike, who rose above herself on her bike. But there's something else going on as I spin past the terraced council houses – no longer identical, no longer alternating plain red, blue, green doors. I'm going to see someone I shouldn't, that's the thing.

They're not good thoughts to have, are they, thoughts about your friends' mothers? Best kept to yourself. Remember when my school-friends shrieked, that time when we were all drunk at Maura's flat, because they thought I was going to kiss Linda?

Imagine if they knew I'd rather snog her mum. Imagine if *I* knew it, that clearly, at that age. Now it's a year since the wedding, since we danced together: me in my cream linen trouser suit, her in a t-shirt with Mother Of The Bride across it, her ex-husband out of his depth. And then my dad came to fetch me and they called each other Mister and Missus and she turned away. Maybe, if I'd had a car, it would have turned out differently. I could have stayed a while. But I've never learnt to drive.

Imagine if I'd followed her up the red staircase

to her hotel room, after the happy couple left for Bali. And you must never ever tell.

When a visitor fails to phone ahead, she is likely to get as much of a surprise as the unwitting hostess.

But then, what did she expect? Did she imagine I'd spent the last year alone in my four-bedroom house, pining for my lost family? As for her, she looked as if she'd spent it on a sponsored ride. There was oil on her trousers, which is perhaps understandable, but on her shirt? I recognised the bicycle as the one she had when they were girls, when she and Linda went out on their rides to Lyme Park - if that *is* where they went. Looking back, how do I know what anyone was doing? They might be a little taken aback to know what *I'd* been doing.

I didn't mind her meeting Harriet, in fact I rather enjoyed the look on her face as she realised. And I could hear her thoughts. Oh, Harriet's not butch, no. But there are advantages to that. She doesn't give up on things the way the butches do. The way this one would.

This one thinks she can have any woman she wants if she just keeps up her confidence, but it is not a trick that a grown woman will fall for when sober. First her face is uncertain, then she fixes it in an arrogant look like Mr Darcy, and then she builds up some momentum until she's sure you're taken in by the performance. But I have seen her cry when Linda snapped at her, then cover it up with a joke; I have seen her stuff herself with chocolate biscuits because she couldn't think of a word to say to my husband. She is not all that, as they say. Smoother at thirty than at fifteen, by a whisker, but still transparent.

I let her in and I gave her tea and biscuits like in the old days and she had to talk to Harriet while I answered the telephone. Eventually I wandered back in with the handset in a particularly awkward silence and presented her with it.

'It's Linda,' I said. 'Would you like to speak to her?' I almost managed to sound innocent.

She looked into my eyes with an expressionless intensity. 'Of course,' she said. 'Of course.'

Perhaps I'll be a teenager forever. I won't have kids. I won't buy a house. I'll pedal round whichever town I find myself in. The women my age will wave as I pass. And the older women...

See how it tips? See how it alters? The air turns cool, the sky turns violet, there are no lights on this bike, look in the window of that shop, its sign unchanged in twenty years and the same khaki trousers and my reflection moving darkly across the glass as I slow at the lights. Home soon to my dad and we'll watch TV and he'll put the subtitles on and refuse to let me dry the dishes. He'll cover them in a tea towel and go up to bed with a cup of whisky tea, and tell me not to worry about something and to check something else. 'Don't worry about locking the back door, I've done that; turn off the kettle at the socket would you lovie.' Something like that.

And after he's gone, after he's taken himself to his bed until his bladder wakes him, I'll look out at the garden through the velvet curtains that replaced those brown and orange ones, at the shed and the lawn and the revolving clothes dryer and the borders full of flowers that I can't name, and I'll see the bicycle lying on its side, colourless under the purple sky.

HELEN SMITH

That's Adolescence

Our Chinese New Year card arrived today. Katie always sends us a card with Chinese writing on the front. My name was on the envelope, along with Maeve and Polly, so I opened it and then left it by the front door for them to find when they got up.

They've got up late the last two weekends, pleased with themselves, looking younger and not bothering with the chores much. We all went out for breakfast last Sunday and called for Navy and took her too. I gave her the thumbs up when she opened the front door.

'Bed death averted?' she asked. 'Nice one, Jake.'

We're both concerned about lesbian bed death. Navy found out about it when Mary P and Mary split up.

'They lived together for ten years, everyone reckoned they had a perfect relationship, they threw a party for their anniversary and that was it, curtains. Turned out they hadn't had sex for four years. Classic case of l.b.d.'

Maeve and Polly have been together for nine and a half years, Navy's mums for nine and a quarter and all of them go without sex for months at a time. I don't want Polly and Maeve to split up and to have my stuff shared out between three homes, and them going through months of depression and spending all their money on therapy for themselves instead of on new trainers for me. Navy hates the idea of having step siblings teasing her about her name.

'It's bad enough getting teased at school. I don't want my home to get broken.'

A lot of our friends are from broken homes. Navy and I do what we can to keep our mothers happy, staying over at each other's houses to give them time together. Its a strain though, lately, on account of Navy starting her periods. Our friendship isn't the same easy thing any more.

Jawad said, 'That's adolescence for you. You'll catch up with Navy again in a few years' time.' The things Jawad says make him sound like an adult already, even though he's shorter than me and his voice hasn't started breaking. Navy doesn't patronise him but I'll have to grow a beard before she stops patronising me.

'I need to catch up with her now, though.' That was the nearest I got to telling him how I feel about Navy. Jawad punched me in the arm so I think he knows what I'm on about.

Katie's not Chinese but she grew up in Hong Kong and she speaks Cantonese. We're not Chinese either but Maeve and Polly appreciate other cultures and make diversions when we're in town to look at the Chinese Arch. Part of my multicultural education.

'Let's take a left here,' one of them will say.

'Will that bring us out at the Chinese arch?' I say. 'Goody goody.' But they don't register sarcasm.

'They're too nice,' says Jawad.

'Too naïve,' says Navy.

I'm busy forgetting that it used to be me who said, 'Let's go by the Arch.'

'Have you had a nice morning?' Navy asked Maeve

and Polly as she got into the car.

'Lovely,' said Maeve with a big smile.

Polly blushed but made a big effort to look Navy in the eye and say, 'Very nice, thank you.'

Sex is not a taboo subject in our house. Nothing's meant to be secret. In fact secrets are frowned upon, unless they're birthday surprises, short term secrets that don't involve shame. If there's any shame involved, get it out in the open, that's the line in this house.

Jawad approves of secrets. 'And I'd rather my parents didn't have sex,' he says. 'All that noise – and why don't you go out and play in the garden, darling? The swing's a death trap and I can't get on with my maths, that's why not.'

The Year of the Dragon's over and it's the Year of the Snake again. I'm a dragon and my mother, Maeve, is a dragon too, because she's thirty six years older than me. There are twelve different animal years, they're listed on the back of the card. When Polly came down to make a cup of tea she brought the card through into the kitchen to show it to me again.

'Which animal are you?' I asked.

'I'm a horse,' she said. I remembered as soon as I asked. She used to tell stories about a dragon and horse when I was a kid.

'What about Dad?' I said. And suddenly she was busy with the kettle and I didn't get an answer.

'What's that about?' I wondered.

Mum wandered down the stairs, humming. It was a song Polly made up for me when I was about nought. They're creative types, my parents, Maeve and Polly, that is, not my Dad. He's more the sort of person who can make money, so I get mega presents off him, and songs and pictures off 'the girls' as Dad calls them. They're all embarassing. The songs, obviously, but the presents off Dad too. I used to boast about them at school when I was little but I don't want that kind of popularity any more.

Mum stopped humming to say, 'We thought we could all wander down to Castlefield, take a picnic, catch some jazz, count bridges?'

Taking a picnic translates as eating our sandwiches furtively on a pub bench and catching some jazz means that the Jazz Festival events at the Dukes are free. Counting bridges is something I used to do.

'If I can take my Game Boy.'

Maeve shot a warning look at Polly who stopped her eyes rolling up to the ceiling at picture rail level.

'Whatever,' Polly says. 'Let's have a nice time. You wouldn't rather have your skate board?' she tries.

Maeve explained to me once about Polly. 'She's wholehearted, Jake. When Polly believes in something she goes for it, she doesn't stop when the going gets tough. She believes in true love, and that sisterhood is powerful. Plus Clause Four of the Labour Party. And she believes in organic carrots and exercise too.'

So I said, 'Maybe next time,' and Polly gave me a nice smile. While they went to get ready I looked at the list of animals on the back of the Chinese New Year card and I thought about my Dad's age and which year he was born and right away I lost confidence in my sums. If Jawad had been there it would have been sorted. All on his own, Jawad reverses our school's underachieving boy scores, but Miss Mann isn't sure she should include him in the figures in case he's an overachieving Asian. I heard her say so to Mr Dunbar on the stairs. Jawad knows if you're meant to minus one or the number you first thought of, without even thinking about it.

There's no point asking Dad what Chinese animal he is, because he won't remember unless it's something romantic and flattering. He wouldn't want to be a rat or a pig. Some memory tugged at my brain while I thought about Dad. It was from the time that Dad and Maeve and Polly were in court all the time arguing over me so I pushed it away and lost it. Instead the song that Mum had been singing snuck in. The tune is repetitive and catchy and the words list about twenty of my friends from when I was a baby including some dogs and cats who are on their last legs now.

'Jawad next door, Jawad next door,
Jake's friend, Jawad next door.
Sappho the cat, Sappho the cat,
Jake's friend, Sappho the cat.
Navy the girl, Navy the girl,
Jake's friend...'

I was stuck with it all the way down to Castlefield.

We sat outside Dukes 92 holding our sandwiches under the table and listened to the longest drum solo in the history of jazz. When it ended I couldn't stop myself clapping I was so relieved. My sandwich got caught up in my enthusiasm and the egg mayonnaise fell out on my thigh.

'Did you enjoy that?' Polly asked as I tried to scrape the egg off.

'Dropping egg on my jeans?'

'The drum solo,' said Polly in her patient voice,

but her eyebrows shot up her forehead.

I made a vomiting gesture and Polly looked surprised but I couldn't be bothered to explain. The double bass was soloing and I needed all my strength for that. Polly got distracted by a cloud of smoke at the next table, nudged Maeve and signalled at the smoke with her eyes. She uses them a lot, her eyes.

Mum took a deep breath. 'Very nice.'

Back in Year 5, I'd told them I was the only person in my class whose parents didn't take drugs, hoping to shame them into confession. I was fed up of being sent to bed early when they managed to score, lying in bed and listening to them giggling out in the garden. They think it's unethical to smoke in the house but obtaining Class C drugs for recreational purposes, setting light to them and inhaling is a blow for freedom.

'I do know what you're talking about,' I said, interrupting their whispers about scoring. It's embarrassing when they're so obvious.

'Do you, darling?' said Maeve, sounding alarmed.

'And all the neighbours know what you're doing in the garden at weekends.'

'Have they said anything?' said Polly.

'Why can't you smoke it quietly indoors like everybody else?'

'It's the smoke, darling, the tar levels, your lungs.'

'You'll just mess up my head with your secrets instead.'

Maeve looked really upset suddenly. I backtracked. 'Let's just say it's not a secret anymore.'

'I'm really sorry that we kept it a secret from you,' said Maeve.

'Do you really think the neighbours know?' said Polly.

'We could start going in the shed,' said Maeve.

Another drum solo started.

'I think you're really growing up, Jake,' Maeve said. She sounded surprised and I couldn't think of anything to say.

'Are you and your Dad doing anything nice tomorrow?' she asked after a pause.

'Going to the Match.'

'That's great,' said Polly with enthusiasm. She obviously thought this was bringing me close to physical activity. Freezing on the terraces and having burgers shovelled down my neck can be nearly as trying as egg sandwiches and jazz.

'That reminds me,' said Maeve, 'we need to see a woman about a dog,' and then she and Polly started talking about when could they fit it in.

They say senseless things like this all the time, but this time, because of the Chinese New Year card, I heard what they were saying. It clicked.

When I was that child who wanted to visit the Chinese Arch all the time, Polly used to tell me a story about how I'd been made. I guess she was worried that when I heard how most kids are conceived I'd feel cheated or weird, so I had to have my own special birth story.

Once upon a time, of course, there was a Dragon who was very happy living on the mountainside with her companion the Horse. One thing made her sad, and she told the Horse that she longed to have a baby Dragon to look after. In the morning the Horse went on a long journey and was gone for a long time, but eventually she returned with an egg.

'What's that?' said the Dragon.

I'm cutting the story short, but it turns out that Horse got the egg off a Dog who wanted to hatch the egg himself but didn't know how. Horse promised the Dog that he could come and play with the baby in the egg if he let her take it back to Dragon for Dragon to hatch. Dragon pulled the egg towards her and once the egg felt the Dragon's heat it began to grow until the shell cracked and out crawled a baby Dragon on wobbly legs to lie between the Dragon's feet and look up at both his mothers.

Dad was the Dog. I just knew that Maeve and Polly were going to see their solicitor about my Dad. I went numb first of all and then my mind started racing. Had they been making cryptic comments about my father all my life? Secretly slagging him off without my knowing? Comments about mad dogs, dogs in mangers, muzzles even, it all began to fall into place.

I went round to Navy's when I got home and told her that my mothers had been calling my Dad a Dog behind my back.

'I'm really gutted,' I said to her.

'Worse than that time when you went downstairs with their dildo balanced on your head?' She was laughing at me again.

'I didn't know it was a dildo. I didn't know what a dildo was. That was completely different. That was a kid feeling gutted.' I wanted to say I'm a man now, but I couldn't. 'This is betrayal,' is what I said.

'Yeah, I can see that,' she said and then she paused, for a long time.

'Go on then,' I said. I could see that she was ready

with advice.

'You know what your Dad's like,' she said. 'All that hassle Maeve and Polly had off him. Sure, them calling him the Dog is pretty bad, but he's been bad too. They're all grown ups. Weird. From a different planet. But maybe Maeve and Polly didn't mean it to be bad? Maybe they just didn't want to say hurtful things about your Dad in front of you?'

'Well they did, didn't they. They just kept it secret so I wouldn't know how mean they really were about him. Secrets are hypocritical, and horrible.'

'What secrets?' Navy said. 'You know they speak in code and you've cracked the code. You know where they hide their dildo. You know where they hide their drugs. They're putty in your hands. If they say one word about flea bitten old dogs you're onto them and you can ruin their lives.'

I thought about it. I didn't know if I wanted to ruin their lives, but if their bag of grass got into the washing machine it could spoil their weekend.

'And anyway,' said Navy, 'what about your secrets?' She looked at me meaningfully and laughed. I blushed and had to spend the rest of the day in agony that she knew how I felt about her. As Jawad said, 'Your father's a dog, boy, but life's a bitch.'

- - -

R. STOCKDALE

After The Queen's Head

Most of us have just been served with coffee, wide cups of gloriously sleep-defying, aromatic liquid. The lights go down and a flickering cake hovers out from the kitchen. This is our cue. 'Happy birthday to you...'

The waitress puts the cake down in front of Sarah, then retreats before any of us can think of more smutty witticisms about her piercings. She probably hears the same lines every night of the week but that hasn't stopped us so far.

Sarah blows out her thirty-four candles in four attempts, not bad going for a woman who smokes as many Marlboro as she does. We all cheer and applaud. Sarah starts to cut the cake, at the same time as snogging her partner, Onya.

My friend Jackie says, 'I need a piss,' and heads for the toilets. I move into her chair so I can chat with Lorraine.

'How's it going?' I ask. 'The grapevine informs me you've finally got a new job.'

'Hey, news travels doesn't it? Yep, that's me on the move at last, after twelve years at the same place. More money too. What about you? I heard Lisa's quite ill.'

I'm reminded that this evening's celebration is only a temporary respite from my tough new regime. By day, I'm a civil engineer at Dulvert and Clamp, designing state-of-the-art road junctions, so today's drivers can enjoy well-managed traffic the length and breadth of the UK; by night I'm carer to my partner, Lisa, who recently managed to break her arm, dislocate a shoulder and amass an impressive collection of bruises.

'She's much better than she was, thanks. It's nothing terminal but she's still in quite a bit of pain and getting tired easily. We think she'll be back at work in a couple of weeks or so.'

'Bloody hell, Karen, how did she manage to do so much damage?'

'It was using my clapped-out ladders,' I admit. 'I should've chucked them out years ago. Of course, Super-Woman had to put the camping gear away on her own. I just heard an almighty crash, as she was coming back down from the loft and the ladders collapsed. Lisa, the loft hatch and the ladders all fell onto the banister rail. Luckily, she fell on to the right side of it rather than down the stairs.'

'God, she really was lucky,' Lorraine mutters, shaking her head. Does she want visitors, maybe on one of the nights you have to work late?'

'That's really kind of you but she's still sleeping a lot at the minute. I'll let her know you've offered and maybe one of us could ring you in a few days, to fix something up?'

Jackie arrives back from the toilets and I shift across to my own seat again. 'Don't let me interrupt anything,' she says, winking at me as if her face is in spasm. 'Who am I to stand in the way of casual sex between friends?'

Lorraine snaps back, 'Don't be stupid. We were just talking about poor Lisa.'

'Sorry, I forgot,' Jackie manages to sound contrite. 'Sounds like she's really hurt herself. Worse than her painting and decorating accident last year, or the great TV aerial incident of '98. It's time you just conceded Karen, the butch jobs are yours. Lisa shouldn't be trusted with anything more dangerous than a feather duster and a can of Pledge.'

'You're probably right,' I nod. 'We already have the best-stocked first aid box on the scene. Any time the General Hospital runs short of supplies, they know to call us first.'

Plates of cake are being passed up the table and we refocus on celebrating Sarah's birthday. Onya has made the cake herself. It's in the shape of a mermaid, with disproportionately large breasts and glacé cherries for nipples. Sarah refuses to cut this part of the cake.

Jackie starts to chant. 'We want nipples, we want nipples.'

Soon the whole table has joined in and the occupants of other tables are staring. We don't care. The chant fades anyway, but not before Sarah has started cutting one of the breasts into slices.

'She's got butter cream implants!' Jackie stage whispers to our whole table.

A couple of women have to get back for their baby-sitters and most of us have to get up for work in the morning. As we say our goodbyes and wait our turn to kiss the birthday girl, everyone sends 'get well' messages to Lisa.

*

I let myself in to the house as quietly as possible. It's not that late but Lisa might well be asleep. I dump my coat and bag in the hall and creep up the stairs. I forget to step over the creaky one and it complains, loudly. Lisa calls out, the gravel of sleep in her voice. 'Hi. I'm awake.'

I put on the landing light and go into our bedroom. 'Did I wake you, darling?'

'It's okay,' she says. 'I've slept most of the evening, anyway.'

'How are you feeling?' I lean across to kiss her cheek, careful not to knock any of her injuries. Even so, I feel her flinch. She's more badly hurt than she's letting on.

'Not too bad. The rest is doing me no end of good. Did you have a good night?'

I stare at her for clues of how she might really be feeling but can't see much of anything in the dimness of second-hand light from the landing. I can just make out the tray I'd left her before I went out and it hasn't been touched. 'You have to eat if you want to get better,' I chide her gently. 'Is there something wrong with my cooking?'

'Of course not.' She smiles at me. 'Just not hungry. I've drunk the juice though. How is everyone?'

I lie down on the bed and put my arm around her before answering. 'They're all very concerned about you. Everyone sends their love and they all want to visit.'

I stroke her hair as I speak. 'Oh yes, Sarah sent a piece of birthday cake for you, must get it out of my bag. She had a great time and said to tell you she loves the present. But I'll tell you all the gory details tomorrow.'

I stand up, only slightly unsteady on my feet. In the bathroom, my teeth get a brief scrub. Then I undress and get into bed. Lisa is already deeply asleep and I'm not far behind as I carefully curl myself round her.

*

I stare at the tatty striped wallpaper in the side bar of The Queen's Head, and let that 'start of the weekend' feeling sink in. Despite the décor, this is a good place to meet if you want to talk. There's no juke-box, resident DJ or satellite TV.

'Thank fuck it's Friday!' Jackie greets me as she returns from the bar. 'If I have to be polite to one more person, there could be a very sticky end, and it won't be mine. The trouble with customer service departments is customers expect to get a service from them. It can't be right.'

'God, that's terrible. Isn't there a European court you can complain to?' I join in with her mood.

'No chance. The company's mantra says the customer's always right, even when they're driving the dedicated customer service department staff to drink. How's Lisa?'

I've known Jackie a long time and I pull a face before I answer. She gets a real reply, not just an 'everything's fine'. 'Good and bad. Her shoulder's getting better really fast but the stupid woman is in such a hurry to be back to normal, she's trying to do too much too quickly.'

'This always happens, doesn't it?' Jackie recognises I'm not really up to a session of wisecracking banter.

'Yeah. She doesn't want to be a burden, especially

at the minute with the bypass project at work being such a bloody nightmare – bugger that protest group! Would you believe, she decided to cook dinner last night, one-handed, because I had to work late? Ended up with quite a bad scald. I had to do the full St. John Ambulance routine, arm under the cold tap, ice cubes – Florence Nightingale herself would've been impressed. And she's still got an award-winning blister. At this rate, I'm going to take her to the office, so I can keep an eye on her.'

Jackie looks thoughtful. 'Sounds like it's difficult for her to be a patient. Look, I know you're really strung out just now; you can talk to your friends, you know.' She puts a hand over mine. 'Some of us are experts in not having perfect lives. Are you ready for another drink?'

'Better not. I don't want to get back late, in case she decides to hold a dinner party or re-roof the house. Do you want a lift?'

Jackie declines my offer. She's meeting some of our gang for a few drinks and maybe going on to a club; making a night of it. As I drive home, I'm glad of the late rush-hour traffic, of the extra time it gives me to mull over the things Jackie's not saying. I'd rather be making a night of it too.

*

The next week or so goes by uneventfully enough. I go to work, cook, clean, put the rubbish out, wash and iron our clothes. The weekend approaches and Lisa's due to return to work on the following Monday, so we plan a night out. It's been a fortnight since she's seen anyone except me (and a couple of doctors) and our friends want the chance to sign her plaster cast.

Lisa can't wait to get out of the house after being cooped up for so long. 'I look so pale! Like a bloody zombie,' she wails at the bathroom mirror.

'Here, catch.' My reply is to throw her a tube of foundation. 'That's why this stuff was invented.'

'Thanks to our special correspondent for that fascinating insight into the history of slap.' Lisa pretends to speak into a microphone as she picks up the tube from the carpet.

It's good to see her smile. I perch on the edge of the bath and watch while she applies ritual layers of paint and powder to disguise her paleness and the shadows under her eyes. We joke around until we're both ready to go.

*

Jackie and Lorraine are already soaking up the beer fumes when we arrive at the Queen's Head. They're guarding a table at the end of the room, one of the best vantage points for looking across the various levels, to see who's doing what, and who with. As we make our way through the Saturday evening crush, they cheer and whistle a welcome to Lisa. She's enveloped by their hugs, and Kylie Minogue shouts her approval by making the tinny speakers vibrate on the wall.

While Lorraine goes to the bar, Sarah and Onya arrive. They manoeuvre their way across the room, negotiating the obstacle course of other drinkers. Our friends greet Lisa with a shout of excitement and an embrace. It's her night. Everyone wants to hear the full details of her latest foray into the world of dangerous domestic sports. I'm just happy to have her back again. The thought of how badly hurt she could have been, makes my stomach turn. As Lorraine points out, 'Lisa, you could've lain there for days, if you and Karen didn't live together.'

'I know,' acknowledges Lisa, turning to smile at me. I return the smile and link an arm through her uninjured one while she gives an account of my good behaviour. 'She's been an angel, doing absolutely everything in the house, while I've just been lying on the sofa.'

*

If anyone had put money on us all drinking more than we intended to, they'd have won their bet. By closing time, we were our usual, fast-talking, raucous gang.

It's time to go. Some of the gang are heading for a club, others to their beds. Lisa looks exhausted despite the Max Factor, so we're among the party poopers.

'See you, Our Lady of the Ladders,' calls Jackie.

'Bye Karen.'

'Good to see you Lisa, don't forget to cover up that cast for work,' says Onya. There are several graphic illustrations on the plaster cast which are unlikely to be appreciated by anyone outside the sisterhood.

Lisa and I are too tired to talk much on the way home. We hold hands in the taxi while the driver talks about the weekend's football fixtures and predicts the results. Apparently, Newcastle are guaranteed to trash Leeds and if Sunderland lose to Aston Villa as well, everyone this side of the Tyne will be happy. Lisa puts her head on my shoulder. 'Alright love?' I ask her quietly, so the taxi driver can't hear.

'Yeah thanks. Tired though. Aren't you?'

I realise the extra strain of the last couple of weeks has caught up with me. 'Yes, knackered but I'm glad we went out.'

*

At home, I take Lisa's hand and lead her upstairs to the bedroom. On the landing, the racks of our drying clothes cast shadows on the wall. Among the melee of everyday t-shirts, jeans and underwear, I spot my silk trousers. They're the ones I wear for presentations to Dulvert and Clamp's biggest clients, the ones that cost a fortune and say 'dry clean only' on the label. They've been through a sixty-degree wash cycle and they're fucked.

Anger wells up inside me; I can feel a pulse beating in my temple. How could she? How could she *do* this? The woman must be an idiot!

I look more closely at the matted fabric. Wrecked, absolutely ruined. Beads of perspiration ooze, then trickle down the back of my neck. I'm so pissed off. I can't trust her to do anything, can't even leave her to do *nothing*. She's worse than a child.

On the wall beside me, Lisa's shadow moves away from mine, back towards the stairs. I grab her arm with one hand and point at the shrivelled silk with the other.

'What the fuck have you done? How can you be so fucking useless?' It's as if she does it on purpose, to wind me up. Stupid, stupid cow!

Lisa's voice takes on a pleading, whimpering tone. 'I'm sorry, Karen. I didn't mean to, I swear I didn't. Don't hit me, please don't.' The whining tone and that intermittent sob in her voice, grate on me. When she whinges like this, I can't fucking stand it; I want to scream.

White flashes move in, form a screen over the inside of my eyelids. The screen swirls with splotches of red and black. My voice gets louder. 'You stupid fucking bitch! Fucking useless bitch! Can't you get anything right? Can't you do anything without fucking up? Will I always have to clear up after you, because you're too fucking stupid to do the simplest thing?'

*

When the landing reforms in front of me, I'm breathing heavily. The washing is strewn all over the floor, the glass from a frame containing our montage of holiday photos is in pieces. Against the backdrop of early hours stillness is the sound of moaning. I flick the switch for the downstairs light. Lisa is lying at the bottom of the stairs. Her face is badly bruised and one of her feet is caught between the spindles, her leg bent at an impossible angle. I rush to help her.

'Lisa, are you alright? I'm sorry darling, I'm so sorry. I never meant to. You know I'd never hurt you on purpose. I don't know what happened. I'm so sorry.'

While I'm talking, my brain races to think of a story, an explanation for the outside world.

JUSTIN WARD

Indiscretion #359

I have a secret.

I collect secrets like notches on bedposts. I don't reveal them to just anyone, only people who savour secrets like expensive cheese. I write mine down in my diary and number them like museum exhibits. This one is indiscretion #359 and it involves my best friend Russell Corkingdale. It goes alongside all that fuss about Jeffrey Archer and the time I caught Mr Plumber jacking up in the boys' toilets at school.

I don't know about anyone else, but I love to see something really, y'know, *illusion shattering*. It really gets me off. Call me cruel if you like. I know I am. But there's nothing else like it. And don't deny you've never felt it yourself, when you heard that little bit of gossip about you know what. I'm talking about that feeling of sheer adrenaline coursing through your veins when you just found out about what Richard your next door neighbour does with his cat or that well kept family secret that your granny was a direct descendent of a certain Nazi leader. Well, that's exactly the feeling I had a few months ago, on a night when I was hanging around a disused tram-shed on the local industrial estate with my buddy, Russell Corkingdale.

*

Russell's mother doesn't know that her son is gay. Or, at least she knows her son well enough not to ask stupid questions. She knows that I'm his closest friend. She likes to think that after six pints of male bonding down the local pub we crash out in Russell's bed, when really, I'm fucking him senseless.

Mrs Corkingdale knows she's happily married and that her husband has been totally in love with her since the day they met.

She knows that it doesn't pay to know too much.

That's why she doesn't know what I know.

*

Consider the scene:

Midnight. A man, in his early fifties, but very good looking, wearing a baseball cap. It's a blue Nike one with frayed edges.

He's alone, on the east, derelict side of the city. In his left pocket he's got a handful of rubbers and lube. In his right, he's got two neatly rolled up spliffs and a small plastic bag of Es. He's taken one already, and he'll sell the rest later to the guys in the disused tram-shed. It helps them to forget their other lives – those of them who *have* other lives, of course.

He comes here often, to the tram-shed, on his way back from business in Bolton or Skegness or somewhere.

He never gets too close at first, cautious of the police picking him up, but the police never come here. Regardless, he usually parks on the other side of the street in between two deserted old meat packing factories.

The ripened smell of the abattoir cauterises his throat. Broken industry breeds vice. And here the vice is at its most foul. So foul, in fact, even the seven o'clock whores don't come here any more. They sell their wares elsewhere. All this ugliness, but somehow he can't stay away.

He leaves the car and walks across the dimly lit road to the tram-shed.

Inside the tram-shed it is very dark. Only a few narrow shafts of moonlight filtering through the gaps in the boarded sides, and a single torchlight, make a wide concrete pit in the centre of the space visible. This must be the trough where engineers were once able to view beneath the trams. Now it is a pit used for one thing only. The floor is peppered with broken glass, packets of lube and used condoms. Across the room twenty or more figures can barely be seen. Silence, but for the grunts, snorts and spit of men shuffling around in the dark.

The guy in the baseball cap eyes me up and then walks directly to the far side of the tram-shed. He's been here before but due to darkness, I didn't previously recognise him until tonight. I don't think he recognizes me either. Thank God. I am so shocked, my heart almost does a back flip.

I watch him. I can't believe it. He's so cool. He knows what he's doing. He likes to get a piece of the action. He rests against the back wall, drops an E and lights up a cigarette. He's already popular with a few of the young men in there who approach him in an attempt to score drugs. I think some of them like the idea of going with an older guy. Russell and I are already in there and have spotted the most likely fucks.

I've got my eye on a man who has come to stand just next to me. I like to stand in the torch light, where

I can get a good look at them. He's a bit short, but good looking. Rugged, tanned, short neatly-trimmed stubble, cropped brown hair. In the half-light I can see he's wearing jeans and a green t-shirt. He gives the impression of being a bit shy but he knows exactly what he's doing.

Russell's attention is elsewhere. There are a couple of men on the opposite side of the room, near the guy with the baseball cap, passing a small bottle of GHB around. We've only been in there about an hour and the guy who followed us in has got the whole tram-shed coming up. We've both dropped an E. I'm wired, Russell's out of it and the guy that I had my eyes on is already beginning to strip. He's taken his t-shirt off and tucked it into his jeans. Jesus – I am absolutely fucking pole-axed. I came up quickly. These Es are really good.

Sweaty palms.

Tingly neck.

Up, up and away.

It's really quiet, all I can hear are the fetid whispers of strangers in the dark, the sound of heavy breathing and the scattering of gritted glass. I can smell indiscriminate sex and amyl nitrate in the air. The noxious scent of stale armpits and beer breath fills my nostrils.

Someone kicks an empty tin can across the floor and suddenly the air is ripe with tension again.

The tanned guy is unbuckling his belt and unzipping his jeans. He rubs his chest with one hand and fingers his left nipple which is pierced. His other hand has slipped into his jeans, and is gently rubbing his cock.

*

Consider me:

My heart, pounding.

Legs like jelly.

Head like water.

Fucked.

And fluffy.

Our eyes meet and he smiles.

He pulls that hard cock out of his trousers. Russell has moved away, but I can still see him, so I move over to the tanned guy. Close up his face is a little red. His eyes sparkly in the half-light. He must have taken some GHB, he's panting with excitement. He pulls me toward him with a firm but gentle hand.

His skin is so smooth. Chest shaved. His upper arms are big and muscular. Oh, he's lovely.

His cock makes me shudder to touch. He's got a huge one. His balls are tight and sweaty. His cock is warm in my hands.

I lick his neck. He groans. He likes it. I kiss the shallow part and move to his nipples. A little suck. He groans even more. He's a nipple man. I nibble on them and pinch one between my fingers. He gasps with delight and squeezes my shoulders. Then I work my tongue down past his stomach to his hard cock. I slip my lips down the fleshy shaft. He passes me a condom and a sachet of lube. He wants me to fuck him.

Jeans around our ankles, his arse in the air, I give it to him hard. And over his shoulder, I see the guy with the baseball cap climbing down into the engineer's pit in the middle of the room. He's getting it on with the guy who has the vial of GHB. He's completely out of it. If I hadn't been so pilled-up, I might have given a fuck. But I just watch...

*

Now, consider his son... Russell.

'*RUSSELL*!' Where the fuck has he gone? He's moved away from me to the centre of the tram-shed. He wants a piece of the action. There's just enough light for me to see him jump down into the pit. I want to call his name, but no, crap idea, that would never do. I cough loudly but he's oblivious, so I just carry on watching. My fuckee wants it bad but I can't take my eyes off of Russell. He is a law unto himself. He's kissing the guy with the baseball cap. It's beautiful and divine and fucked up all at the same time. A moment of sheer intimacy between two men.

He's getting all lubed up. Slips a condom onto the guy. Turns his back on him. The guy drops the baseball cap on the floor... And that, as they say, is that! Russell is getting fucked like a pig by his own father. What a mess? And neither of them will ever know, it's *that* dark.

*

All that said, consider his wife, and Russell's mother, Mrs Corkingdale:

A decent woman, preparing breakfast the following morning. She's been married to her one and only for thirty years and she's never once strayed. Good girl. See, she has all those very admirable characteristics: loyalty, self-respect, honesty and above everything else, discretion. And she probably has a very good idea about her husband's *indiscretions*, but says nothing. What's the point? Mr Corkingdale loves her very much. And in all honesty, they seem very happy.

I take my hat off to the woman. She's one of a dying breed, born of a family who 'just got on with it'. As I watch the three of them sitting around the breakfast table together, however, it gives me a little kick. Still... her secret is safe with me.

Looking at Mr Corkingdale, I can't help a cruel smile flicker across my face.

Russell's father sits, trying to read my face. But I give nothing away. Behind my eyes I can feel a catalogue of indiscretions unravelling – Mr Corkingdale's indiscretions. He needs to take more care in covering his tracks. I caught him once buying a copy of *Torso* in a local sex shop, and slipping into that filthy place they call a 'gentleman's health spa'. Then I saw him leaving the STD clinic. I wonder what he went in for. And poor Mrs Corkingdale! Whatever it was, she must have thought she'd caught it from the lavatory seat.

He stares at me. I stare at Russell.

Russell stares at his father.

Neither of them have any idea. The only thing they recognize is the mischief on my face.

'You courting yet, Josh?' asks Mrs Corkingindale.

'No,' I smile. 'You ask me that every time I come here.'

'A young boy like you deserves to be in love.'

'There's no love anymore.'

'Cynical bastard,' says Russell.

'Russell! Not at the dinner table,' snaps Mrs Corkingdale.

Mr Corkingdale rustles his newspaper. 'How you feeling today, Josh?' he asks me.

'Bit odd.'

'Odd?'

'Oh you know, sweaty palms, palpitations, that sort of thing.'

'Huh?'

'Been playin' too hard, I guess.' I fake trembling palms to him.

He laughs. 'A late night, huh?'

'Yes,' I sigh and grin. I can't hold back. It's just killing me. 'Actually, you look a bit shakey yourself.' I say.

'I look ill?'

'There's something wrong with your eyes.'

'What?' He looks surprised.

'And you look like you haven't slept for days.'

Pulling the frayed blue Nike baseball cap out of my back pocket, I decide to go in for the kill.

A little wink.

Ready, aim...

'Russell was telling me you're gonna buy him a car for his birthday.'

Mrs Corkingdale looks surprised but pleased.

Fire!

Cap on head.

Mr. Corkingdale is paralysed.

Direct hit.

Adrenaline rush.

'Wish I had a Dad like yours.'

JAN WHALEN

Lester Leaps In

I followed Stella home once. I hid behind a tree in a park across the road and watched her letting herself in. Later, when it got a little darker, I crept up and looked through her window. The room was sparse, tidy and modern, subtly lit and delicately furnished with things that had been bought specially for it. No hand-me downs here. But what struck me immediately, and most forcefully, were the posters.

She likes jazz. The coolest of music, bristling with discord, discreet but exciting – she has a wild side! Charlie Parker, Thelonious Monk, Charles Mingus. A side she keeps hidden beneath her cool, pedestrian business-like manner. A smoky, dark intelligent side. Her heroes are men from the other side of the fence. I imagine her snapping those well-manicured fingers to *'Round Midnight*, bobbing her neat little head to *April in Paris*.

Of course, I went after jazz myself like a newly-evangelised convert. Bought as many CDs as I could manage and tried to memorise *Lester Leaps In* so I could hum it to myself as previously I might have hummed something by Travis. I even obtained a Charlie Parker poster of my own from that intimidating jazz shop on Deansgate. All black and white, tortured genius and smoke and sweat. It made me feel sophisticated and somehow closer to Stella. If only she knew. We are joined by Bird!

The music was another thing though – the taste took some acquiring. Not exactly music to relax to. In fact, if I'm honest, it gave me a bit of a headache. Sometimes I'm ashamed to admit, I'd find it downright annoying. My dad would shout, 'What's that bloody racket?' up the stairs and at other times sneer at me as if he knew something I didn't. When you add that to the, let's be honest, sheer *unfriendliness* of the music – all that squeaking and honking, it felt as if my nerves were going through a shredder.

Around this time I began trying to disguise the ugly furniture in my room with the use of 'throws' – two for ten pounds from one of those here-today-gone-tomorrow shops on Market Street. The wallpaper is hideous royal blue flock, the sort that makes passers-by catch their breath in disbelief. My furniture is the cast-offs from dead relatives. Charlie Parker sweats all over the place from his own spot above the white dressing table. I feel my heart grow heavier whenever I come through the door. I would like to be surrounded by beautiful things and in my mind these have somehow become Stella's things. Her angular metallic table lamp with green shade, her smoked glass coffee table, her ash bookshelves on which classics and modern writers rubbed spines.

I wonder if she has a boyfriend or is maybe even married. I imagine her talking to her husband, the easy casual way they have with each other, the affectionate names they call each other. She likes him. Throws him an easy smile over her shoulder as she washes the dishes. Or she doesn't like him, she is afraid as she washes the dishes. She resents him. Maybe her beautiful mind is elsewhere and she smiles a secret smile into the blackened kitchen window, her arms up to the wrists in soap suds, her head awash with

Goodbye Pork Pie Hat. The music she loves, her only refuge from a man who scares her. I don't know which I prefer of the two but I feel a pang of pain that she should wash dishes at all. She is meant for other things.

I admit I've become obsessed with her. Obsession isn't necessarily dangerous, frightening. It doesn't always have to end in murder and misery splashed across the *South Manchester Reporter.* Obsession is as everyday as cleaning your teeth. Surely everyone has some object of fanatical devotion. Cigarette cards, Dosteyevsky, Elvis.

We were playing that game in Home Ec. once. 'What would *you* do if you won the lottery?' This one girl said without a second thought: 'Yeah, I'd buy lots of really nice shoes.' Shoes? That's right. Shoes. 'Yes I *love* shoes, I'd have whole closets full if I could.' Shoes with slim blue straps around the ankle, shoes that go high up the leg, shoes with glorious buckles, shoes with needle-like stiletto heels, different colours for different moods, a different style of shoe for every style of music, different shoes for different tunes. Rows and rows and rows of shoes. It was like suddenly hearing a different language. I never think of shoes other than as things to walk around in and when they wear out - buy more. But I was more surprised by the ease with which she confessed it. She had no shame. And why should she? She was a woman who took righteous pride in her obsession.

Maybe some people's fantasies are more acceptable than others. Sometimes the feeling of not being completely in control scares me. But deep down I enjoy it, down in a secret, scared breathless little place. There, I can take Stella by the hand, she leads me to the dance floor and there we groove seductively together. We ride the waves of a coaxing, sardonic music together in our special place.

*

Monday, nine am still at the bus stop and I'm now past caring whether the bloody thing comes or not. It's warm for November. The year, caught on the hop has just remembered it's Autumn and started hurriedly throwing leaves down on top of us in great handfuls. The traffic is tedious, hypnotic even, and my watch ticks the late minutes away, the rubbish blowing down the gutter of the old home town.

At times like this my mind evaporates, drifts towards her like a ghost. Though I try to stop it. I prefer to savour these moments – our precious time alone in my head, and I hate to waste my complex, indulgent, glorious thoughts on such grim surroundings. I like to choose the right time, the right circumstances, to relax with her, to indulge. But she comes to me anyway on the warm breeze with the ease of a leaf blowing. I feel weak and floaty, I slip back to the time when she was off college on 'family business'.

I imagine she's visiting her elderly but fiercely independent mother, see over and over, her slender figure clipping down the avenues in a strange faceless town, somewhere in Wales. A seaside town, I decide, with a fog rolling in off the sea and the seagulls calling eerily. At eight o'clock, church bells ring in the solitary dark and she passes through the wrought iron gates and privets, crunches up the gravel path, suitcase in hand. A dutiful daughter visiting an ageing mother. I speculate what sort of reception she'll get. Naturally the whole family love her and are so pleased she's here. They take her bag and hug her in the hallway before she's even had time to take off her raincoat. Her cheek is cold against their faces. She is welcomed in for tea and fruit loaf, butter served in a porcelain dish with a lid. She is a welcome part of that big friendly family. Or, they can't stand her! They're jealous. Jealous of her success, of her big escape from Llandrubadidug or wherever it is. Upstairs she's shaking, alone, combing her hair in the mirror, trying to be strong.

I don't know how her hair feels to the touch or how it smells but I can imagine. I think all the time about the colour of her hair, its dark beautiful reddish brownness, then its feel, its smell, like conkers. She has it short and neat. I pick out people in the street who could be her, maybe are her, but they're not. I meditate for ages on how it will feel if I ever get close enough. How I wish my own hair was as luxurious and fascinating.

Stella is a lecturer at my college. I walked into English one day to find Mr Hughes was History, so to speak, and Ms Warner was here to take over. I noticed immediately her warm confident manner. She seemed to enjoy what she did and she looked adorable. Sophisticated but casual. Painstakingly, I collected scraps of information about her from the other students and staff. They think I'm above gossip. They're easily fooled by my disinterested 'hm?' as I look up from a book. Secretly I'm slicing up the details like a butcher with a raw kidney, parcelling it up for later. I fall upon each new piece eagerly and when I've sucked it dry as a bone, I am free to place it in the picture, the jigsaw puzzle I'm fitting together about her. The one that has her and me in it. Together.

*

Unfortunately, I can't relax on the bus when it finally deigns to show its ugly unwashed face; it's full and I have to stand up. I stare out the windows trying to see through the condensation. Shop windows juddering past, their seedy boards and misspelt signs one after the other. I consider trying to memorise them so I can notice with the eye of a fanatic which ones change from time to time and which don't. Would it be worth it as a conversation starter? 'Do you remember that used to be a Butchers and now it's a Hairdressers?' Probably not. Forget it.

Pauline from my course gets on the bus. I don't want her next to me, forcing me into conversation. I stare out of the window looking as if someone I know is out there semaphoring at the bus with an urgent message but Pauline spots me, makes a bee-line and I feel guilty then because she's so nice and I should be grateful.

'What a laugh we had last night!' she starts joyfully. 'Went down to Cruz 101. Ever been? It's great!'

'Yes,' I say quickly so I don't get detailed instructions of how to get there followed by a description of what the dance floor looks like.

'...really really really really dead friendly and I met the devil – well, y'know – a bloke dressed like the devil with horns, in red and everything, so we were dancing 'n' all and when I came out my face was totally covered in red paint! The others were all killin' themselves!'

'Ha ha ha!' I roar on cue, more convincingly than it sounds. I swim in a different element. I don't really understand other people's lives. Pauline, bless her, reminds me of this, so I'm glad to see the back of her.

*

I imagine Stella likes me. I think she does, it's the way she speaks to me – kindly interested. She says my name a lot when she sees me around college. 'Kit, how are you today?' 'How is your assignment coming along, Kit?' 'Good morning Kit!' See what I mean? It's personal. I love my name the way she says it. It means I'm alive. I'm alive for just a tiny moment.

I never say hers of course. I'd blush, and I know that I'm just one among many to her. I've heard she describes me as 'eccentric' (overheard by one of the girls who laughed when she told me, though not unkindly). I don't think I'm in love with her. 'I don't think I am in love with you,' I whisper. Her face rises in my dreams and when I'm awake I drift off into some romantic notion: 'Drink?' she asks and when I nod breaking my concentration on the furious beat that is pounding down from the stage and breaking over us like waves on a hot Mediterranean beach, she smiles and drifts off to the bar. I'm soaked in sweat from the heat and the dancing and the intense concentration it requires to follow every nuance of the music. When she returns I seize my tall ice-cold amber beer and gulp it down while she rests her arm on my shoulder.

I'm brought to by Pauline again, this time in the café bar, raucously reliving her night out. Apparently she's arranged to see the devil again and is very much looking forward to it. I listen as if I might finally understand this strange talk of 'mates' and 'blokes' and 'clubs'. Maybe I'll meet a devil of my own one day? Just as I'm mulling over this strange thought, Stella herself, Queen of my world, passes regally by. And the sun is eclipsed.

'Hello Kit, how's the course going?' she asks breezily. I have an ill-timed mouthful of spaghetti to deal with so I splutter something obscure. She looks puzzled, but in a friendly way I think, and sweeps on to be snapped up by other more deserving students. I wanted to show her my new Charlie Parker CD which I just happen to have with me. She'd be interested, we could discuss Charlie. His music, his effect on my life and so on... she'd be impressed. Maybe we'd start swapping CDs, who knows? Too late.

I watch the way the others fall over themselves to talk with her, dying to ask her this and that about the essay she set. What does she think about this, what does she expect from that. I'm jealous, of course, but don't crowd her. She knows I'm here if she wants me.

Sometimes I want her so much I ache. It's a kind of ache I don't really understand. Like a long smooth note from a sax, so sad it hurts. If I were to make love to her I would do so slowly, easing myself gently, reverentially, against her and smoothing her soft pale skin, sliding my hands down her stomach and holding off long enough to make her want me. Moonlight would illuminate the room, music curl like smoke in the corners. When, finally, I make her come with the slow teasing movements of my fingers, I watch her face intently, watching for a sign that she needs me as much as I need her. She leans into me like an animal, hungry for me, ready for me. Odd when I remember she's so much older than me. A woman in fact and me just a daft girl.

*

I'm hanging around the gates, pretending to look for something in my bag. It's getting dark earlier and earlier these days. Beautiful Stella comes out and looks over in a friendly way and notices my new CD

'Hey, that's my boyfriend's favourite! Lester loves Charlie Parker!'

'Lester?' I say faintly, as if the name has killed me somehow, but the actual dying is still to come.

'Yes, my boyfriend. It's funny we're so alike in some ways but that jazz music it's just so, well, *awkward*. I prefer Mahler myself, we try to convert each other but we never do.'

I feel sick at all these revelations in one go. She smiles, waves, eases herself across the road as gracefully as a cat, swinging herself up, up into a waiting car. A huge four-wheel drive jeep thing with bull bars on the front, electric blue. The man driving looks competent and sensible. He has a large Seventies-style moustache. Stella is clearly pleased to see him because they kiss each other like new lovers, as if they can't wait to tear each other's clothes off.

I feel a huge sharp pang inside, when I see that kiss. It's as if something vital has been snipped and the world is suddenly swinging by a thread. Such a little act.

I watch them drive away.

I can see my bus coming, lights on in the gloom, and I know full well there won't be another for at least an hour, or perhaps ever, but I don't even move one single step towards the bus stop.

ABOUT THE AUTHORS

Jack Berry a.k.a John Joseph Bibby (born Liverpool, 1/6/82) moved away to Blackpool in 1998. After three years of very hard work he moved on once again. This time he followed the bright lights all the way to London and contributed a piece to *The Next Wave* (Gay Times Books 2001). He is now writing a novel, more short stories, lyrics and poems. If asked to sum up his life so far in a sentence, Jack says it would be, 'Absolutely no regrets.' He dedicates this piece to all the people who 'have helped me deal with a lot of shit recently'.

Cathy Bolton (born Stoke on Trent, 18/3/64) spent her early years in a caravan travelling round construction sites but now lives a very static life in Manchester. She works as a development worker for Commonword. Her poems and stories have been published in many magazines and anthologies, including: *The Rialto*, *Rain Dog*, *Multi-Storey* and *The Diva Book of Short Stories*. She has never found Jesus.

Sean Burn has just finished touring *FATBASTARD* – a novella written for Demotext 2001. Author of three poetry pamphlets *(leery* received a Northern Arts writers award in 1997), the most recent was *voltairechoruses* – a collaboration with photographer Andrew Hardie. He belongs to *Paternoster* – a collaboration between northern writers and international musicians. Their 2000 anthology *Paternoster* included an excerpt from his novel *margin walkin*. His prose has been widely published with further novel excerpts appearing in *Whitenoise* and *Route*. Plays include *in an age of double-glazin* commissioned by Plaines

Plough (1999).

Wayne Clews (born Congleton, Cheshire, 6/11/72) spent many years toiling in theatres and bookshops around Manchester until he stumbled into journalism. He is currently a contributing editor at *City Life* and *Attitude* magazines and writes regularly for *Gay Times* and *Metro*. A graduate of Manchester University's M.A. in Novel Writing, *Eczema In Gothenburg* is his first published fiction but he has a drawer full of novels that have yet to see the light of day.

Julia Davis (born Nottingham, 18/05/56) grew up in Manchester and is presently exiled in York. She mostly writes and performs poetry but every so often enjoys the odd short story burst! Works freelance in the live literature scene and dabbles in ceramics.

Simon De Courcey (born Rochdale, 24/2/75) is a writer and teacher. He read English at The University of Wales, Aberystwyth and has had poetry and short stories published regularly for the last six years. Until recently, he was a creative writing tutor for Open College North West. He won the *Queer Words* Poetry Prize in 1997. Poems to be found in *Pennine Ink*, *Rain Dog*, *Interchange*, *Queer Words* and *Nailing Colours*, published by Crocus. Short fiction to be found in *Queer Words*. Some articles to be found in the now sadly defunct *Queer Soul* magazine.

Lewis Gill (born Chesterfield, 8/7/81) lived with his mother and sister in various little terraces until he was eighteen. He then moved to Blackpool to study for his A-levels. During this time he developed a love of literature and wrote his first piece of fiction, *A Picture Of James,* that was published in 2001 by Gay Times Books. After a long jaunt to London, he is back in Chesterfield, writing his first novel and looking forward to starting an English degree in the autumn.

Robin Graham (born London, 30/4/60) is a performance poet and playwright. His plays include *Growing Pains,* a monologue for schoolchildren, toured by M6 Theatre Company as part of *Double Six; A Better Place,* produced by Stop Gap Theatre Company in Guildford; *Club Nemesis* at the Green Room, Manchester; *Children of Abraham*, produced by Manchester Sangeet Academy; and *Guardians,* for the Abraham Moss Youth Theatre. As Poet In Residence at Clitheroe Castle Museum during *The Year Of The Artist*, he wrote *Crikey Mikey's Summer Holiday;* this was performed for local schoolchildren and published by *Ribble Valley Council. A Better Place* is published in the *Journal of Consciousness, Literature and the Arts* (July 2001) at http://www.aber.ac.uk/tfts/journal. Currently he is associate writer at the Green Room.

Michelle Green (born Portsmouth, 05/04/76) has moved between England and Canada four times so far, but plans to stay on this side of the Atlantic for a while this time. She started her artistic life as an actor and began writing and performing her own material four years ago. She has since published some of her writing in the Canadian fanzine *Back of the Bus*, has written and performed with Contact Theatre's *Queer Contact* for the last two years, and has appeared behind the mic at various poetry and storytelling events around Manchester.

P-P Hartnett (born London, 15/06/58) grew up in a residential home for the elderly until the age of seven. His photography and journalism has featured in *The Sunday Times Magazine*, *The Independent*, *i-D*, *Attitude*, *City Life* and *Time Out* – amongst others – broadcast on *VH1* and *RTL*, plus exhibited in London, New York and Tokyo. Hartnett is the author of three novels and a book of short stories: *Call Me* (Pulp Books, 1996), *I Want To Fuck You* (Pulp Books, 1998), *Sixteen* (Sceptre, 2001) and *Mmm Yeah* (Pulp Books, 1999). Previous to *City Secrets*, he has edited two anthologies of short fiction, *The Gay Times Book Of Short Stories: New Century, New Writing* (Gay Times Books, 2000) and *The Next Wave* (Gay Times Books, 2001). P-P Hartnett lives alone. Home is a terraced house on a hill in Colne, Lancashire. His next novel, *Rock 'n' Roll Suicide*, will be published by Sceptre in November 2002.

Robin Ibbeson (born Sheffield, 30/4/77) raised in Sheffield until his late teens when he finally packed in his job at the local steelworks to move to Manchester. Since then, he has worked in a variety of occupations ranging from tarot phone line operator to medical testing volunteer in an attempt to fund his writing habit. An erotic novel about footballers created by one of his alter egos was published in March of last year, and he recently contributed to *The Gay Times Book of Short Stories: The Next Wave*. Robin was also awarded an annual North West Arts Board's Writer's Bursary in recognition of his talents.

Maisie Langridge (born Wolverhampton, 12/3/1960) gained a first class degree in English and obtained her MA in Theatre both at Leeds University. After some theatre work she now lectures in Performing Arts at a college in North

Wales. She has other work published and has won literary prizes for her favourite form, the Short Story. She adores cats and cooking and is a qualified Iyengar Yoga teacher. Maisie is a sharp dresser and would love to be able to be half way decent as a gardener and admires the green fingers of her dear friend Ann.

Mary Lowe (born Bath, 1959) moved to London when she was four to seek her fortune. She has done a variety of jobs including teaching, training, health promotion and youth work. Since 1984 she's been living in Newcastle with partner Maggie and two computers (one for each hand). She is currently writing a novel with her left hand and a musical with her right. She is involved in the organisation of Proudwords, the UK's only creative writing festival for lesbians, gay men and bisexuals.

Rosie Lugosi (born London, 08/05/65) has an eclectic writing and performance history, ranging from singing in 80s Goth band *The March Violets*, to her current incarnation as *Rosie Lugosi the Vampire Queen*, electrifying performance poet and host of the *Creatures of the Night* Poetry Slam at The Green Room, Manchester. As well as two solo collections of poetry, *Hell and Eden* and *Coming Out At Night*, her short stories, poems and essays have been widely anthologised. Her chilling short story *You'll Do* appeared in the *Diva Book of Short Stories. Host*, her first novel, is currently with an agent. She recently won the Erotic Oscar Award for Performance Artist of the Year 2001.

Susannah Marshall (born Zambia, 1968, the Year of the Monkey). She has had a variety of 'day jobs', teaching English, working in community arts and currently works in mental health, but throughout has written stories and poems and produced paintings. She has had works published in *Iron, Mslexia, New Writer* and in a collection of lesbian erotica. She lives with her dog and any girlfriend who happens to be passing. She was a pirate in a previous life.

Mark Michalowski (born Chesterfield, 7/3/63) is the editor of the Yorkshire gay paper, *Shout!* and lives in Leeds. His first published fiction was in the science fiction anthology *The Dead Men Diaries* (Big Finish, 2000) and since then he's had work published in a couple of charity anthologies. His first novel, *Doctor Who – Relative Dementias* (BBC Worldwide) was published in January 2002.

Keith Munro (born West Lothian, Scotland, 14/12/76) is a graduate of the Manchester Metropolitan University and earns a living as a writer, composer and performer. His fiction has been published in *The Gay Times Book of Short Stories: The Next Wave*, and much of his spare time is taken up with the unfashionably long novel he's been writing for the last four years. Keith currently lives in Crewe, Cheshire.

John Myatt (born Warrington, 22/8/73) is a resident of Hulme. His short fiction has appeared in *New Century/ New Writing: The Gay Times Book of Short Stories* (published by Gay Times Books, 2000) and *The Illustrated Ape* magazine. Other work includes *Great Monsters of Western Street*, a homo-erotic horror play, which received a First Scene Award from North West Playwrights and two nominations for *Manchester Evening News* Drama Awards in 1998. His second play, *Edgar Allan Who?*, was short-listed for the 1999 International Playwriting Competition.

He is currently studying for an MA in Creative Writing at Manchester Metropolitan University, whilst working on his fourth play and first novel.

Jenny Roberts (born a boy, Bridlington, 1944) changed to her more correct gender in 1996 at the London Bridge Hospital. She identified as lesbian shortly afterwards and founded the *Libertas! Women's Bookshop* in York in 1998. Her debut thriller, *Needle Point*, the first Cameron McGill Mystery, was published by Diva Books in 2000 and her second, *Breaking Point* in 2001. The third book in the series, *Reckoning Point,* is due out in late 2002. She is also a contributor to the *Diva Book of Short Stories* (Diva Books 2000). Her web site is: www.jennyroberts.net and she welcomes e-mails from her readers.

Helen Sandler (born Manchester, 25/08/67) left for the Smoke at eighteen and never found her way back home. But she did find a smoke. She is the author of *Big Deal* (Sapphire) and *The Touch Typist* (Diva), and the editor of two Diva short story anthologies – the second will be published in late 2002. *The Ride* was inspired by a real wedding and a real bike but the people in it are made up and not to be confused with the innocents in her real life. She has no secrets.

Helen Smith (born Hackney Hospital, 1954) had early adventures in Nigeria followed by a dull childhood in suburban London. Her story, *That's Adolescence*, draws on her life in Manchester, bringing up her baby son with her partner, but some of it is imagined. She has a few secrets and is getting better at keeping some and setting others free.

R. Stockdale (born Dartford, 9/2/61) went to school in Dartford, Lincolnshire, Norfolk and Bath. She completed a degree in sociology, then spent time in Israel, followed by a succession of bar jobs back in the UK. She has worked in the fields of welfare rights advice, community development and more recently with homeless young people. She lives in Newcastle upon Tyne and now works for the local council. She has not been published before.

Justin Ward (born Wolverhampton, 2/3/75) lives and works in London as a writer and a teacher. Among his interests are film, literature, the music of Tori Amos and to his mother's despair, anything dark and black. He was considered a perverted weirdo at school and has remained so ever since.

Jan Whalen (born Manchester, 18/12/1963) lives with a bicycle and two black cats. She works for Manchester University Library, writes poems and stories and is co-editor of the poetry magazine *Rain Dog*. She's had stories published by Crocus Books and poems in *Tandem*, *The Affectionate Punch* and *Panda*. She's performed her poetry on the radio, the sideboard and the kitchen table including one entirely in Latin accompanied by slapping herself on the head with a dead fish.